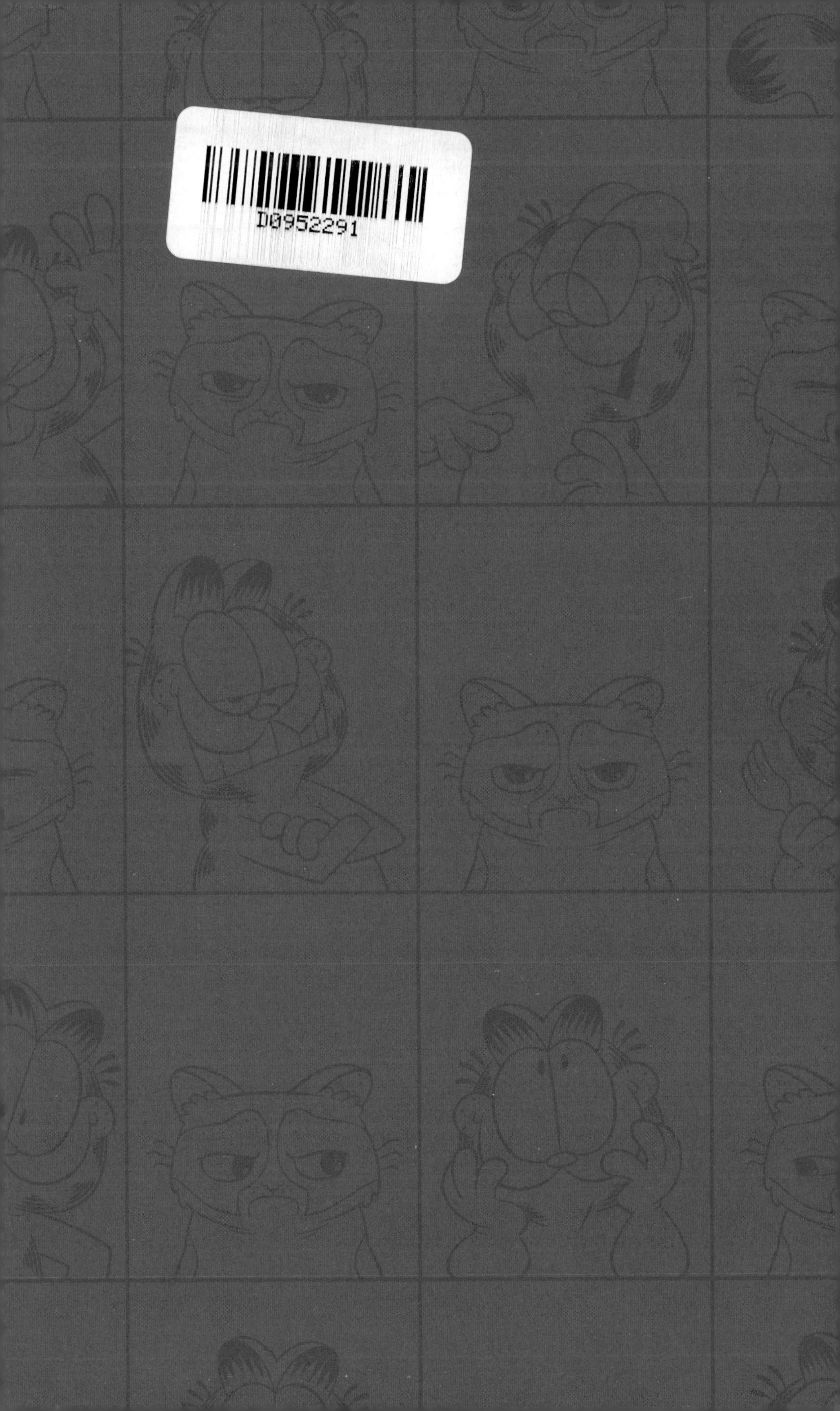

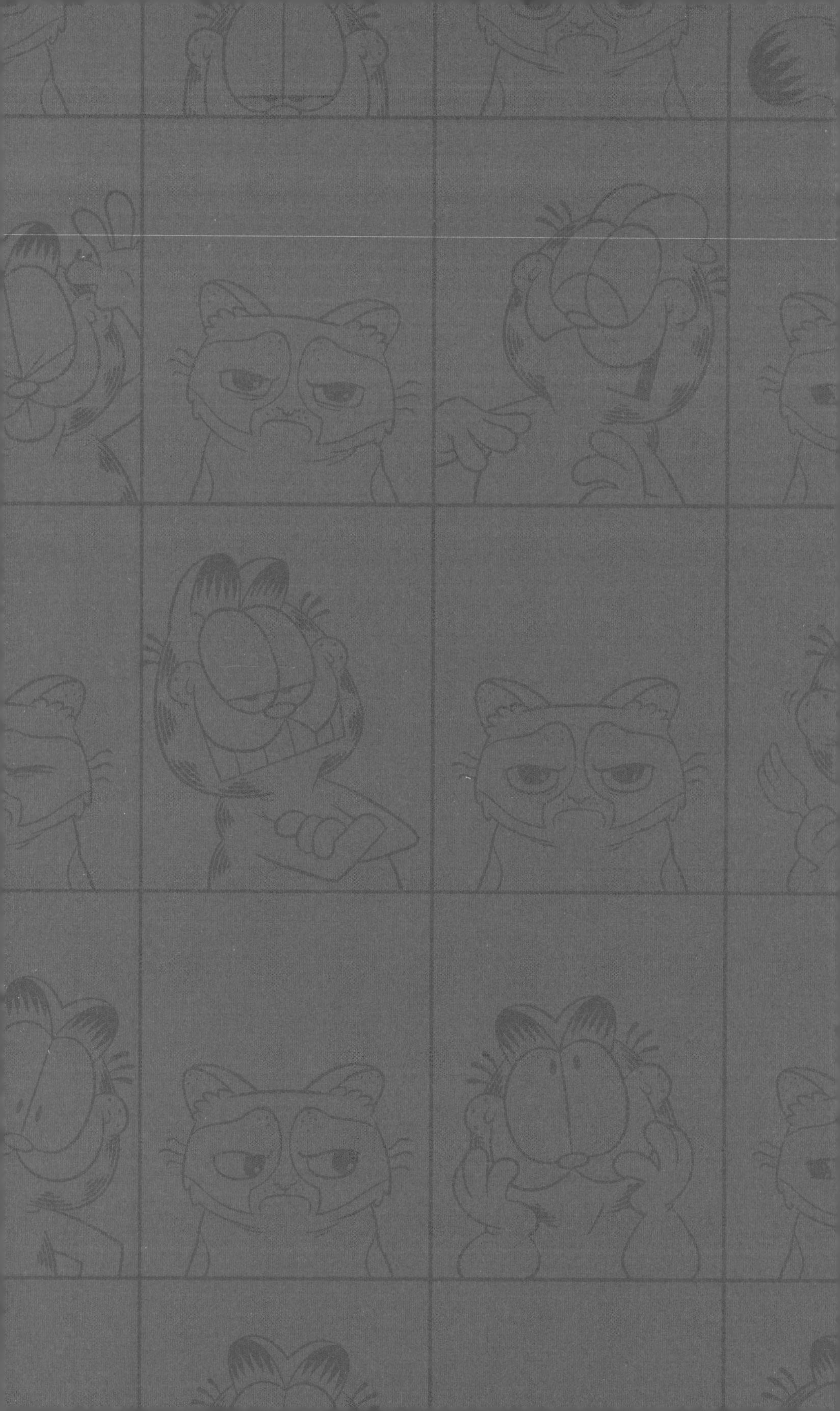

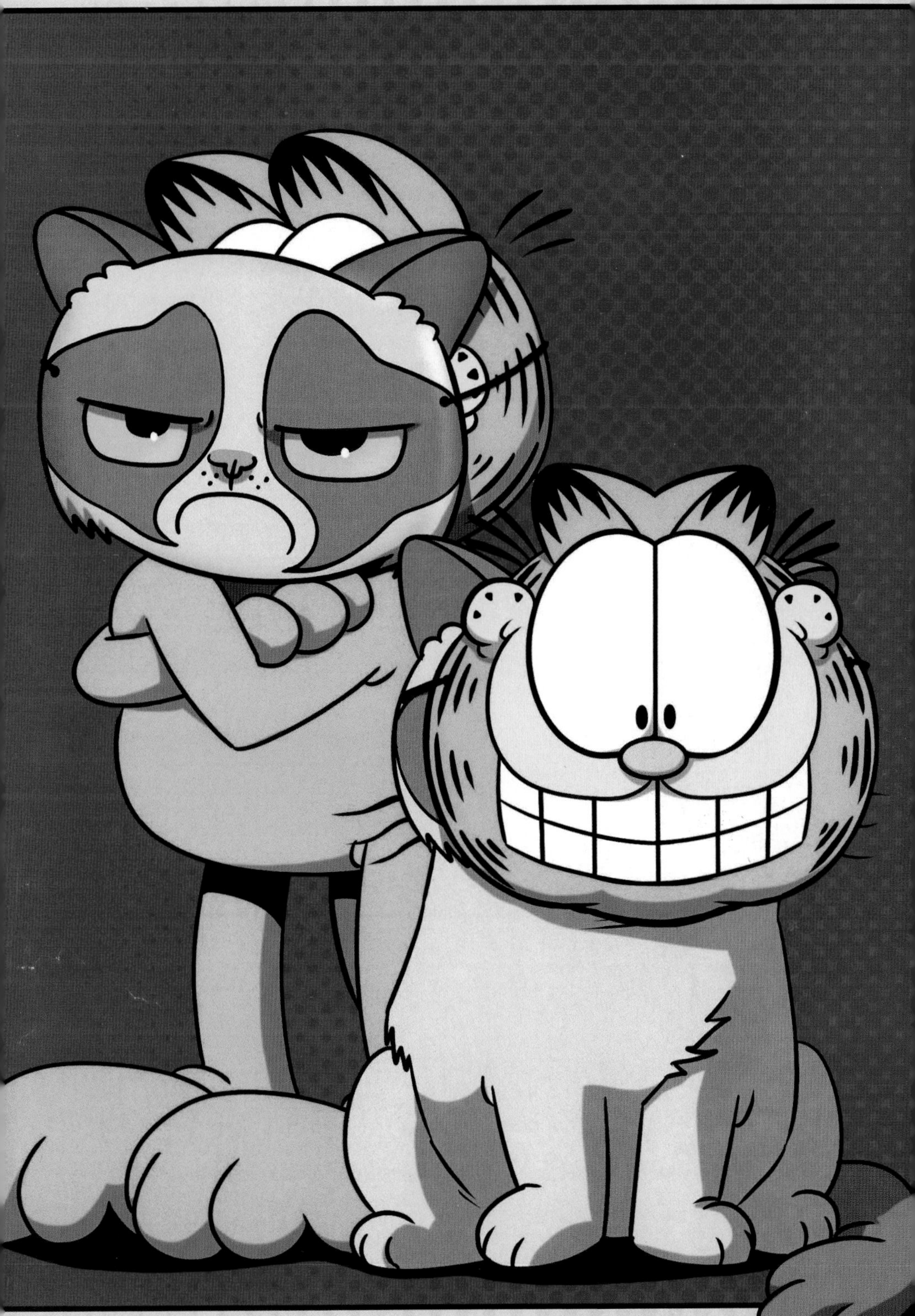

Grumpy Cat®

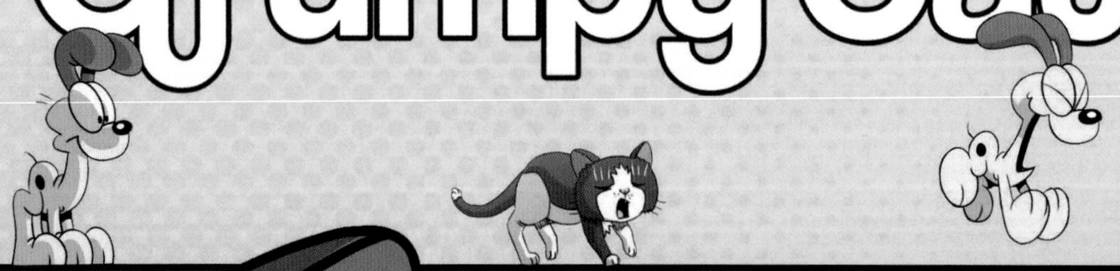

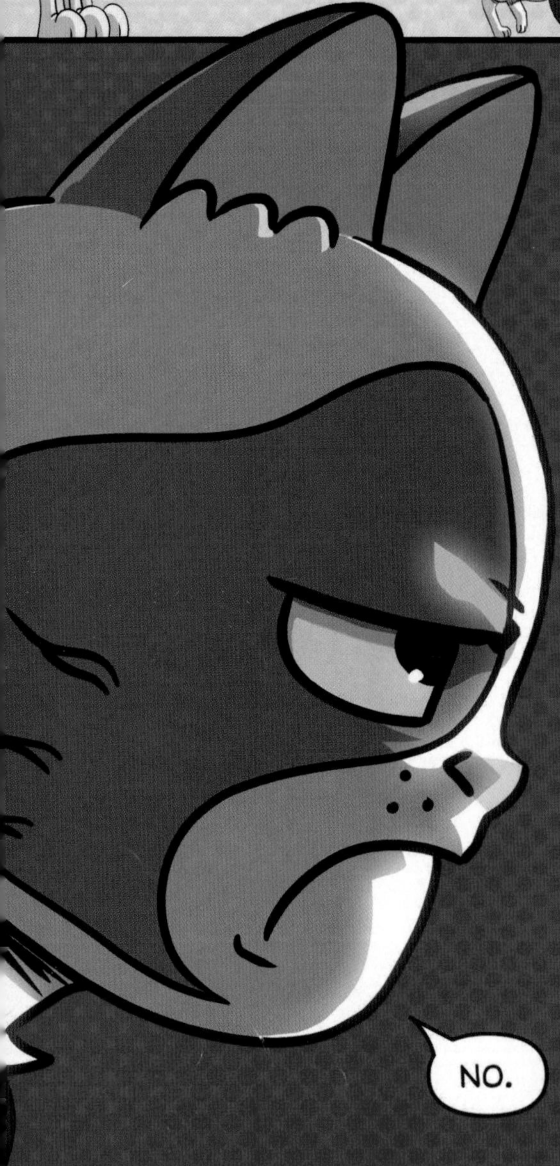
NO.

WRITTEN BY
MARK EVANIER

ART BY
STEVE UY

LETTERS BY
TOM NAPOLITANO

ORIGINAL SERIES EDITED BY
ANTHONY MARQUES

COLLECTION COVER ART BY
STEVE UY

COLLECTION DESIGN BY
JASON ULLMEYER

Garfield

BY JIM DAVIS ®

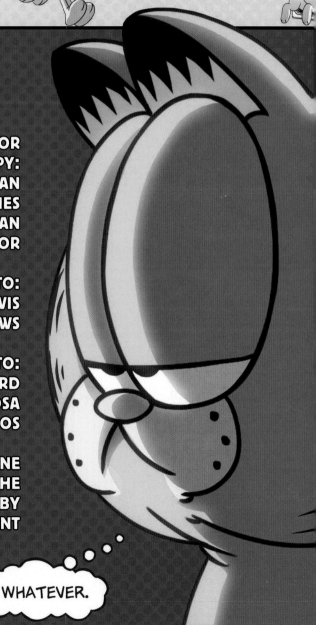

SPECIAL THANKS FOR
TEAM GRUMPY:
TABATHA BUNDESEN BRYAN
BUNDESEN BEN LASHES
KIA KAMRAN
HEATHER TAYLOR

SPECIAL THANKS TO:
JIM DAVIS
AND PAWS

SPECIAL THANKS TO:
WHITNEY LEOPARD
AND CHRIS ROSA
AT BOOM! STUDIOS

COLLECTING ISSUES ONE
THROUGH THREE OF THE
SERIES PUBLISHED BY
DYNAMITE ENTERTAINMENT

WHATEVER.

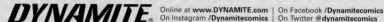

DYNAMITE®
Online at www.DYNAMITE.com | On Facebook /Dynamitecomics
On Instagram /Dynamitecomics | On Twitter @dynamitecomics

Nick Barrucci, CEO / Publisher • **Juan Collado**, President / COO

Joe Rybandt, Executive Editor • **Matt Idelson**, Senior Editor • **Anthony Marques**, Associate Editor • **Kevin Ketner**, Assistant Editor

Jason Ullmeyer, Art Director • **Geoff Harkins**, Senior Graphic Designer • **Cathleen Heard**, Graphic Designer
Alexis Persson, Graphic Designer • **Chris Caniano**, Digital Associate • **Rachel Kilbury**, Digital Assistant

Brandon Dante Primavera, V.P. of IT and Operations • **Rich Young**, Director of Business Development

Alan Payne, V.P. of Sales and Marketing • **Janie Mackenzie**, Marketing Coordinator • **Pat O'Connell**, Sales Manager

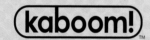
Online at www.BOOM-STUDIOS.com | On Facebook /BOOMStudiosComics
On Instagram @boom_studios | On Twitter @boomstudios

ROSS RICHIE CEO & Founder • **MATT GAGNON** Editor-in-Chief • **FILIP SABLIK** President of Publishing & Marketing
STEPHEN CHRISTY President of Development • **LANCE KREITER** VP of Licensing & Merchandising
PHIL BARBARO VP of Finance • **ARUNE SINGH** VP of Marketing • **BRYCE CARLSON** Managing Editor
MEL CAYLO Marketing Manager • **SCOTT NEWMAN** Production Design Manager • **KATE HENNING** Operations Manager
SIERRA HAHN Senior Editor • **DAFNA PLEBAN** Editor, Talent Development • **SHANNON WATTERS** Editor
ERIC HARBURN Editor • **WHITNEY LEOPARD** Editor • **CAMERON CHITTOCK** Editor • **CHRIS ROSA** Associate Editor
MATTHEW LEVINE Associate Editor • **SOPHIE PHILIPS-ROBERTS** Assistant Editor • **AMANDA LAFRANCO** Executive Assistant
KATALINA HOLLAND Editorial Administrative Assistant • **JILLIAN CRAB** Production Designer
MICHELLE ANKLEY Production Designer • **KARA LEOPARD** Production Designer • **MARIE KRUPINA** Production Designer
GRACE PARK Production Design Assistant • **CHELSEA ROBERTS** Production Design Assistant
ELIZABETH LOUGHRIDGE Accounting Coordinator • **STEPHANIE HOCUTT** Social Media Coordinator
JOSÉ MEZA Event Coordinator • **HOLLY AITCHISON** Operations Coordinator • **MEGAN CHRISTOPHER** Operations Assistant
RODRIGO HERNANDEZ Mailroom Assistant • **MORGAN PERRY** Direct Market Representative • **CAT O'GRADY** Marketing Assistant
LIZ ALMENDAREZ Accounting Administrative Assistant • **CORNELIA TZANA** Administrative Assistant

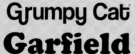
Online at www.GRUMPYCATS.com | On Facebook /TheOfficialGrumpyCat
On Instagram @RealGrumpyCat | On Twitter @RealGrumpyCat

Online at www.GARFIELD.com | On Facebook /GARFIELD
® On Twitter @Garfield

PEFC Certified
Printed on paper from
sustainably managed
forests and controlled
sources
PEFC/01-31-106   www.pefc.org

ISBN: 978-1-5241-0496-2
First Printing
10 9 8 7 6 5 4 3 2 1
Printed in Canada

CHAPTER

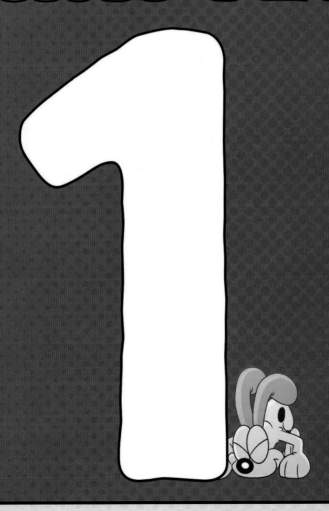

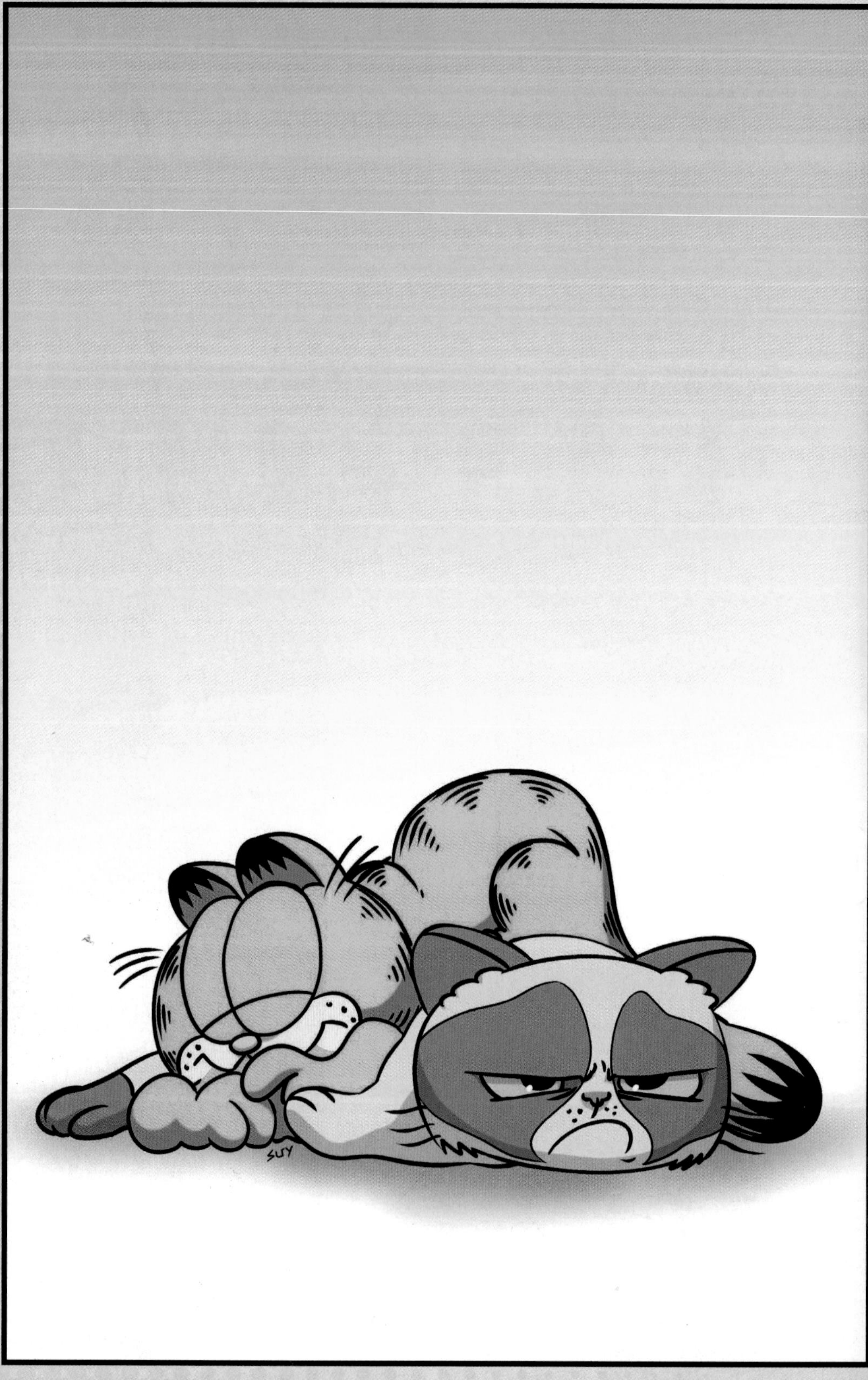
SUY

ISSUE 1 COVER BY: **STEVE UY**

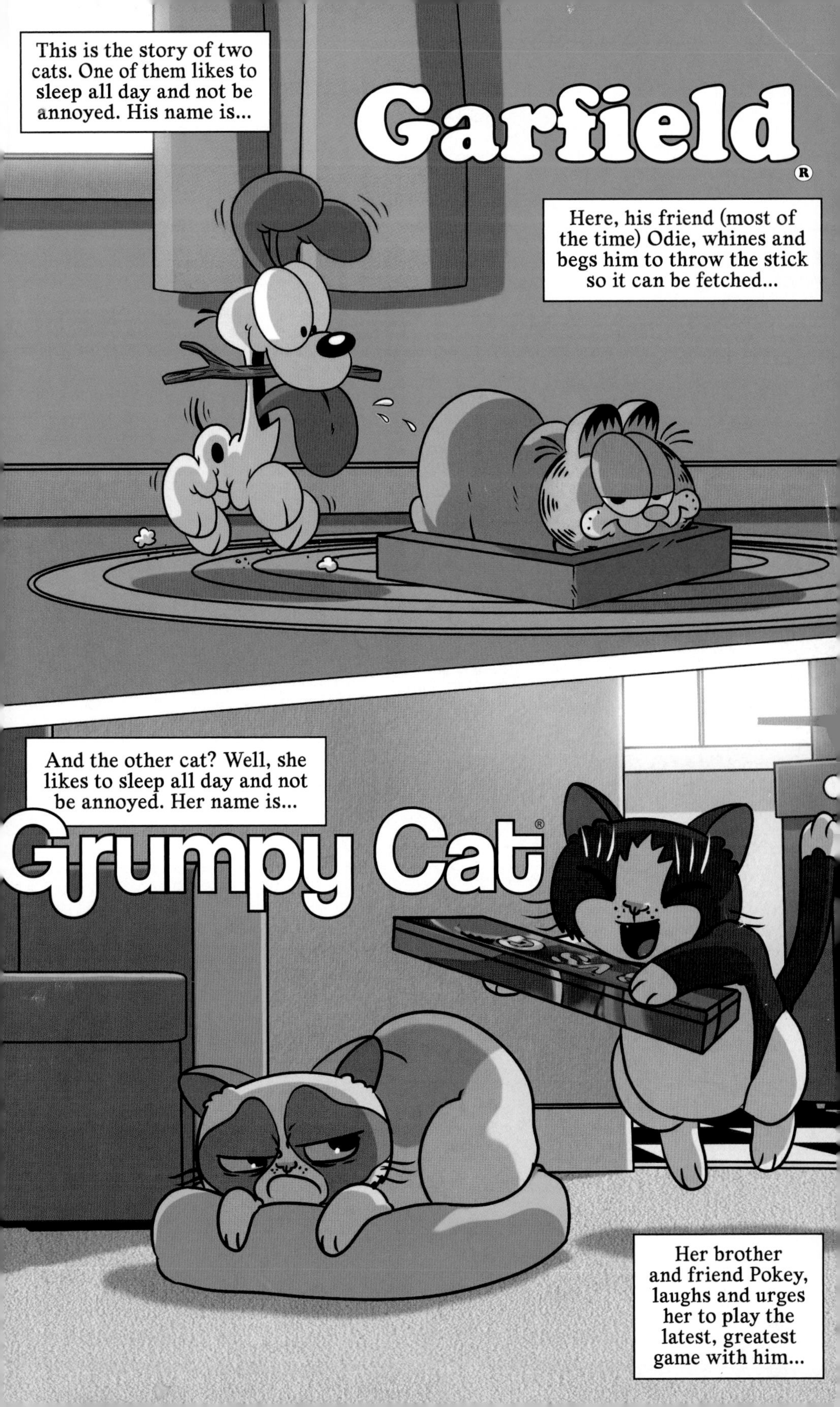

This is the story of two cats. One of them likes to sleep all day and not be annoyed. His name is...
Garfield®
Here, his friend (most of the time) Odie, whines and begs him to throw the stick so it can be fetched...
And the other cat? Well, she likes to sleep all day and not be annoyed. Her name is...
Grumpy Cat®
Her brother and friend Pokey, laughs and urges her to play the latest, greatest game with him...

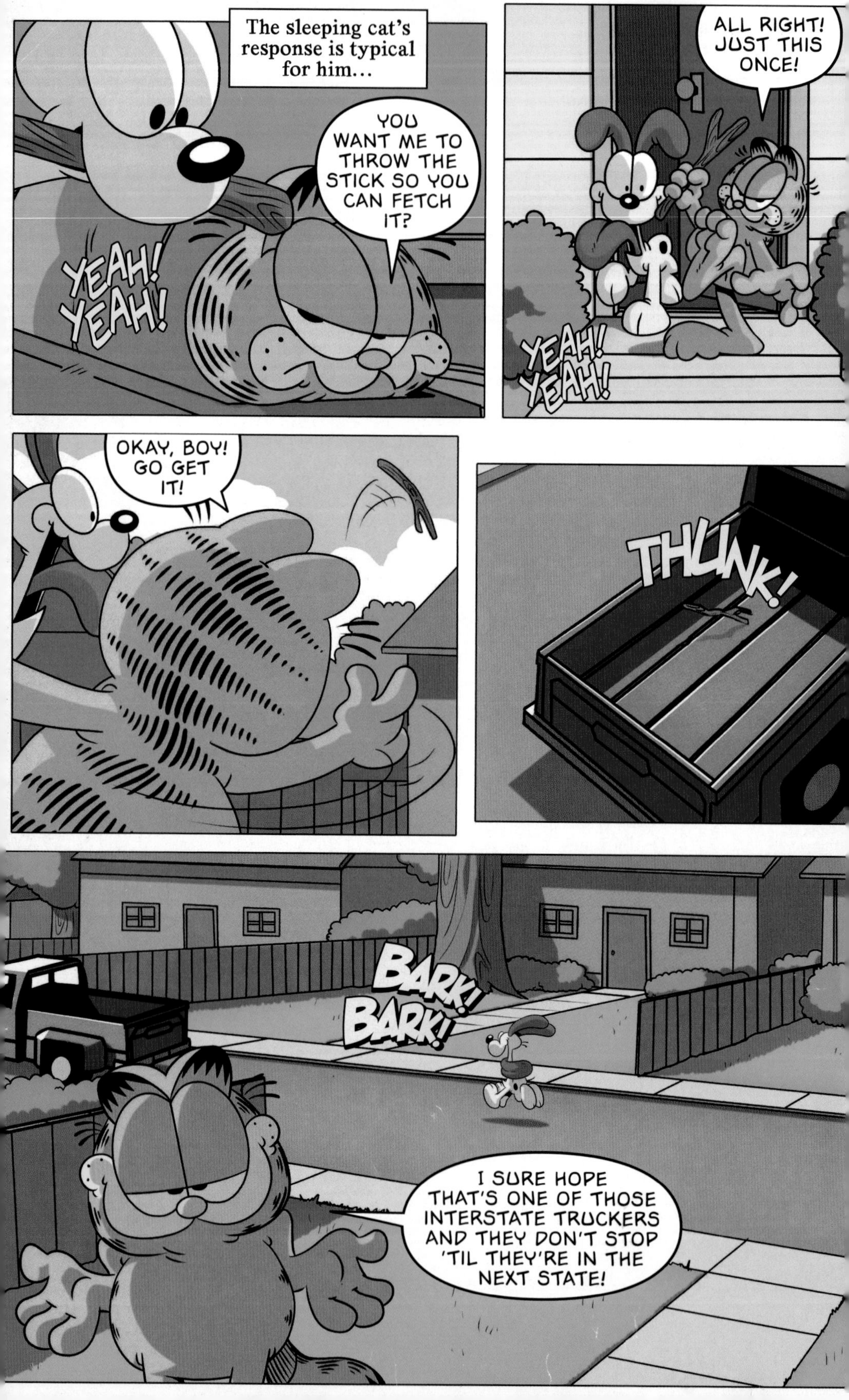

The sleeping cat's response is typical for him...
YOU WANT ME TO THROW THE STICK SO YOU CAN FETCH IT?
YEAH! YEAH!
ALL RIGHT! JUST THIS ONCE!
YEAH! YEAH!
OKAY, BOY! GO GET IT!
THUNK!
BARK! BARK!
I SURE HOPE THAT'S ONE OF THOSE INTERSTATE TRUCKERS AND THEY DON'T STOP 'TIL THEY'RE IN THE NEXT STATE!

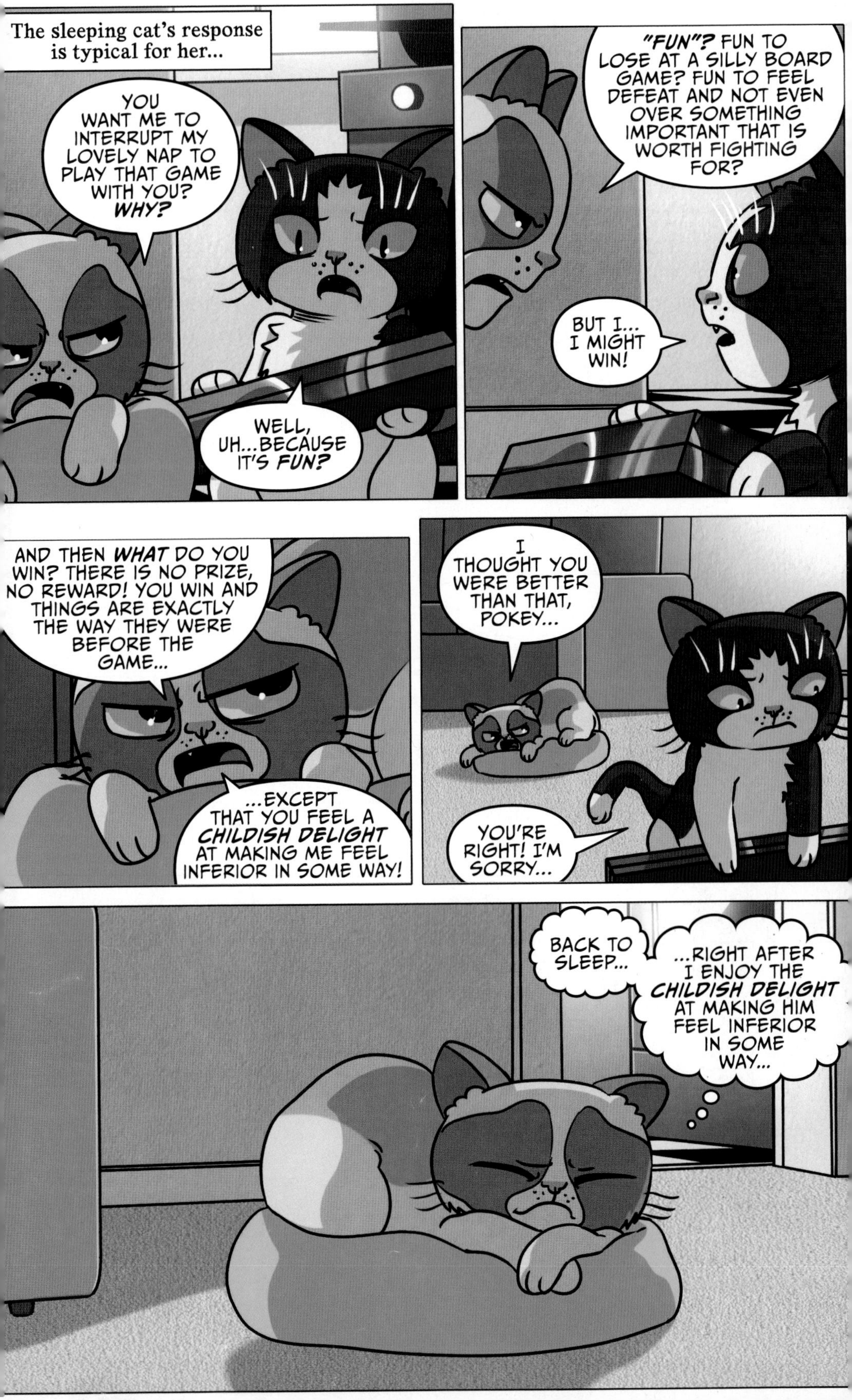
The sleeping cat's response is typical for her...
YOU WANT ME TO INTERRUPT MY LOVELY NAP TO PLAY THAT GAME WITH YOU? WHY?
WELL, UH...BECAUSE IT'S FUN?
"FUN"? FUN TO LOSE AT A SILLY BOARD GAME? FUN TO FEEL DEFEAT AND NOT EVEN OVER SOMETHING IMPORTANT THAT IS WORTH FIGHTING FOR?
BUT I... I MIGHT WIN!
AND THEN WHAT DO YOU WIN? THERE IS NO PRIZE, NO REWARD! YOU WIN AND THINGS ARE EXACTLY THE WAY THEY WERE BEFORE THE GAME...
...EXCEPT THAT YOU FEEL A CHILDISH DELIGHT AT MAKING ME FEEL INFERIOR IN SOME WAY!
I THOUGHT YOU WERE BETTER THAN THAT, POKEY...
YOU'RE RIGHT! I'M SORRY...
BACK TO SLEEP...
...RIGHT AFTER I ENJOY THE CHILDISH DELIGHT AT MAKING HIM FEEL INFERIOR IN SOME WAY...

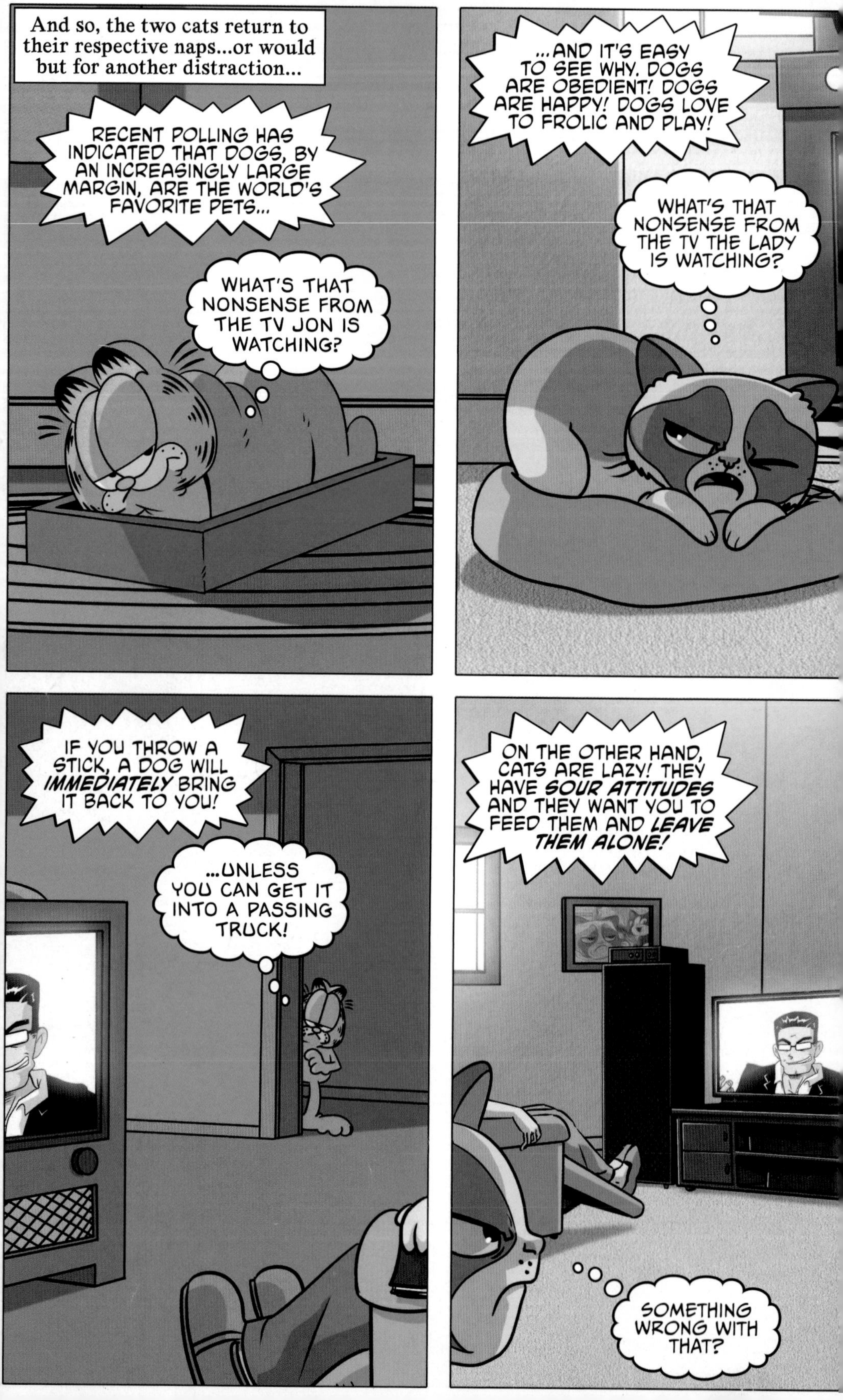
And so, the two cats return to their respective naps...or would but for another distraction...
RECENT POLLING HAS INDICATED THAT DOGS, BY AN INCREASINGLY LARGE MARGIN, ARE THE WORLD'S FAVORITE PETS...
WHAT'S THAT NONSENSE FROM THE TV JON IS WATCHING?
...AND IT'S EASY TO SEE WHY. DOGS ARE OBEDIENT! DOGS ARE HAPPY! DOGS LOVE TO FROLIC AND PLAY!
WHAT'S THAT NONSENSE FROM THE TV THE LADY IS WATCHING?
IF YOU THROW A STICK, A DOG WILL IMMEDIATELY BRING IT BACK TO YOU!
...UNLESS YOU CAN GET IT INTO A PASSING TRUCK!
ON THE OTHER HAND, CATS ARE LAZY! THEY HAVE SOUR ATTITUDES AND THEY WANT YOU TO FEED THEM AND LEAVE THEM ALONE!
SOMETHING WRONG WITH THAT?

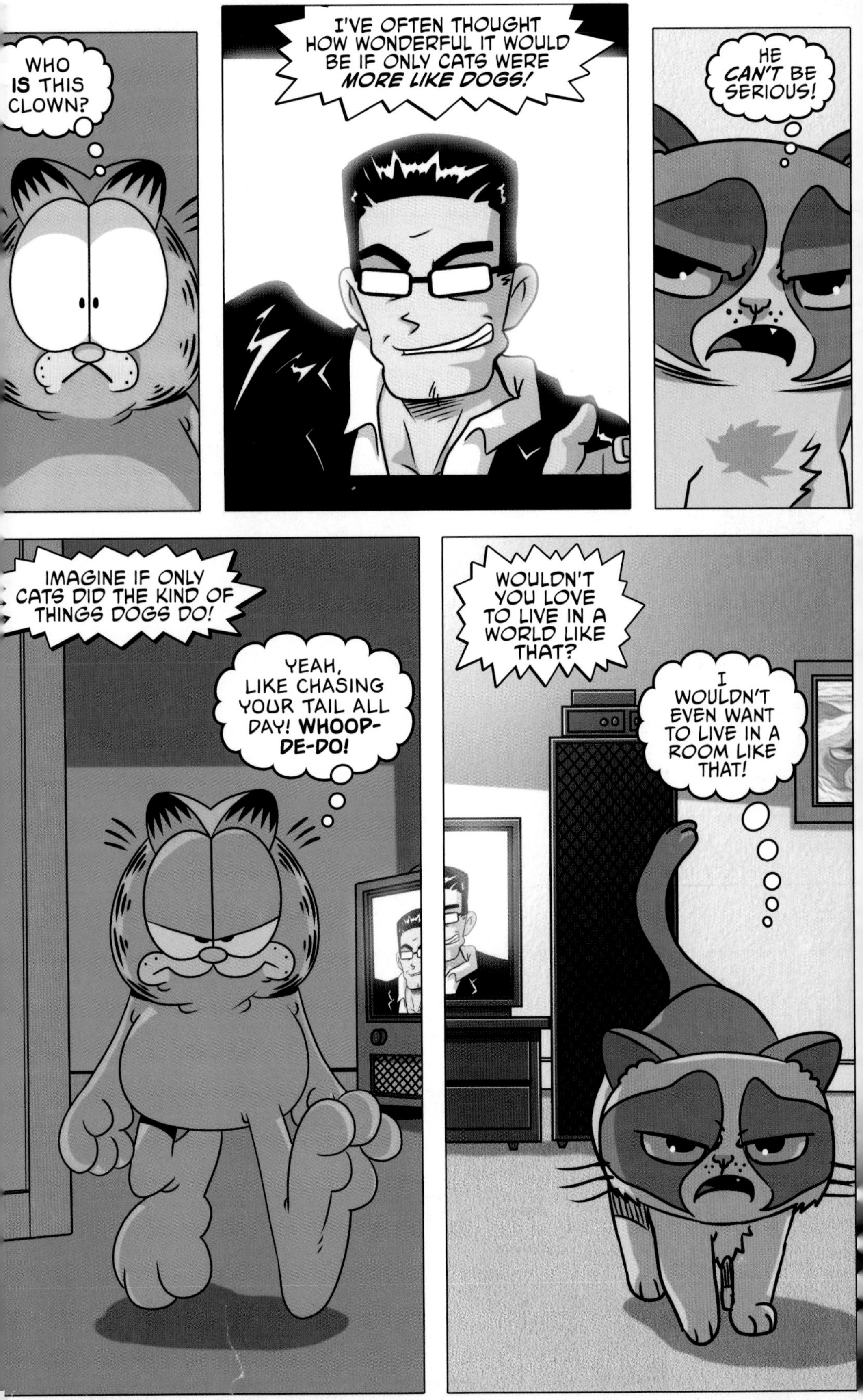
WHO IS THIS CLOWN?
I'VE OFTEN THOUGHT HOW WONDERFUL IT WOULD BE IF ONLY CATS WERE MORE LIKE DOGS!
HE CAN'T BE SERIOUS!
IMAGINE IF ONLY CATS DID THE KIND OF THINGS DOGS DO!
YEAH, LIKE CHASING YOUR TAIL ALL DAY! WHOOP-DE-DO!
WOULDN'T YOU LOVE TO LIVE IN A WORLD LIKE THAT?
I WOULDN'T EVEN WANT TO LIVE IN A ROOM LIKE THAT!

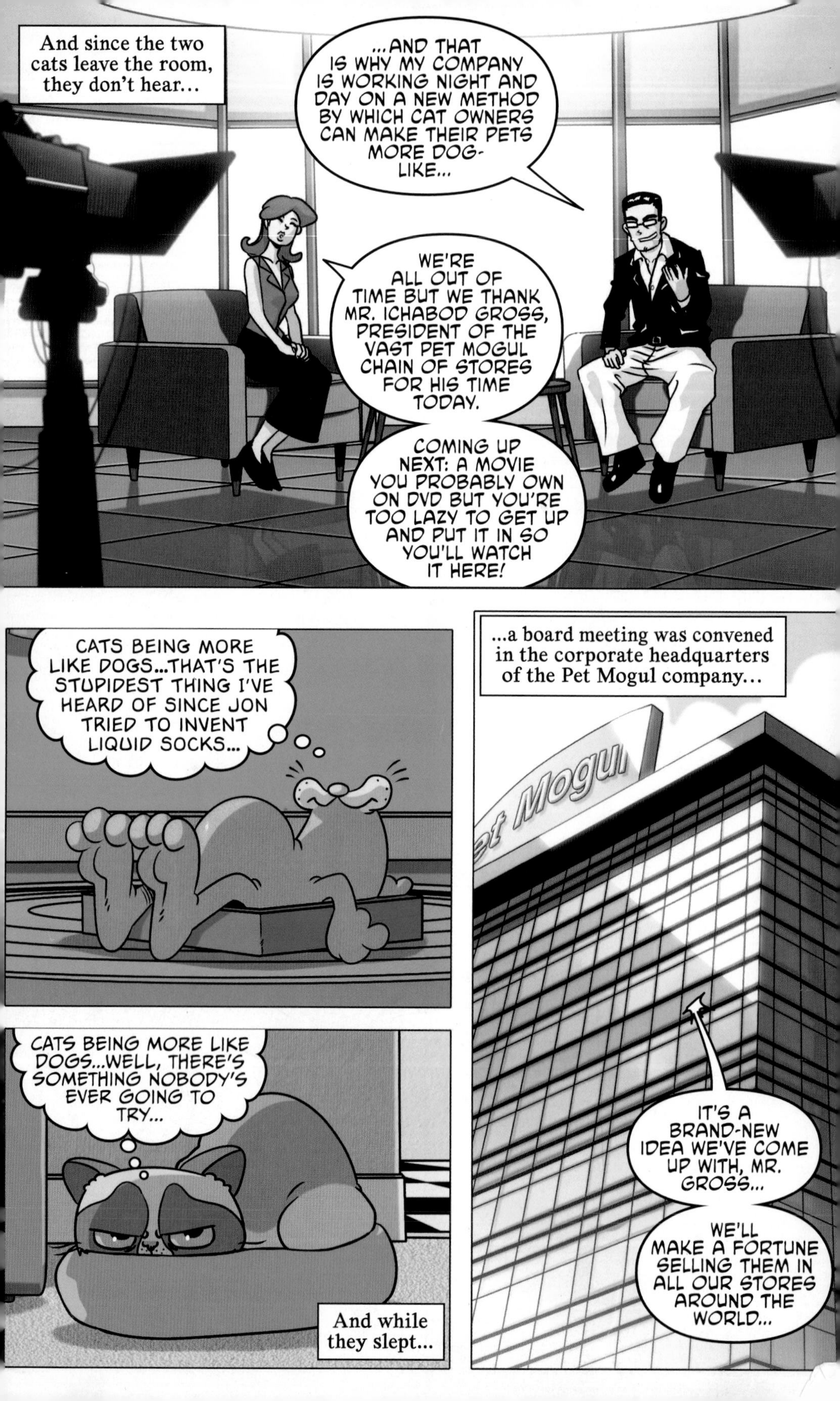

And since the two cats leave the room, they don't hear…
...AND THAT IS WHY MY COMPANY IS WORKING NIGHT AND DAY ON A NEW METHOD BY WHICH CAT OWNERS CAN MAKE THEIR PETS MORE DOG-LIKE...
WE'RE ALL OUT OF TIME BUT WE THANK MR. ICHABOD GROSS, PRESIDENT OF THE VAST PET MOGUL CHAIN OF STORES FOR HIS TIME TODAY.
COMING UP NEXT: A MOVIE YOU PROBABLY OWN ON DVD BUT YOU'RE TOO LAZY TO GET UP AND PUT IT IN SO YOU'LL WATCH IT HERE!
CATS BEING MORE LIKE DOGS...THAT'S THE STUPIDEST THING I'VE HEARD OF SINCE JON TRIED TO INVENT LIQUID SOCKS...
CATS BEING MORE LIKE DOGS...WELL, THERE'S SOMETHING NOBODY'S EVER GOING TO TRY...
And while they slept...
...a board meeting was convened in the corporate headquarters of the Pet Mogul company…
et Mogul
IT'S A BRAND-NEW IDEA WE'VE COME UP WITH, MR. GROSS...
WE'LL MAKE A FORTUNE SELLING THEM IN ALL OUR STORES AROUND THE WORLD...

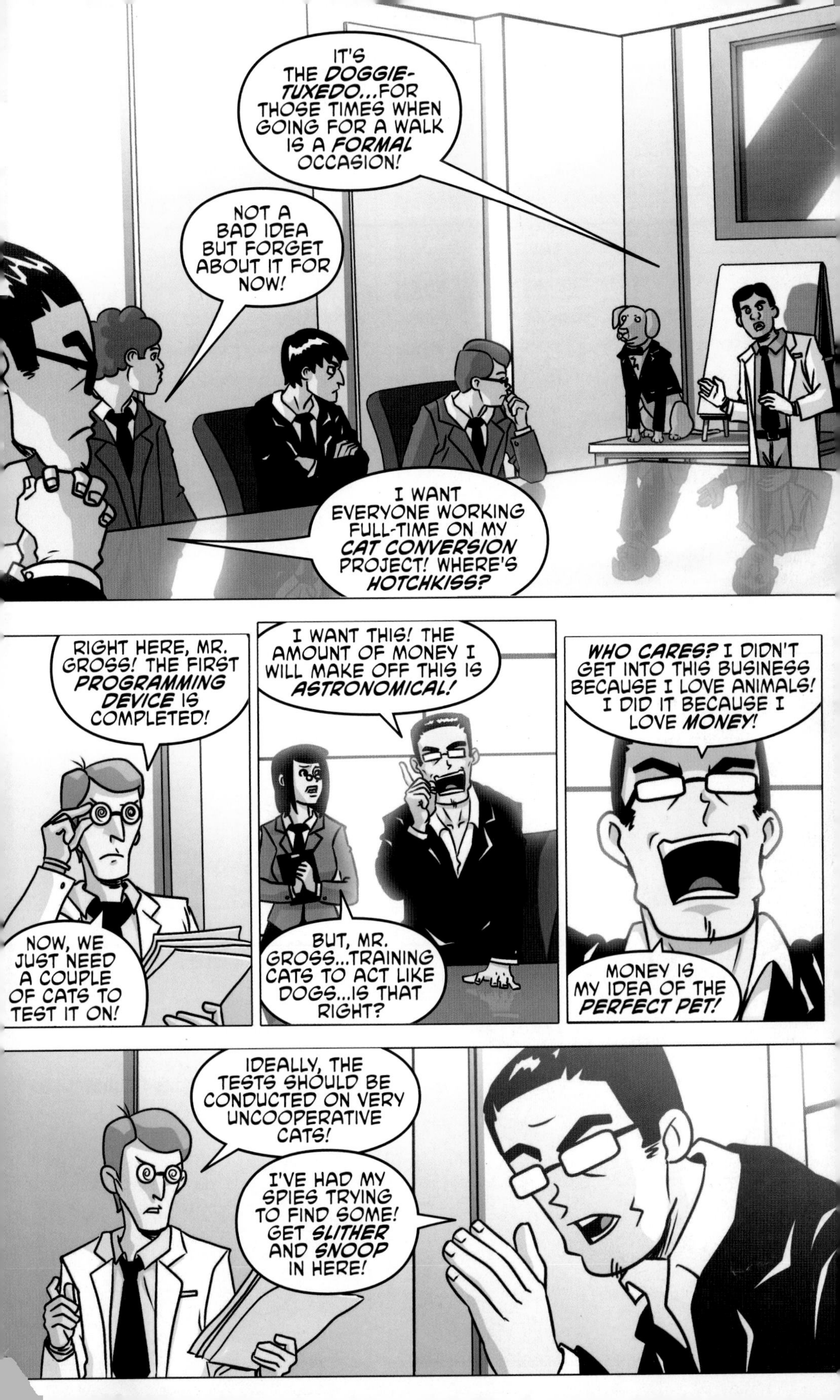
IT'S THE DOGGIE-TUXEDO...FOR THOSE TIMES WHEN GOING FOR A WALK IS A FORMAL OCCASION!
NOT A BAD IDEA BUT FORGET ABOUT IT FOR NOW!
I WANT EVERYONE WORKING FULL-TIME ON MY CAT CONVERSION PROJECT! WHERE'S HOTCHKISS?
RIGHT HERE, MR. GROSS! THE FIRST PROGRAMMING DEVICE IS COMPLETED!
NOW, WE JUST NEED A COUPLE OF CATS TO TEST IT ON!
I WANT THIS! THE AMOUNT OF MONEY I WILL MAKE OFF THIS IS ASTRONOMICAL!
BUT, MR. GROSS...TRAINING CATS TO ACT LIKE DOGS...IS THAT RIGHT?
WHO CARES? I DIDN'T GET INTO THIS BUSINESS BECAUSE I LOVE ANIMALS! I DID IT BECAUSE I LOVE MONEY!
MONEY IS MY IDEA OF THE PERFECT PET!
IDEALLY, THE TESTS SHOULD BE CONDUCTED ON VERY UNCOOPERATIVE CATS!
I'VE HAD MY SPIES TRYING TO FIND SOME! GET SLITHER AND SNOOP IN HERE!

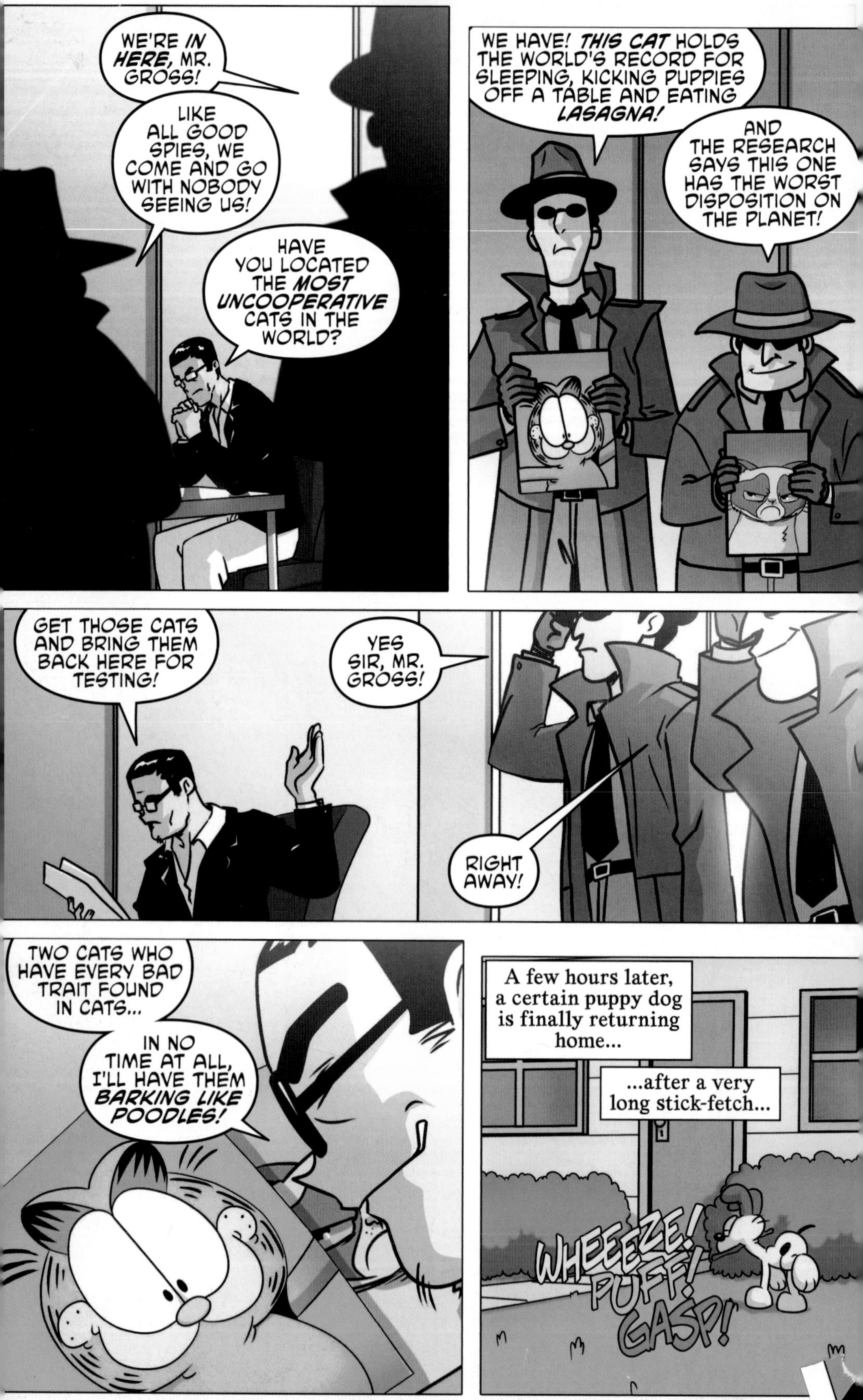
WE'RE *IN HERE,* MR. GROSS!
LIKE ALL GOOD SPIES, WE COME AND GO WITH NOBODY SEEING US!
HAVE YOU LOCATED THE ***MOST UNCOOPERATIVE*** CATS IN THE WORLD?
WE HAVE! ***THIS CAT*** HOLDS THE WORLD'S RECORD FOR SLEEPING, KICKING PUPPIES OFF A TABLE AND EATING ***LASAGNA!***
AND THE RESEARCH SAYS THIS ONE HAS THE WORST DISPOSITION ON THE PLANET!
GET THOSE CATS AND BRING THEM BACK HERE FOR TESTING!
YES SIR, MR. GROSS!
RIGHT AWAY!
TWO CATS WHO HAVE EVERY BAD TRAIT FOUND IN CATS...
IN NO TIME AT ALL, I'LL HAVE THEM ***BARKING LIKE POODLES!***
A few hours later, a certain puppy dog is finally returning home...
...after a very long stick-fetch...
WHEEEZE! PUFF! GASP!

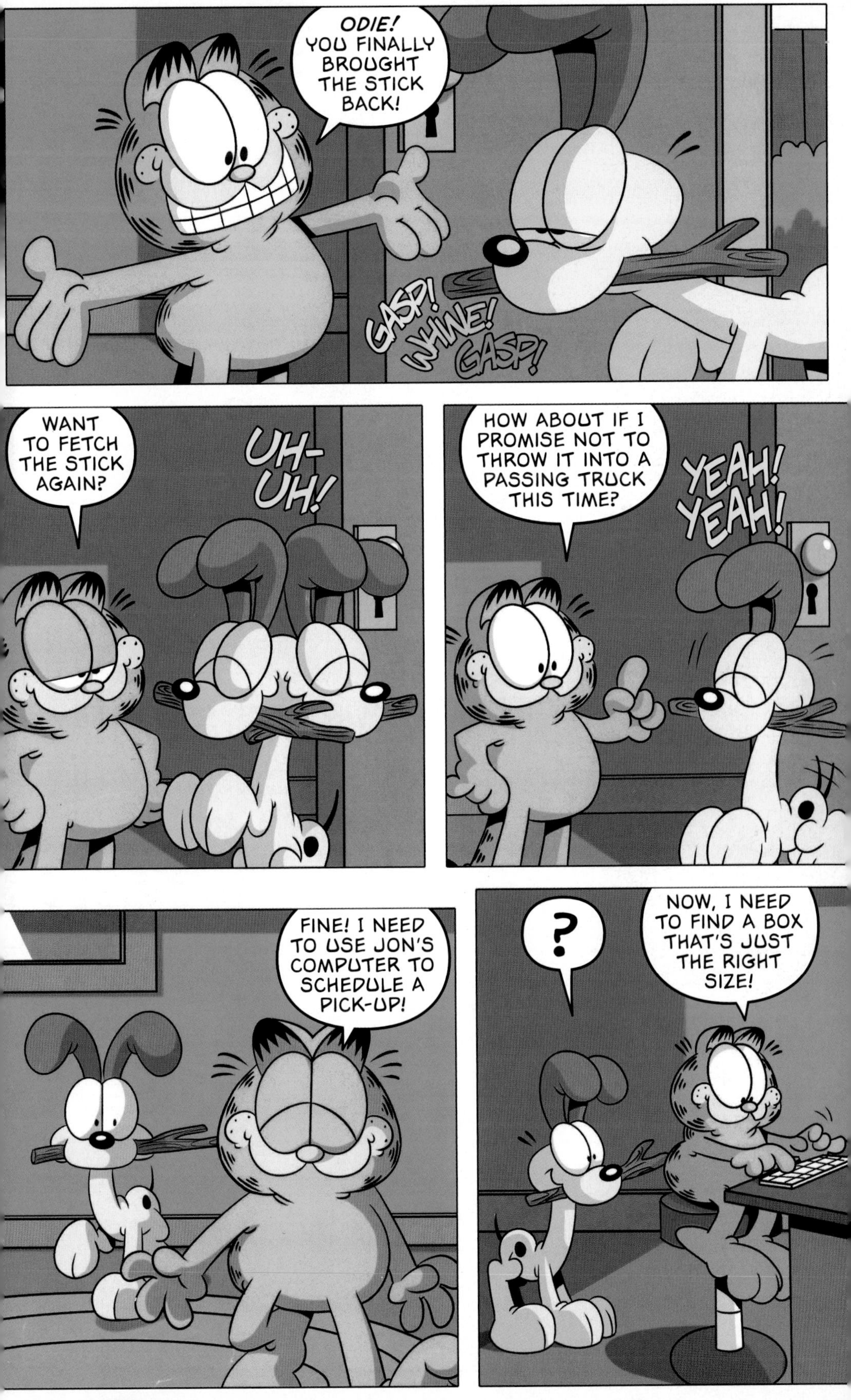

ODIE! YOU FINALLY BROUGHT THE STICK BACK!
GASP! WHINE! GASP!
WANT TO FETCH THE STICK AGAIN?
UH-UH!
HOW ABOUT IF I PROMISE NOT TO THROW IT INTO A PASSING TRUCK THIS TIME?
YEAH! YEAH!
FINE! I NEED TO USE JON'S COMPUTER TO SCHEDULE A PICK-UP!
?
NOW, I NEED TO FIND A BOX THAT'S JUST THE RIGHT SIZE!

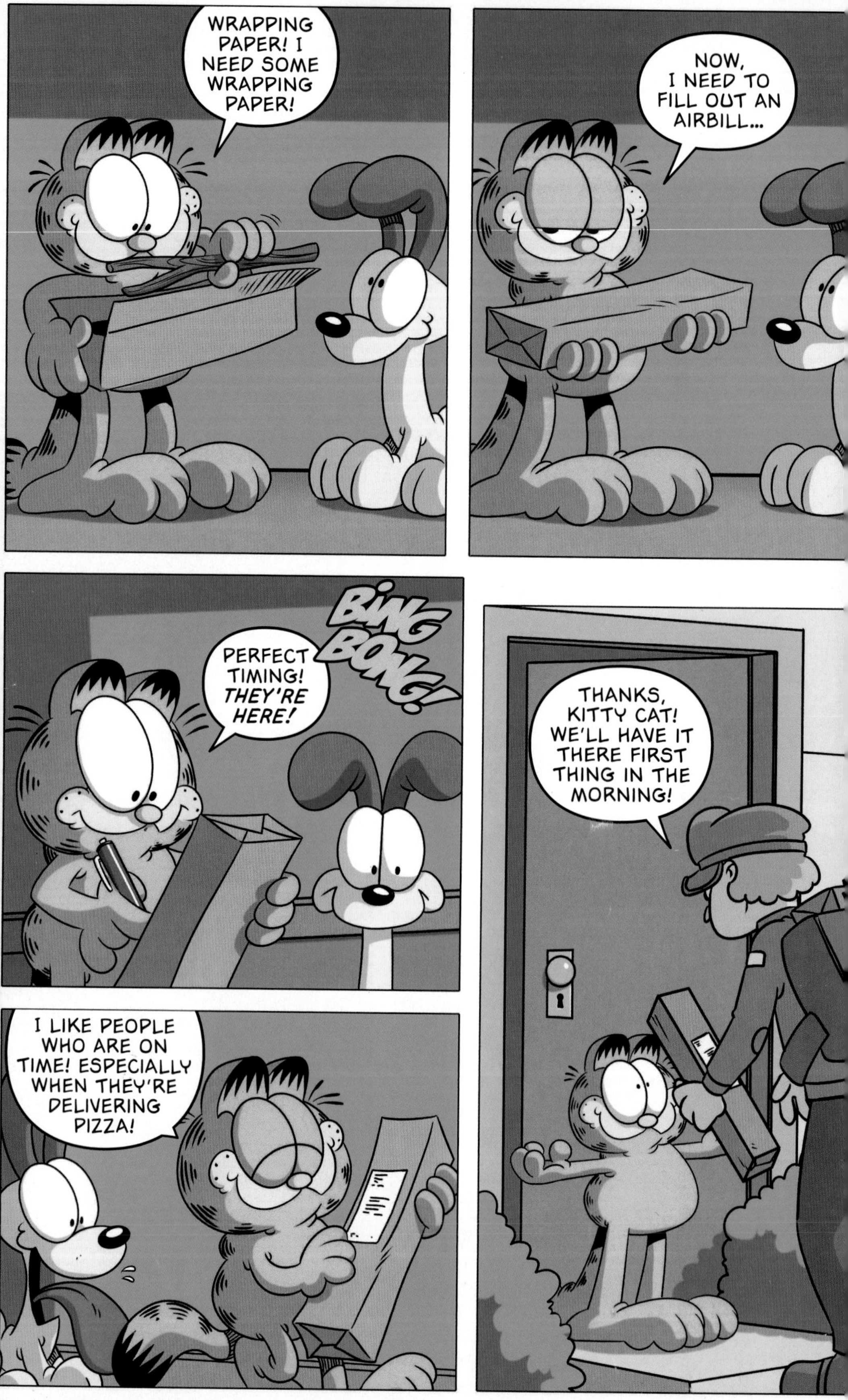
WRAPPING PAPER! I NEED SOME WRAPPING PAPER!
NOW, I NEED TO FILL OUT AN AIRBILL...
PERFECT TIMING! *THEY'RE HERE!*
BING BONG!
I LIKE PEOPLE WHO ARE ON TIME! ESPECIALLY WHEN THEY'RE DELIVERING PIZZA!
THANKS, KITTY CAT! WE'LL HAVE IT THERE FIRST THING IN THE MORNING!

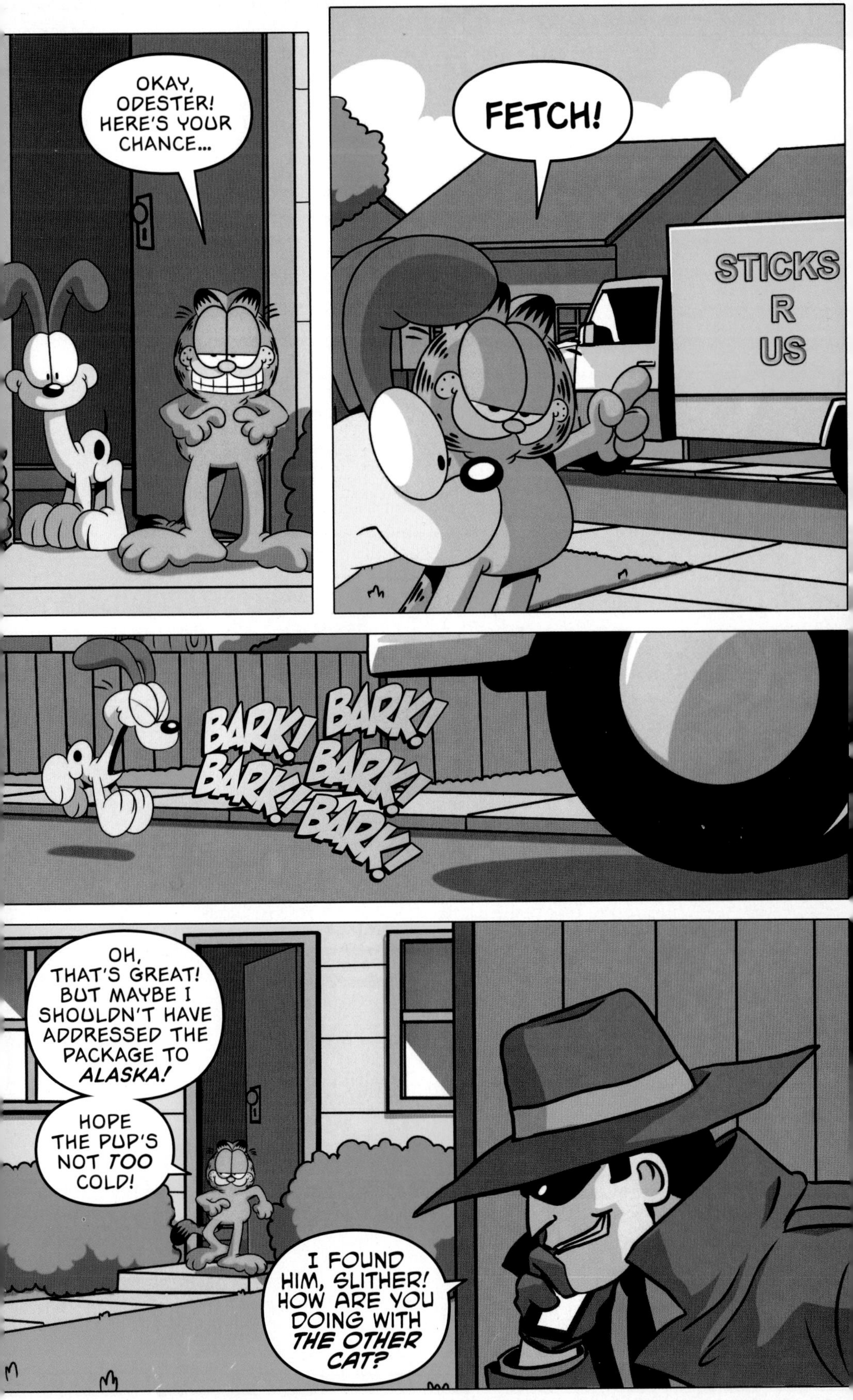
OKAY, ODESTER! HERE'S YOUR CHANCE...
FETCH!
STICKS R US
BARK! BARK! BARK! BARK! BARK! BARK!
OH, THAT'S GREAT! BUT MAYBE I SHOULDN'T HAVE ADDRESSED THE PACKAGE TO *ALASKA!*
HOPE THE PUP'S NOT *TOO* COLD!
I FOUND HIM, SLITHER! HOW ARE YOU DOING WITH *THE OTHER CAT?*

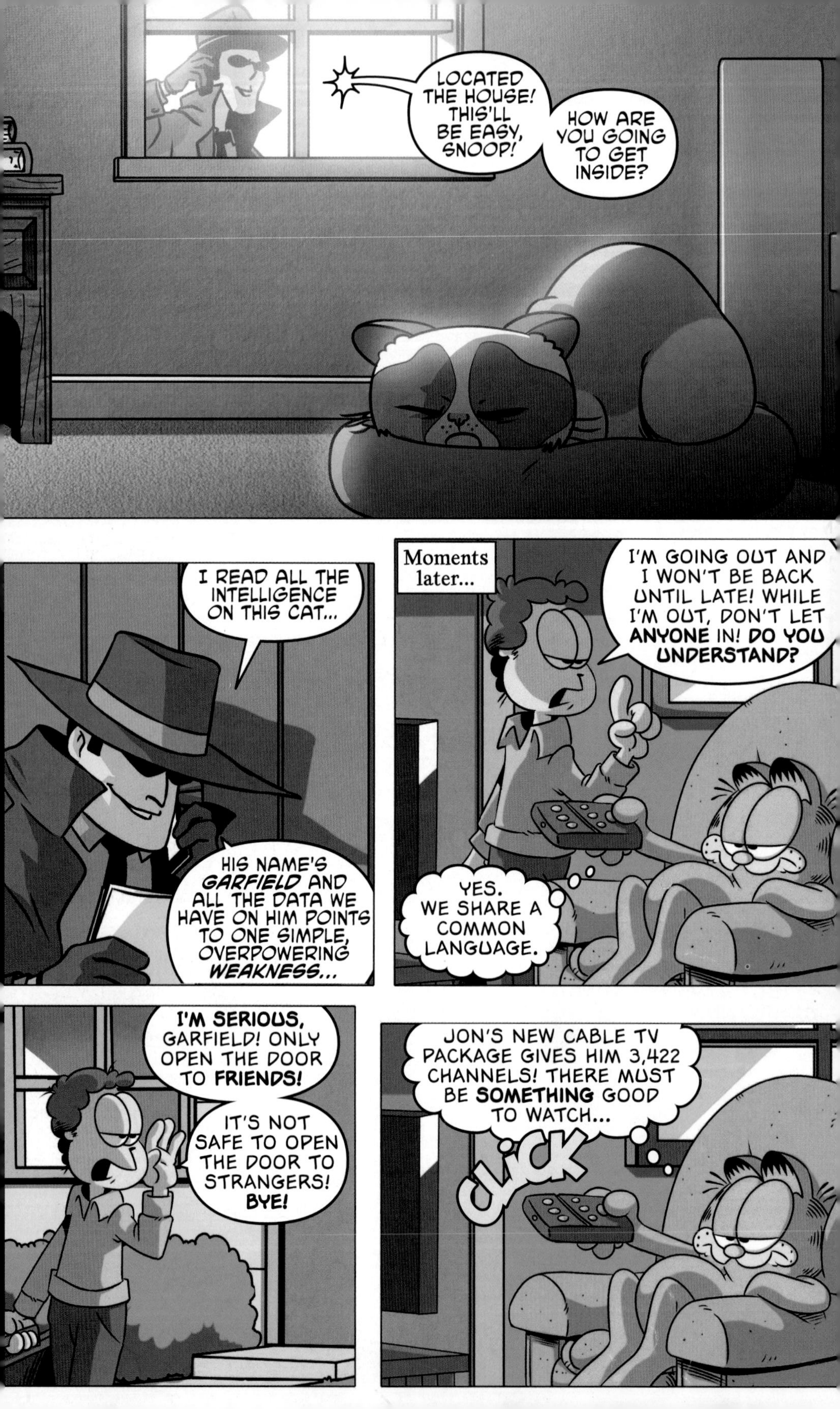
LOCATED THE HOUSE! THIS'LL BE EASY, SNOOP!
HOW ARE YOU GOING TO GET INSIDE?
I READ ALL THE INTELLIGENCE ON THIS CAT...
HIS NAME'S GARFIELD AND ALL THE DATA WE HAVE ON HIM POINTS TO ONE SIMPLE, OVERPOWERING WEAKNESS...
Moments later...
I'M GOING OUT AND I WON'T BE BACK UNTIL LATE! WHILE I'M OUT, DON'T LET ANYONE IN! DO YOU UNDERSTAND?
YES. WE SHARE A COMMON LANGUAGE.
I'M SERIOUS, GARFIELD! ONLY OPEN THE DOOR TO FRIENDS!
IT'S NOT SAFE TO OPEN THE DOOR TO STRANGERS! BYE!
JON'S NEW CABLE TV PACKAGE GIVES HIM 3,422 CHANNELS! THERE MUST BE SOMETHING GOOD TO WATCH...
CLICK

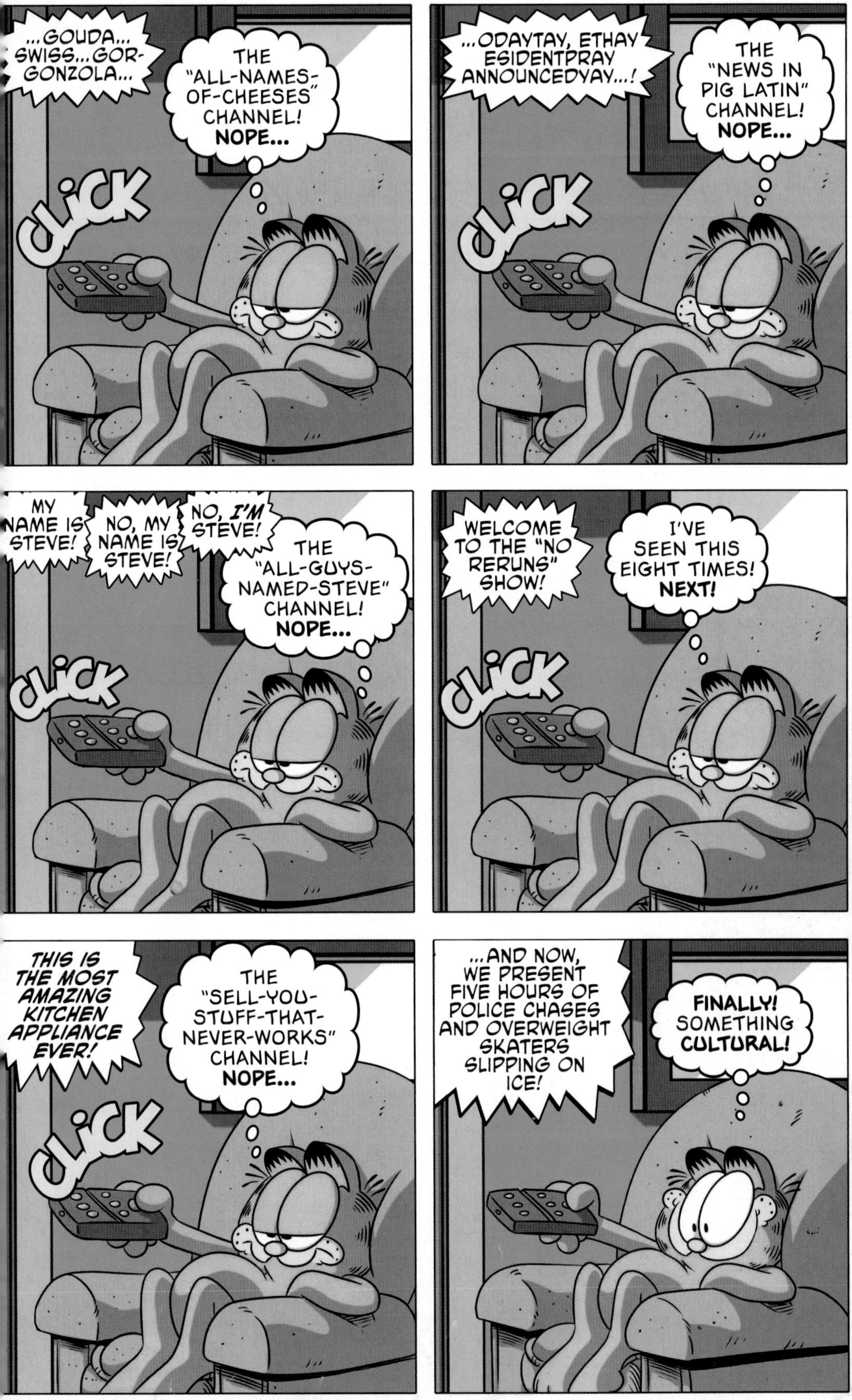

...GOUDA... SWISS...GOR-GONZOLA...
THE "ALL-NAMES-OF-CHEESES" CHANNEL! **NOPE...**
CLICK
...ODAYTAY, ETHAY ESIDENTPRAY ANNOUNCEDYAY...!
THE "NEWS IN PIG LATIN" CHANNEL! **NOPE...**
CLICK
MY NAME IS STEVE!
NO, MY NAME IS STEVE!
NO, *I'M* STEVE!
THE "ALL-GUYS-NAMED-STEVE" CHANNEL! **NOPE...**
CLICK
WELCOME TO THE "NO RERUNS" SHOW!
I'VE SEEN THIS EIGHT TIMES! **NEXT!**
CLICK
THIS IS THE MOST AMAZING KITCHEN APPLIANCE EVER!
THE "SELL-YOU-STUFF-THAT-NEVER-WORKS" CHANNEL! **NOPE...**
CLICK
...AND NOW, WE PRESENT FIVE HOURS OF POLICE CHASES AND OVERWEIGHT SKATERS SLIPPING ON ICE!
FINALLY! SOMETHING **CULTURAL!**

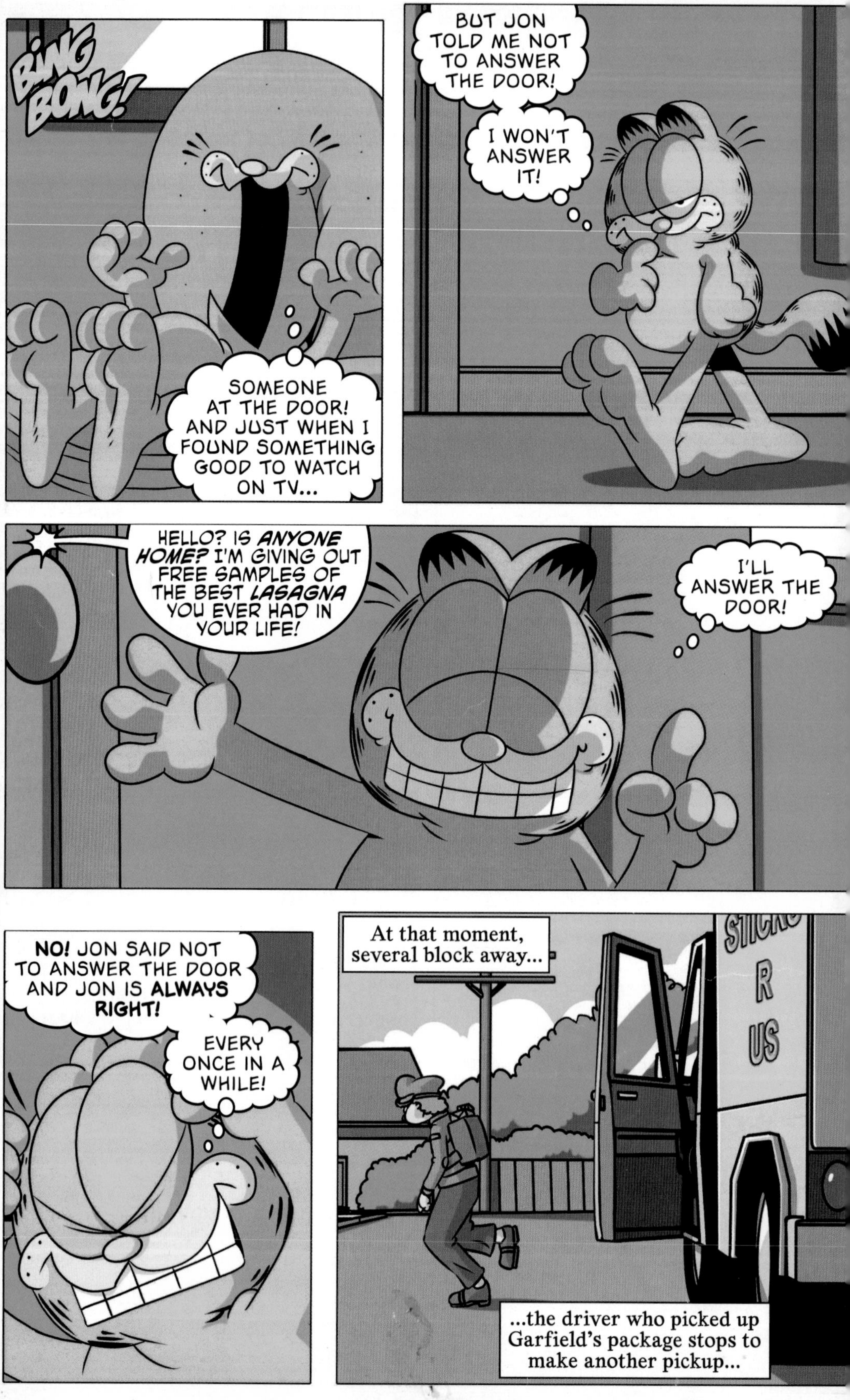

BING BONG!
SOMEONE AT THE DOOR! AND JUST WHEN I FOUND SOMETHING GOOD TO WATCH ON TV...
BUT JON TOLD ME NOT TO ANSWER THE DOOR!
I WON'T ANSWER IT!
HELLO? IS ANYONE HOME? I'M GIVING OUT FREE SAMPLES OF THE BEST LASAGNA YOU EVER HAD IN YOUR LIFE!
I'LL ANSWER THE DOOR!
NO! JON SAID NOT TO ANSWER THE DOOR AND JON IS ALWAYS RIGHT!
EVERY ONCE IN A WHILE!
At that moment, several block away...
R
US
...the driver who picked up Garfield's package stops to make another pickup...

...giving someone the chance to hop on...

...and hop off...

While...

IF YOU'RE IN THERE, OPEN UP!

OTHERWISE, I'LL HAVE TO GIVE ALL THIS *DELICIOUS, FREE LASAGNA* TO SOMEONE ELSE!

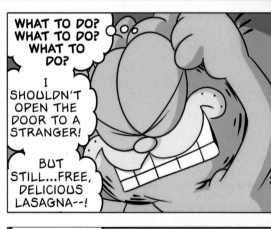

WHAT TO DO? WHAT TO DO? **WHAT TO DO?**

I SHOULDN'T OPEN THE DOOR TO A STRANGER!

BUT STILL...FREE, DELICIOUS LASAGNA--!

WAIT A SECOND! JON SAID I COULD OPEN THE DOOR TO **FRIENDS!**

AND ANYONE WHO GIVES YOU **FREE, DELICIOUS LASAGNA** IS A **FRIEND** IN MY BOOK!

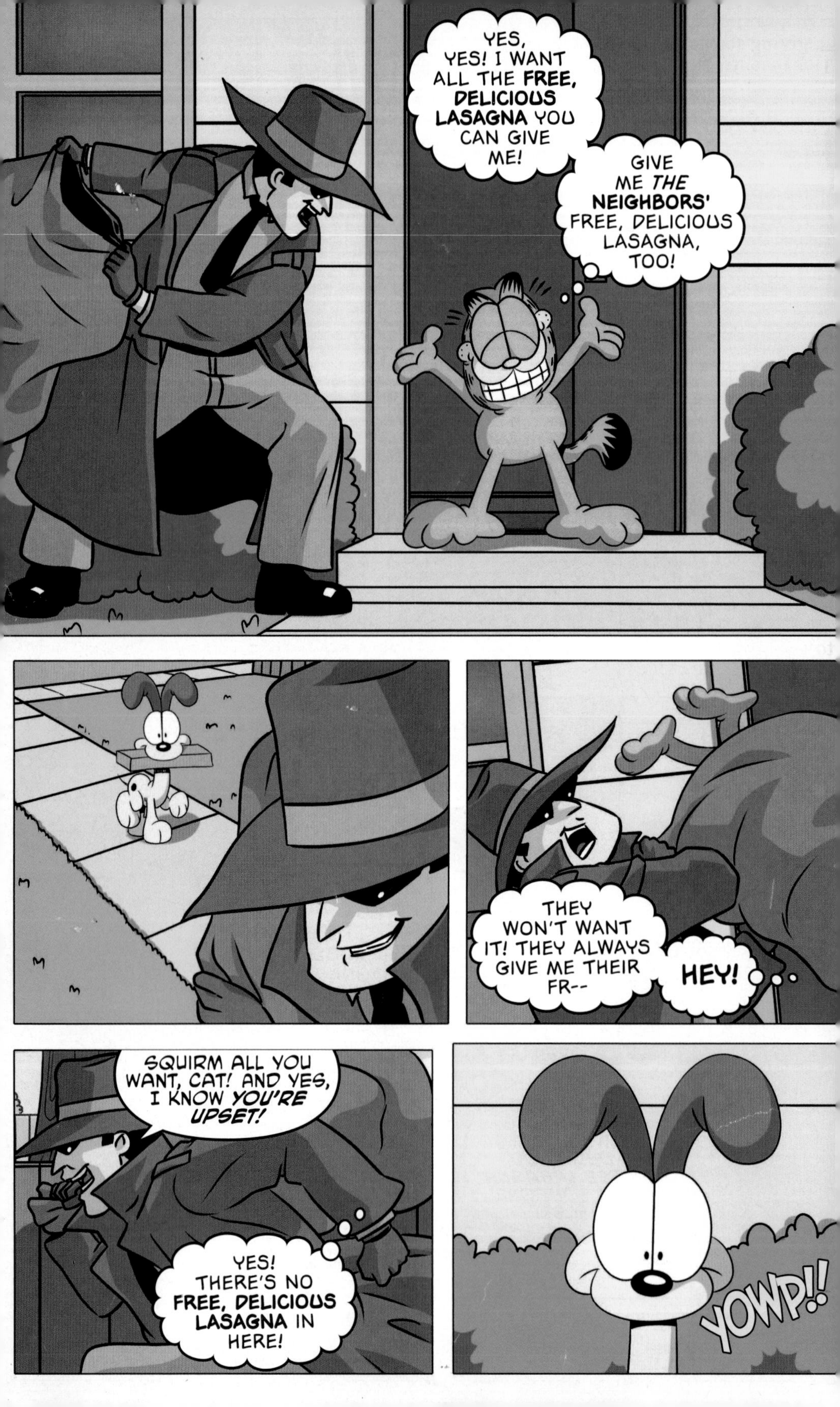

YES, YES! I WANT ALL THE **FREE, DELICIOUS LASAGNA** YOU CAN GIVE ME!
GIVE ME *THE* **NEIGHBORS'** FREE, DELICIOUS LASAGNA, TOO!
THEY WON'T WANT IT! THEY ALWAYS GIVE ME THEIR FR--
HEY!
SQUIRM ALL YOU WANT, CAT! AND YES, I KNOW *YOU'RE UPSET!*
YES! THERE'S NO **FREE, DELICIOUS LASAGNA** IN HERE!
YOWP!!

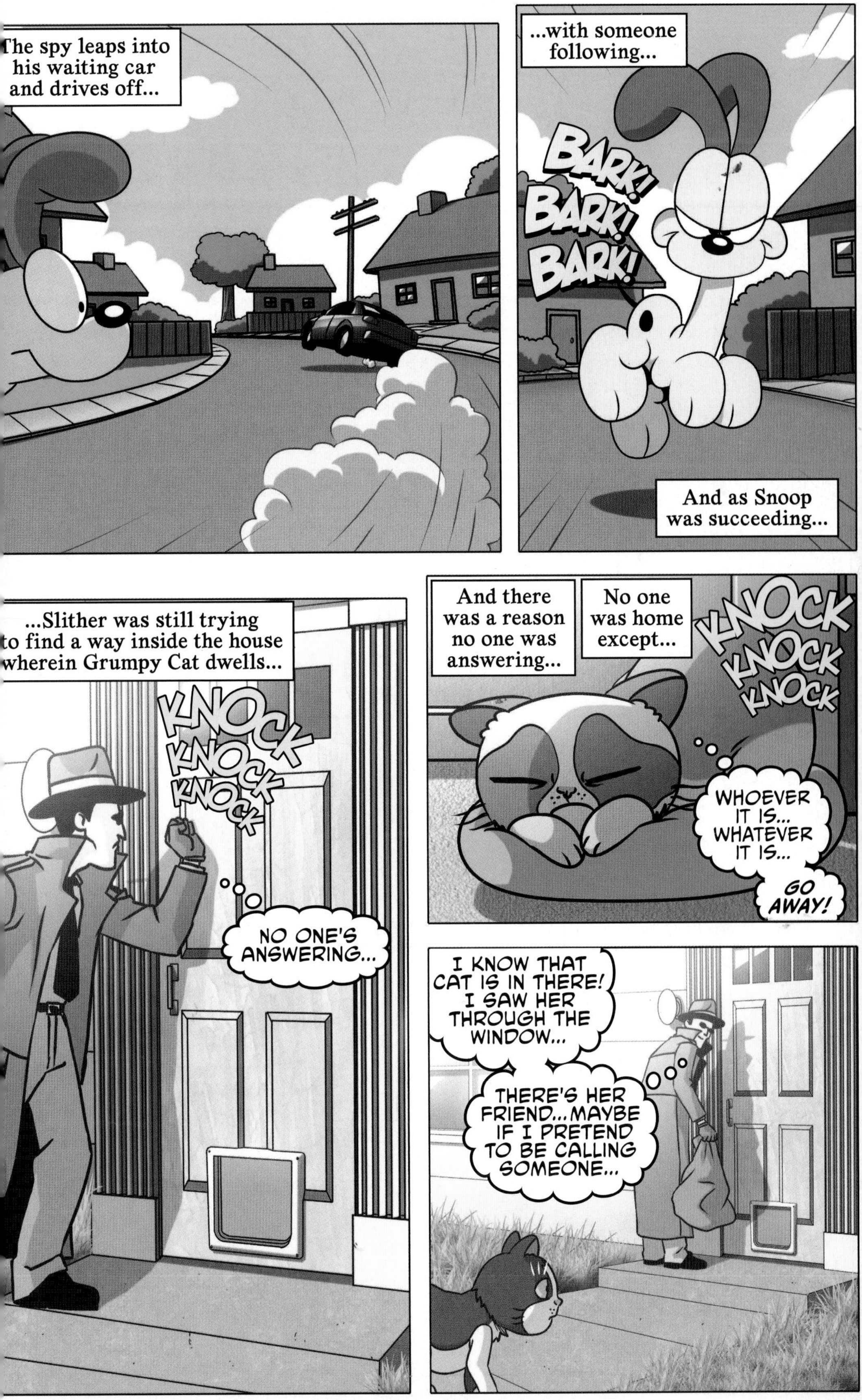
The spy leaps into his waiting car and drives off...
...with someone following...
BARK! BARK! BARK!
And as Snoop was succeeding...
...Slither was still trying to find a way inside the house wherein Grumpy Cat dwells...
KNOCK KNOCK KNOCK
NO ONE'S ANSWERING...
And there was a reason no one was answering...
No one was home except...
KNOCK KNOCK KNOCK
WHOEVER IT IS... WHATEVER IT IS...
GO AWAY!
I KNOW THAT CAT IS IN THERE! I SAW HER THROUGH THE WINDOW...
THERE'S HER FRIEND... MAYBE IF I PRETEND TO BE CALLING SOMEONE...

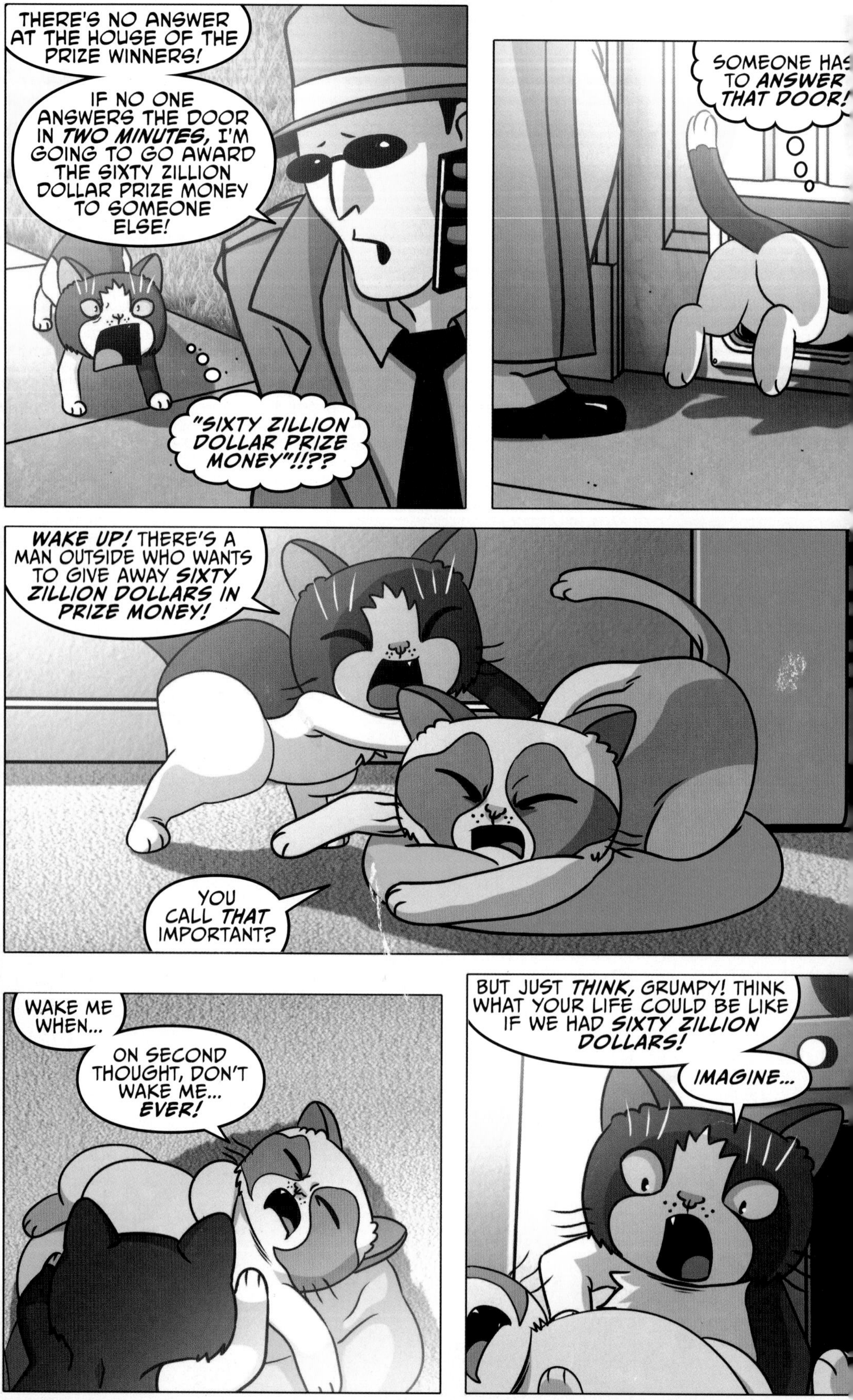
THERE'S NO ANSWER AT THE HOUSE OF THE PRIZE WINNERS!
IF NO ONE ANSWERS THE DOOR IN TWO MINUTES, I'M GOING TO GO AWARD THE SIXTY ZILLION DOLLAR PRIZE MONEY TO SOMEONE ELSE!
"SIXTY ZILLION DOLLAR PRIZE MONEY"!!??
SOMEONE HAS TO ANSWER THAT DOOR!
WAKE UP! THERE'S A MAN OUTSIDE WHO WANTS TO GIVE AWAY SIXTY ZILLION DOLLARS IN PRIZE MONEY!
YOU CALL THAT IMPORTANT?
WAKE ME WHEN...
ON SECOND THOUGHT, DON'T WAKE ME... EVER!
BUT JUST THINK, GRUMPY! THINK WHAT YOUR LIFE COULD BE LIKE IF WE HAD SIXTY ZILLION DOLLARS!
IMAGINE...

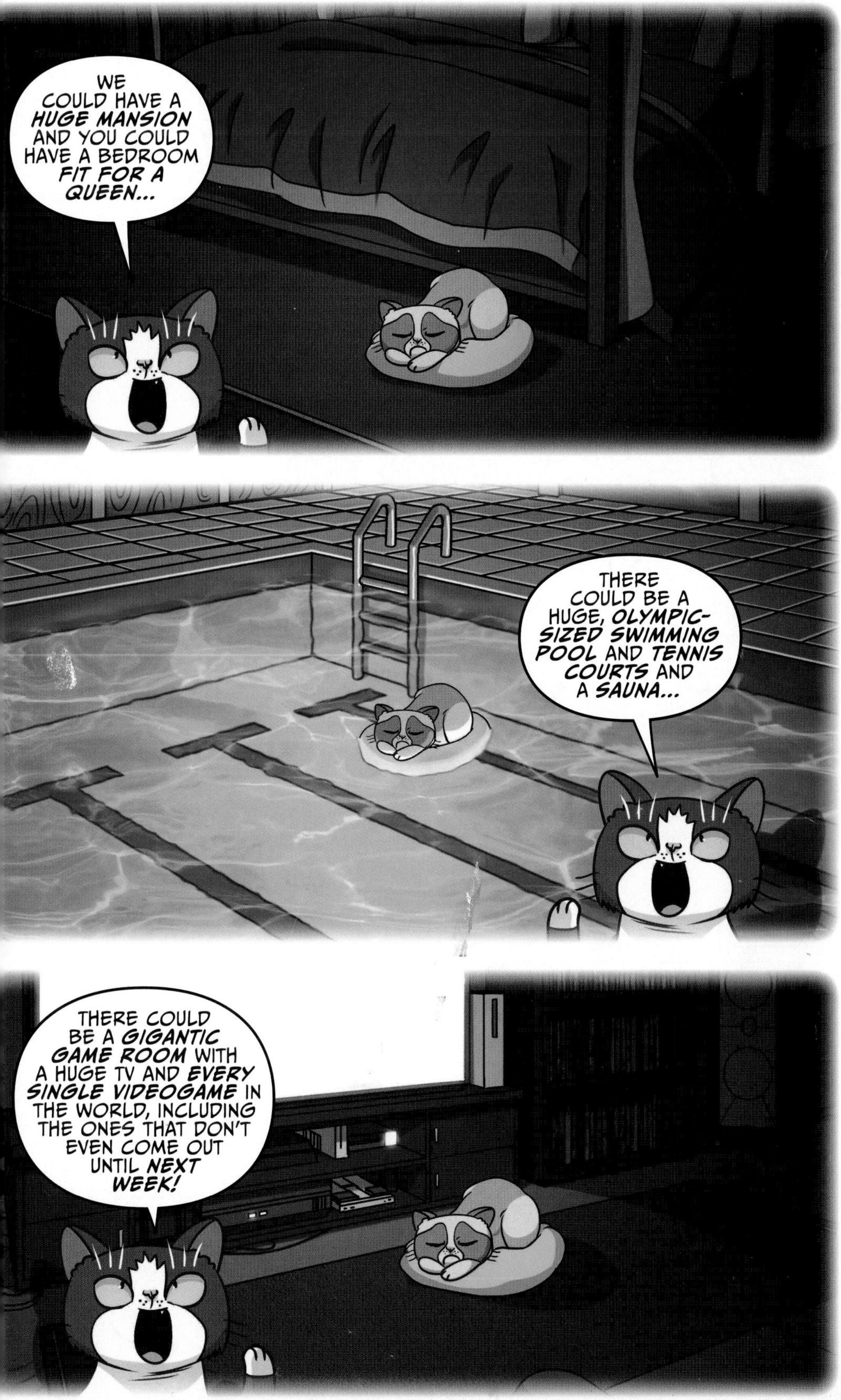
WE COULD HAVE A HUGE MANSION AND YOU COULD HAVE A BEDROOM FIT FOR A QUEEN...
THERE COULD BE A HUGE, OLYMPIC-SIZED SWIMMING POOL AND TENNIS COURTS AND A SAUNA...
THERE COULD BE A GIGANTIC GAME ROOM WITH A HUGE TV AND EVERY SINGLE VIDEOGAME IN THE WORLD, INCLUDING THE ONES THAT DON'T EVEN COME OUT UNTIL NEXT WEEK!

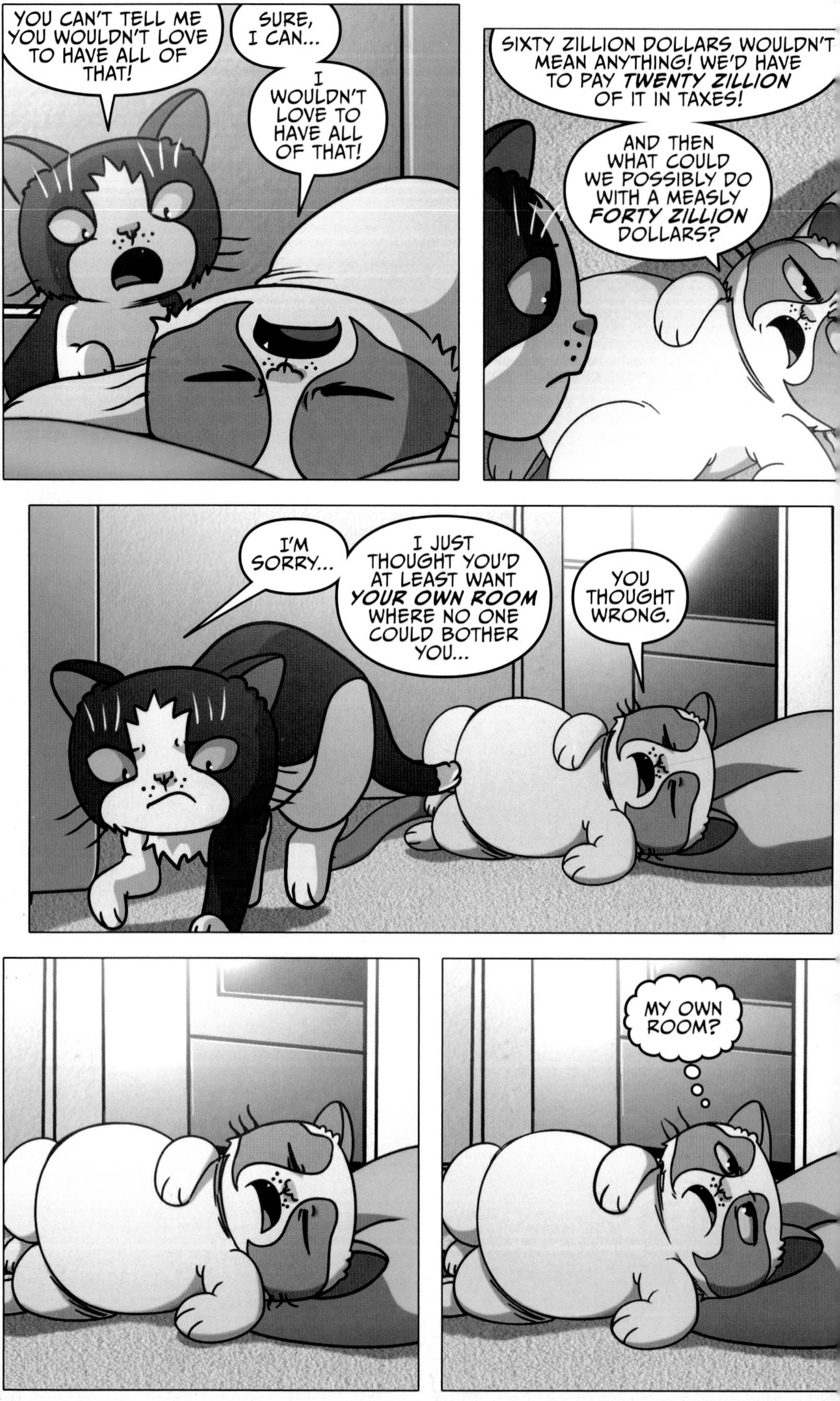
YOU CAN'T TELL ME YOU WOULDN'T LOVE TO HAVE ALL OF THAT!
SURE, I CAN...
I WOULDN'T LOVE TO HAVE ALL OF THAT!
SIXTY ZILLION DOLLARS WOULDN'T MEAN ANYTHING! WE'D HAVE TO PAY *TWENTY ZILLION* OF IT IN TAXES!
AND THEN WHAT COULD WE POSSIBLY DO WITH A MEASLY *FORTY ZILLION* DOLLARS?
I'M SORRY...
I JUST THOUGHT YOU'D AT LEAST WANT *YOUR OWN ROOM* WHERE NO ONE COULD BOTHER YOU...
YOU THOUGHT WRONG.
MY OWN ROOM?

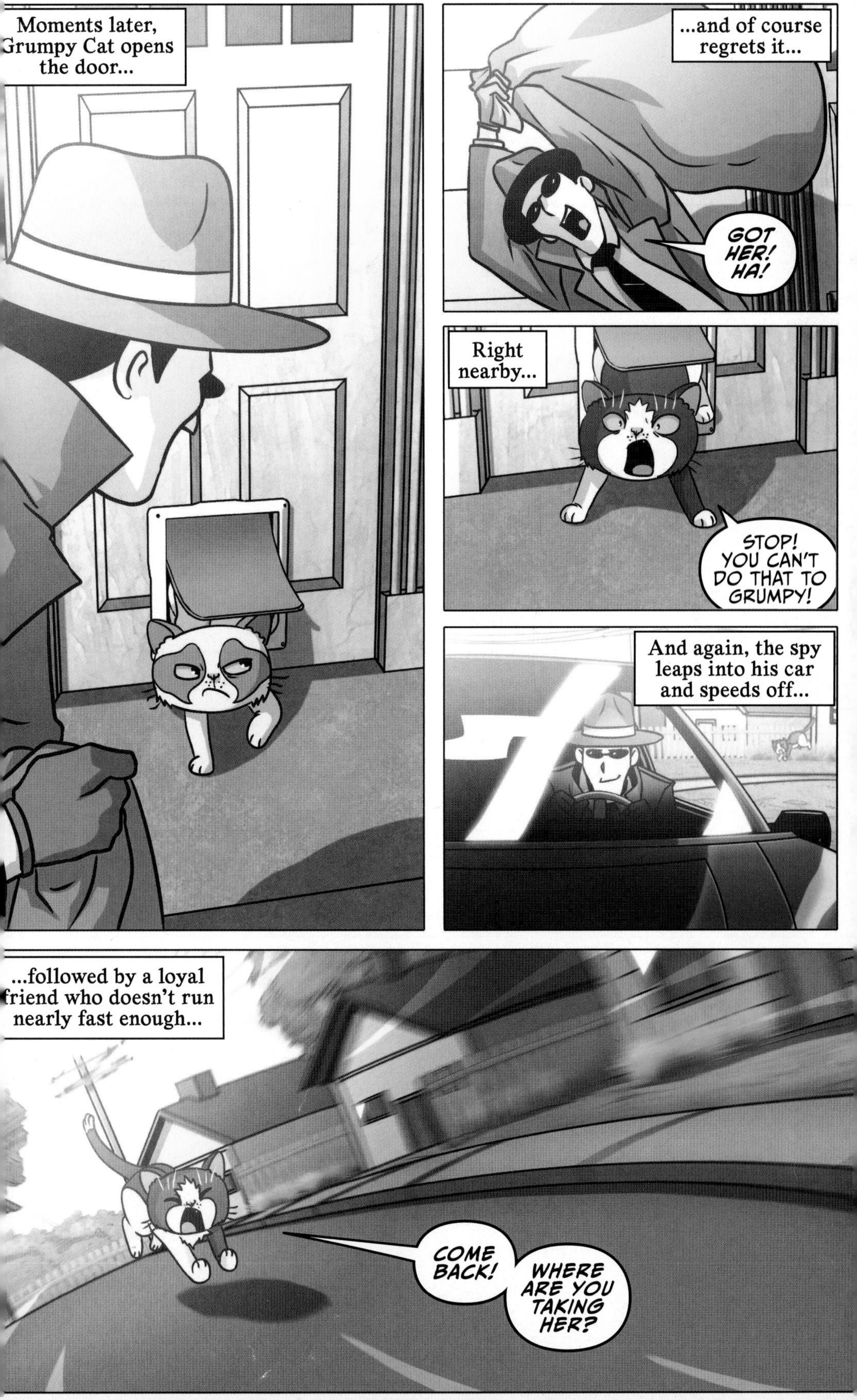
Moments later, Grumpy Cat opens the door...
...and of course regrets it...
GOT HER! HA!
Right nearby...
STOP! YOU CAN'T DO THAT TO GRUMPY!
And again, the spy leaps into his car and speeds off...
...followed by a loyal friend who doesn't run nearly fast enough...
COME BACK!
WHERE ARE YOU TAKING HER?

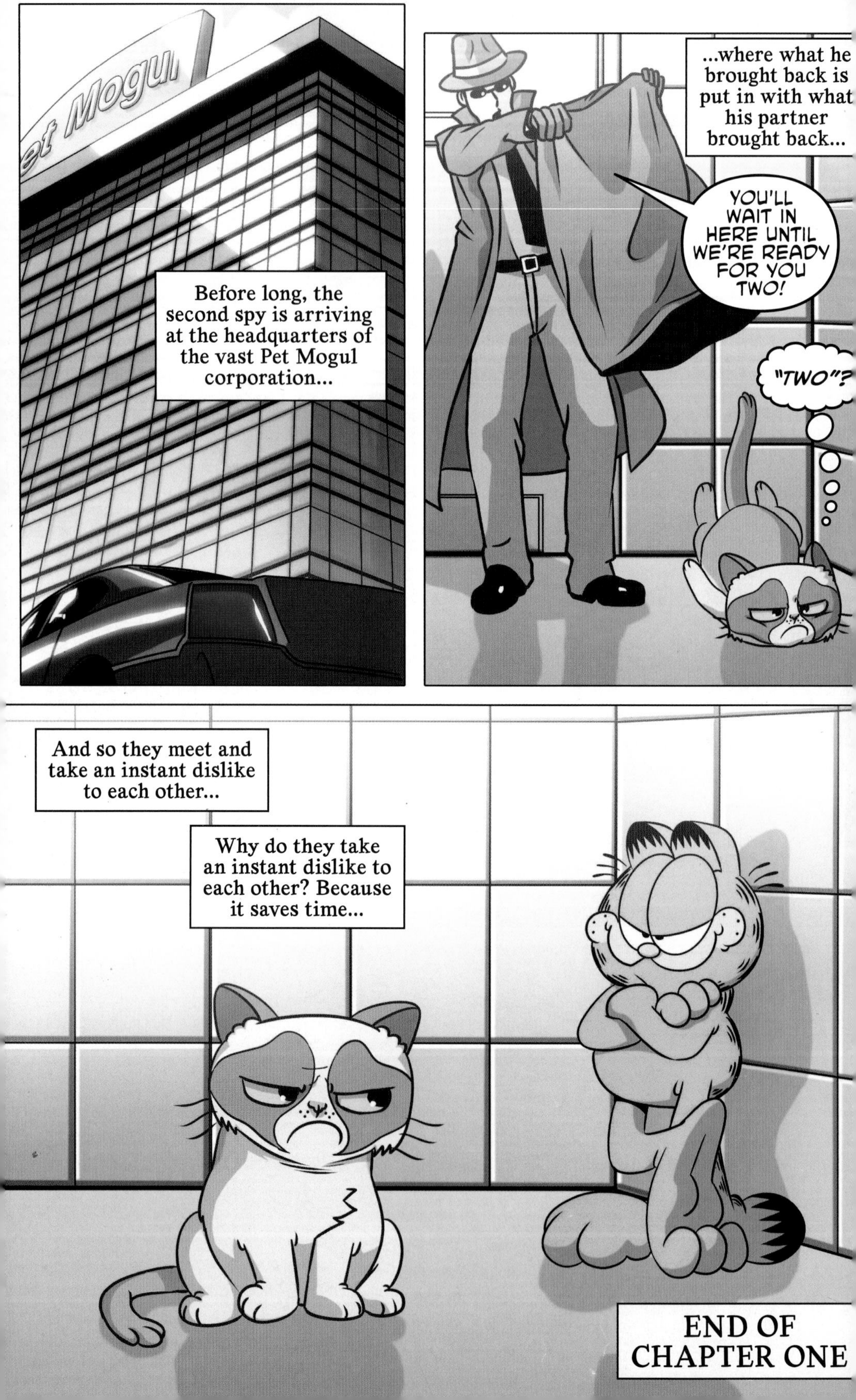
Pet Mogul
Before long, the second spy is arriving at the headquarters of the vast Pet Mogul corporation...
...where what he brought back is put in with what his partner brought back...
YOU'LL WAIT IN HERE UNTIL WE'RE READY FOR YOU TWO!
"TWO"?
And so they meet and take an instant dislike to each other...
Why do they take an instant dislike to each other? Because it saves time...
END OF CHAPTER ONE

CHAPTER

2

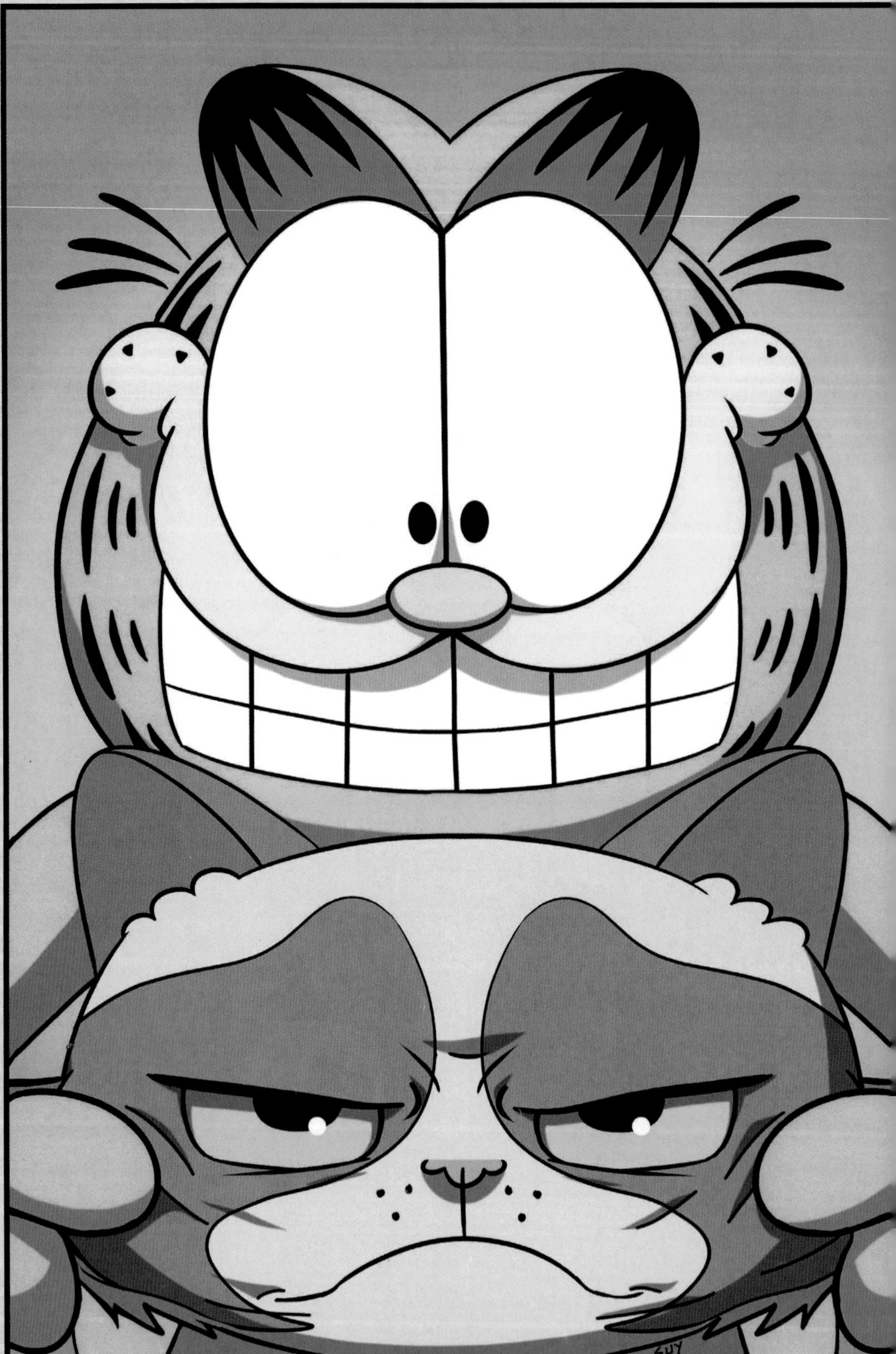
SUY

ISSUE 2 COVER BY: **STEVE UY**

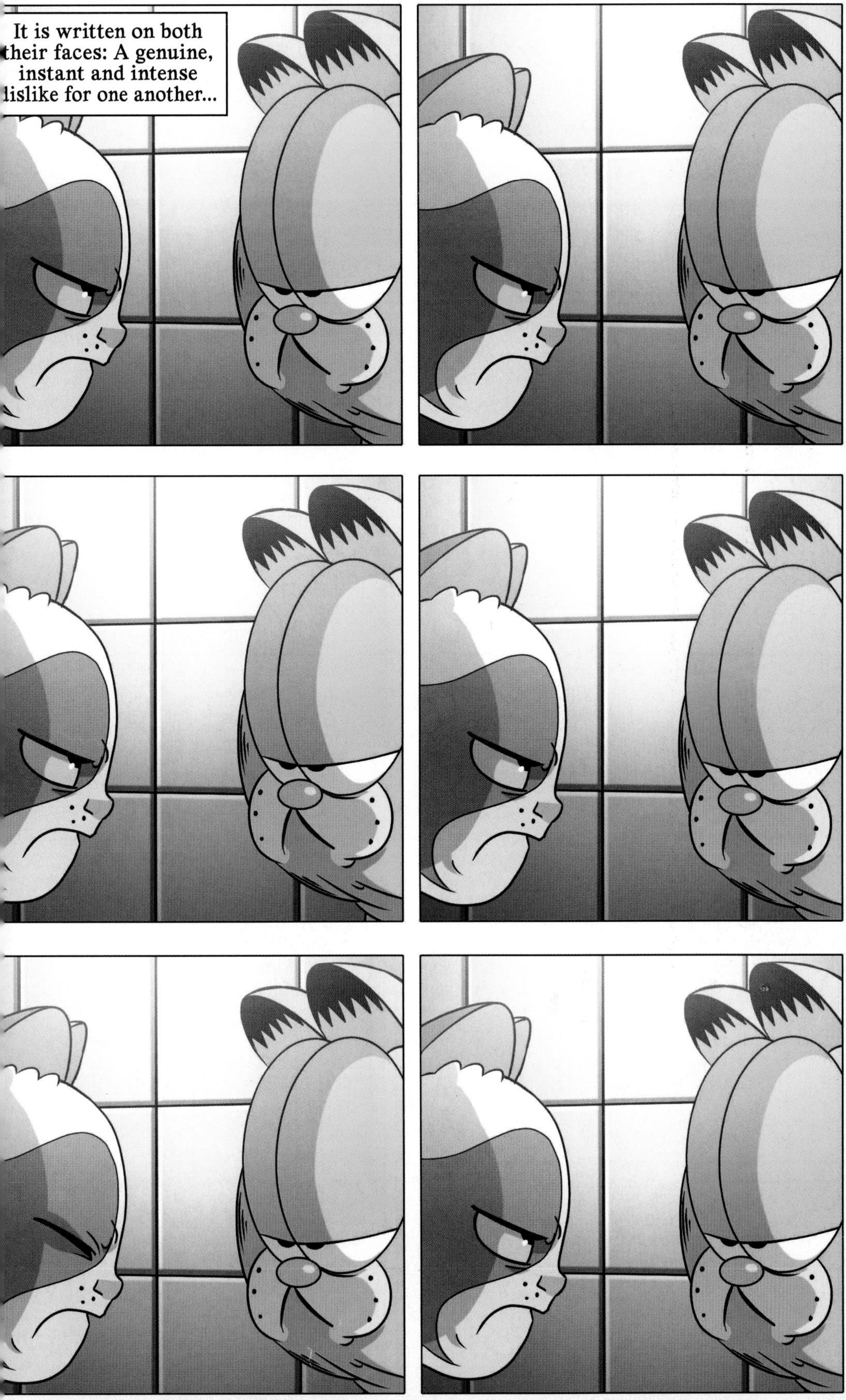
It is written on both their faces: A genuine, instant and intense dislike for one another...

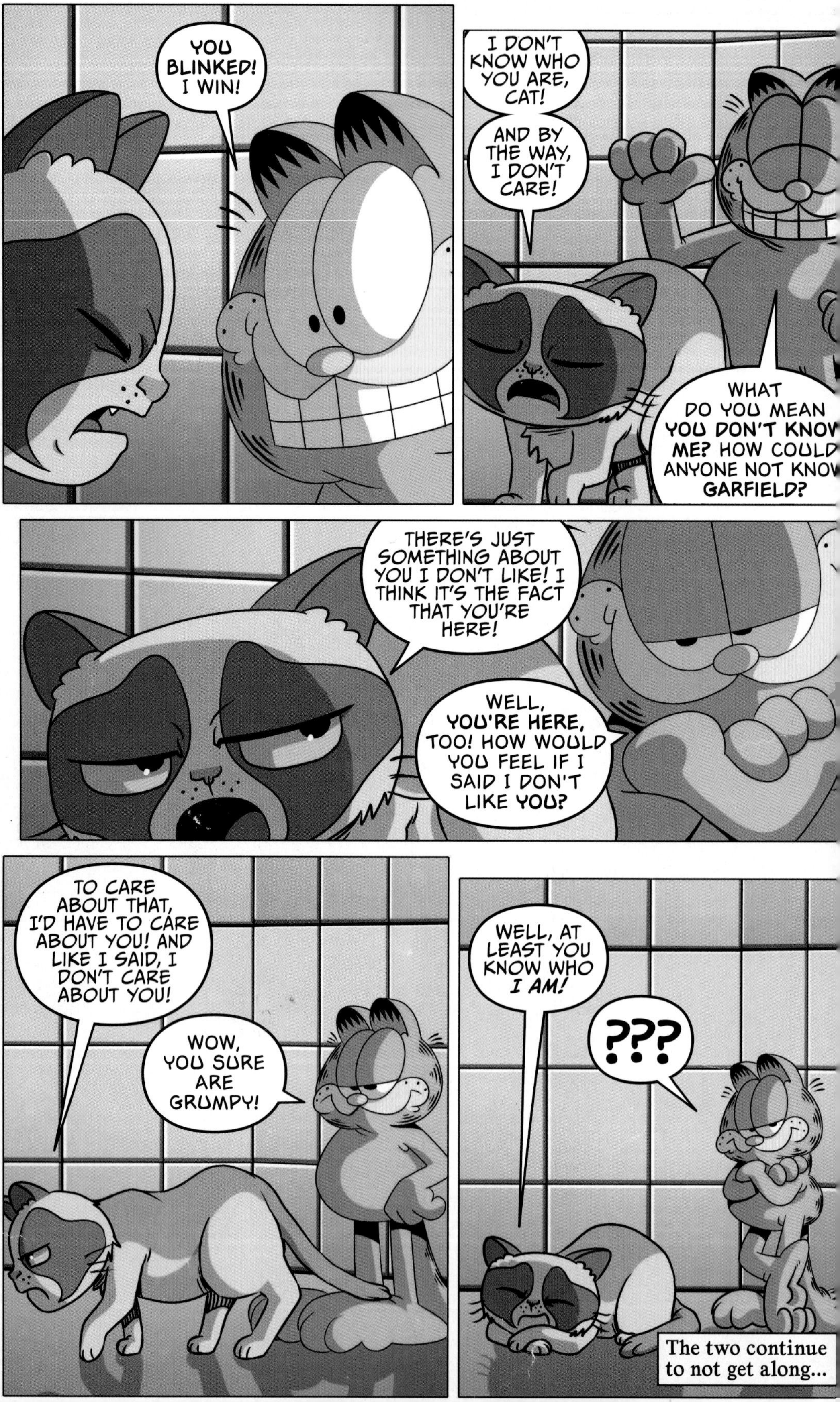

YOU BLINKED! I WIN!
I DON'T KNOW WHO YOU ARE, CAT!
AND BY THE WAY, I DON'T CARE!
WHAT DO YOU MEAN **YOU DON'T KNOW ME?** HOW COULD ANYONE NOT KNOW **GARFIELD?**
THERE'S JUST SOMETHING ABOUT YOU I DON'T LIKE! I THINK IT'S THE FACT THAT YOU'RE HERE!
WELL, **YOU'RE HERE,** TOO! HOW WOULD YOU FEEL IF I SAID I DON'T LIKE **YOU?**
TO CARE ABOUT THAT, I'D HAVE TO CARE ABOUT YOU! AND LIKE I SAID, I DON'T CARE ABOUT YOU!
WOW, YOU SURE ARE GRUMPY!
WELL, AT LEAST YOU KNOW WHO *I AM!*
???
The two continue to not get along...

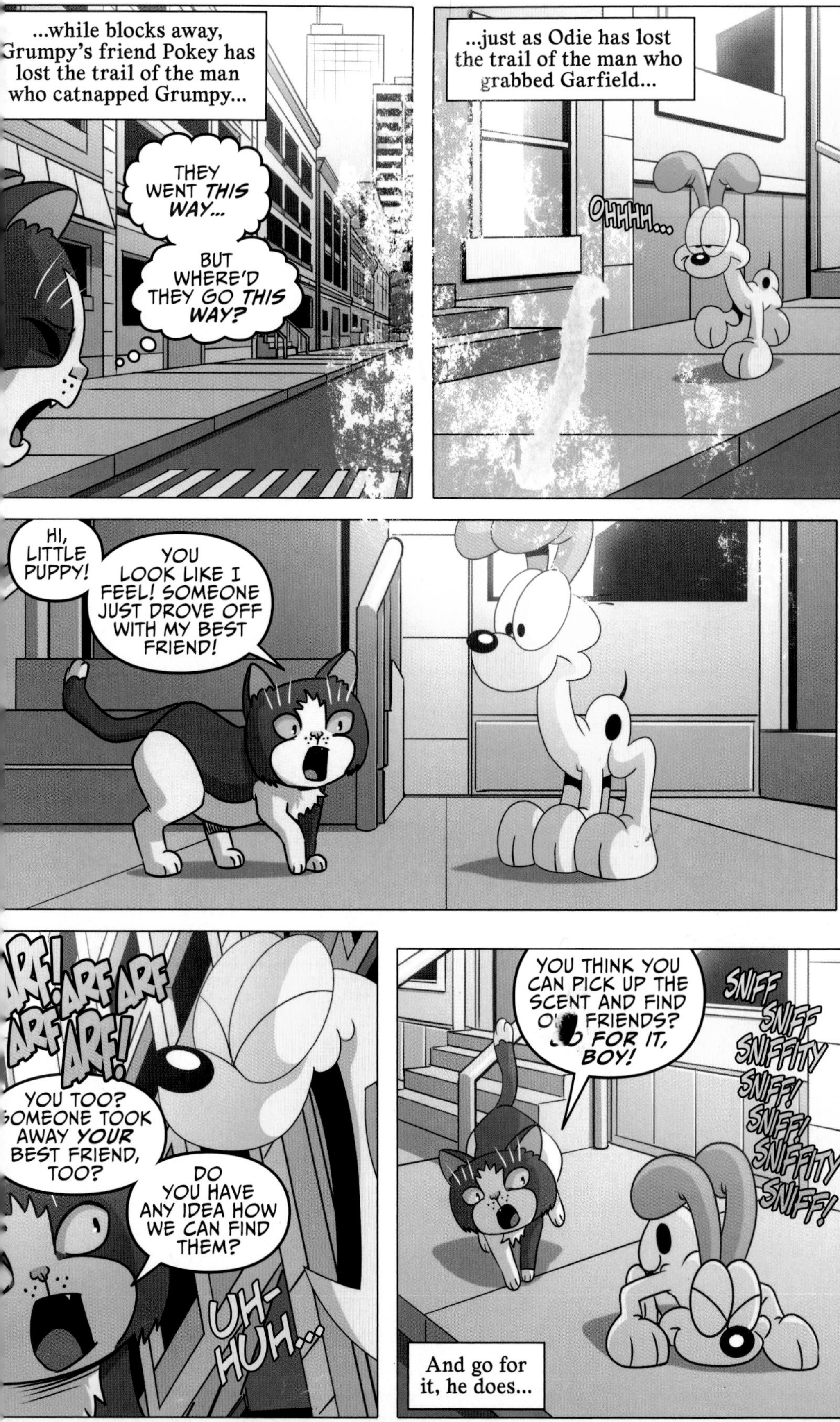

...while blocks away, Grumpy's friend Pokey has lost the trail of the man who catnapped Grumpy...
THEY WENT *THIS* *WAY*...
BUT WHERE'D THEY GO *THIS* *WAY?*
...just as Odie has lost the trail of the man who grabbed Garfield...
OHHHH...
HI, LITTLE PUPPY!
YOU LOOK LIKE I FEEL! SOMEONE JUST DROVE OFF WITH MY BEST FRIEND!
ARF! ARF ARF ARF! ARF!
YOU TOO? SOMEONE TOOK AWAY *YOUR* BEST FRIEND, TOO?
DO YOU HAVE ANY IDEA HOW WE CAN FIND THEM?
UH-HUH...
YOU THINK YOU CAN PICK UP THE SCENT AND FIND
FRIENDS?
FOR IT, *BOY!*
SNIFF SNIFF SNIFFITY SNIFF! SNIFF! SNIFFITY SNIFF!
And go for it, he does...

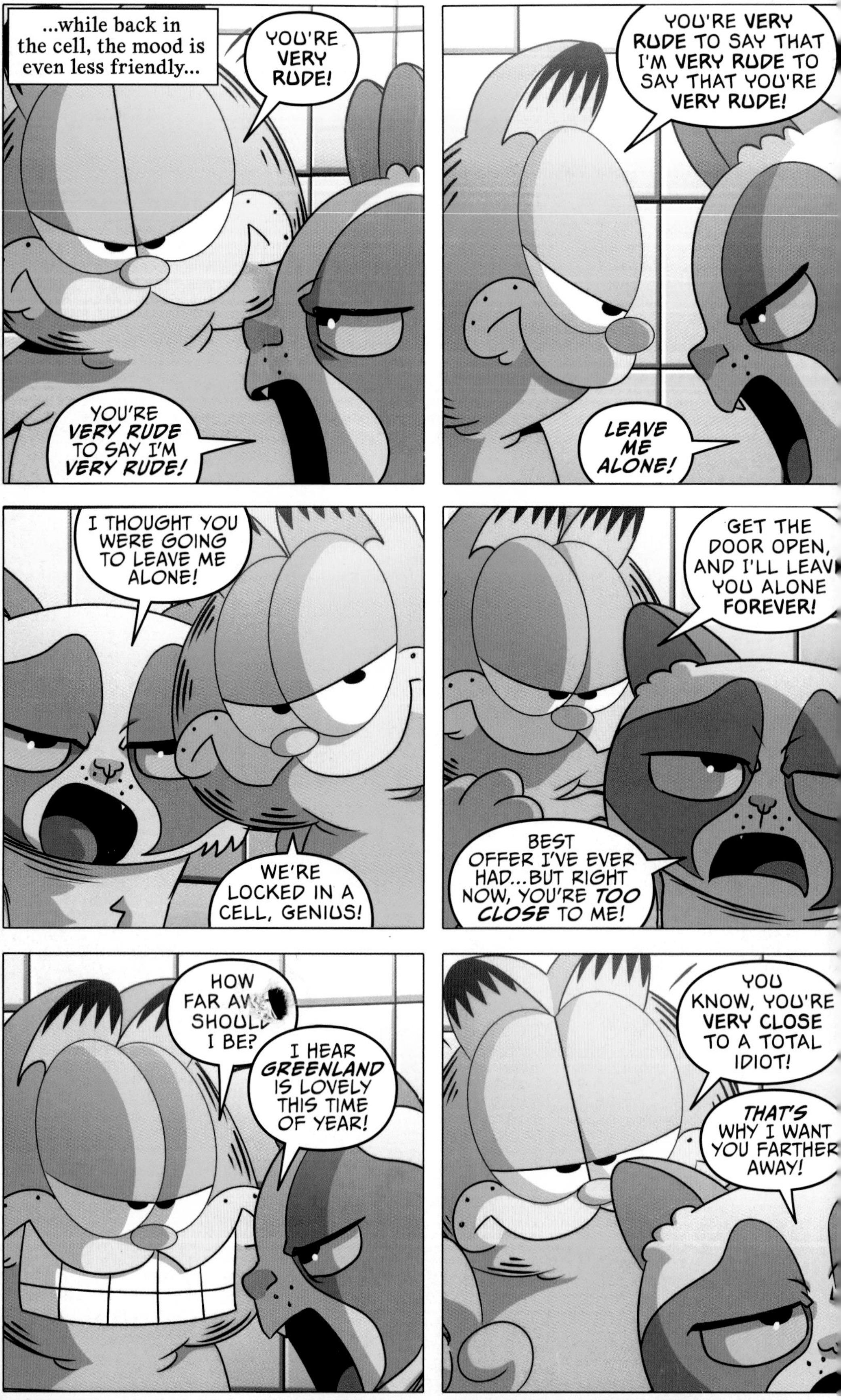
...while back in the cell, the mood is even less friendly...
YOU'RE VERY RUDE!
YOU'RE VERY RUDE TO SAY I'M VERY RUDE!
YOU'RE VERY RUDE TO SAY THAT I'M VERY RUDE TO SAY THAT YOU'RE VERY RUDE!
LEAVE ME ALONE!
I THOUGHT YOU WERE GOING TO LEAVE ME ALONE!
WE'RE LOCKED IN A CELL, GENIUS!
GET THE DOOR OPEN, AND I'LL LEAV YOU ALONE FOREVER!
BEST OFFER I'VE EVER HAD...BUT RIGHT NOW, YOU'RE TOO CLOSE TO ME!
HOW FAR AW SHOUL I BE?
I HEAR GREENLAND IS LOVELY THIS TIME OF YEAR!
YOU KNOW, YOU'RE VERY CLOSE TO A TOTAL IDIOT!
THAT'S WHY I WANT YOU FARTHER AWAY!

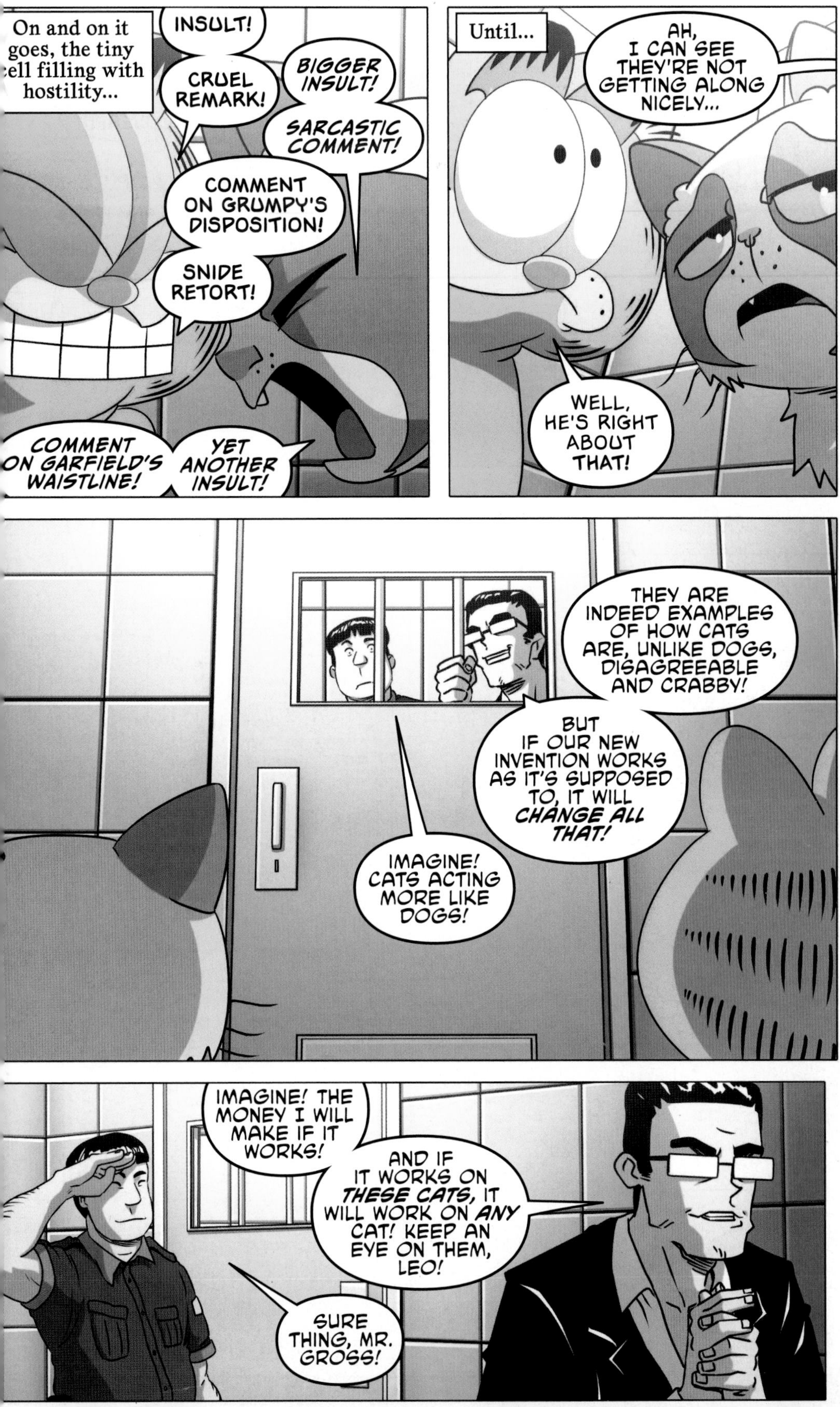
On and on it goes, the tiny cell filling with hostility...
INSULT!
CRUEL REMARK!
BIGGER INSULT!
SARCASTIC COMMENT!
COMMENT ON GRUMPY'S DISPOSITION!
SNIDE RETORT!
COMMENT ON GARFIELD'S WAISTLINE!
YET ANOTHER INSULT!
Until...
AH, I CAN SEE THEY'RE NOT GETTING ALONG NICELY...
WELL, HE'S RIGHT ABOUT THAT!
THEY ARE INDEED EXAMPLES OF HOW CATS ARE, UNLIKE DOGS, DISAGREEABLE AND CRABBY!
BUT IF OUR NEW INVENTION WORKS AS IT'S SUPPOSED TO, IT WILL CHANGE ALL THAT!
IMAGINE! CATS ACTING MORE LIKE DOGS!
IMAGINE! THE MONEY I WILL MAKE IF IT WORKS!
AND IF IT WORKS ON THESE CATS, IT WILL WORK ON ANY CAT! KEEP AN EYE ON THEM, LEO!
SURE THING, MR. GROSS!

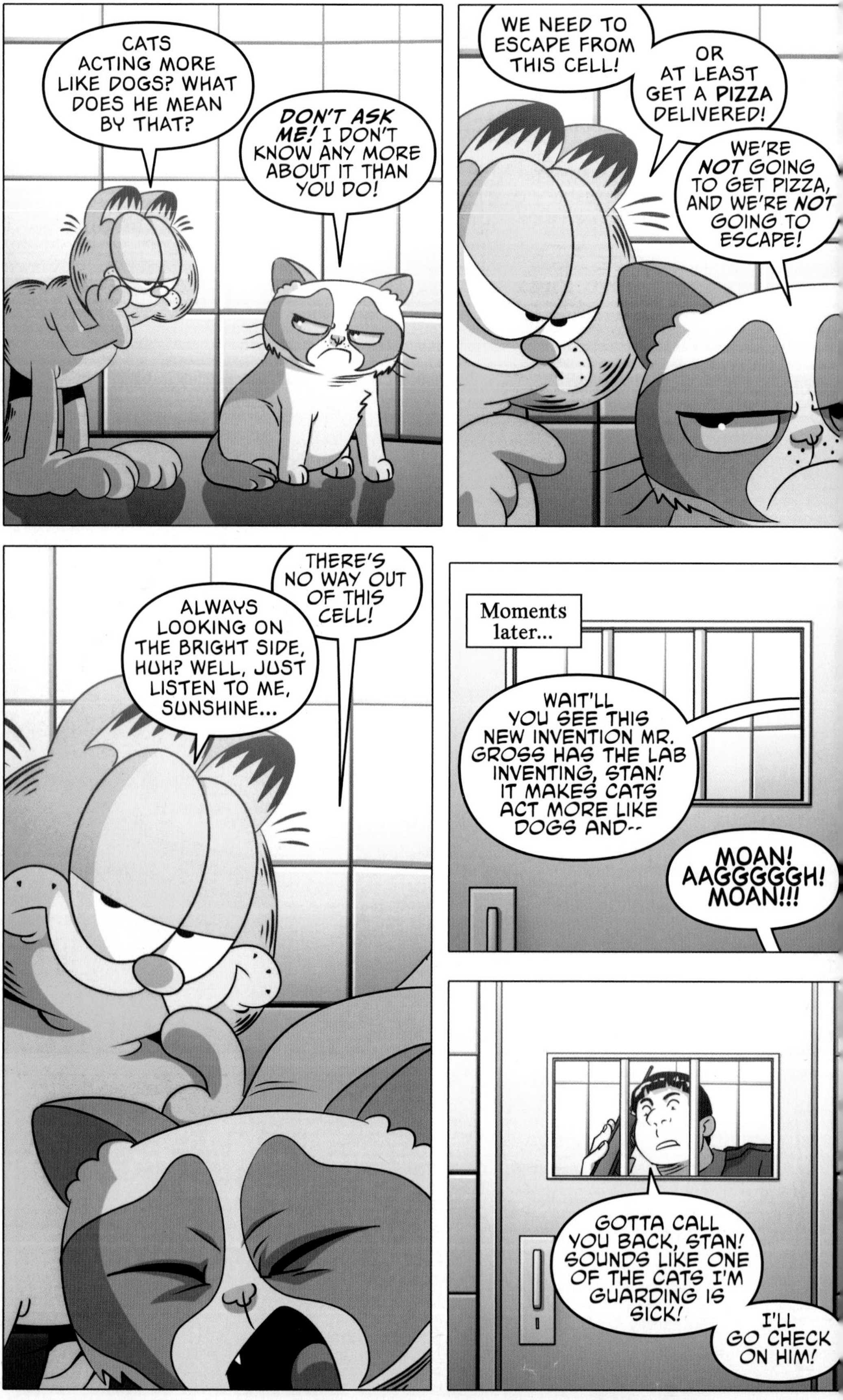

CATS ACTING MORE LIKE DOGS? WHAT DOES HE MEAN BY THAT?
DON'T ASK ME! I DON'T KNOW ANY MORE ABOUT IT THAN YOU DO!
WE NEED TO ESCAPE FROM THIS CELL!
OR AT LEAST GET A PIZZA DELIVERED!
WE'RE NOT GOING TO GET PIZZA, AND WE'RE NOT GOING TO ESCAPE!
THERE'S NO WAY OUT OF THIS CELL!
ALWAYS LOOKING ON THE BRIGHT SIDE, HUH? WELL, JUST LISTEN TO ME, SUNSHINE...
Moments later...
WAIT'LL YOU SEE THIS NEW INVENTION MR. GROSS HAS THE LAB INVENTING, STAN! IT MAKES CATS ACT MORE LIKE DOGS AND--
MOAN! AAGGGGGH! MOAN!!!
GOTTA CALL YOU BACK, STAN! SOUNDS LIKE ONE OF THE CATS I'M GUARDING IS SICK!
I'LL GO CHECK ON HIM!

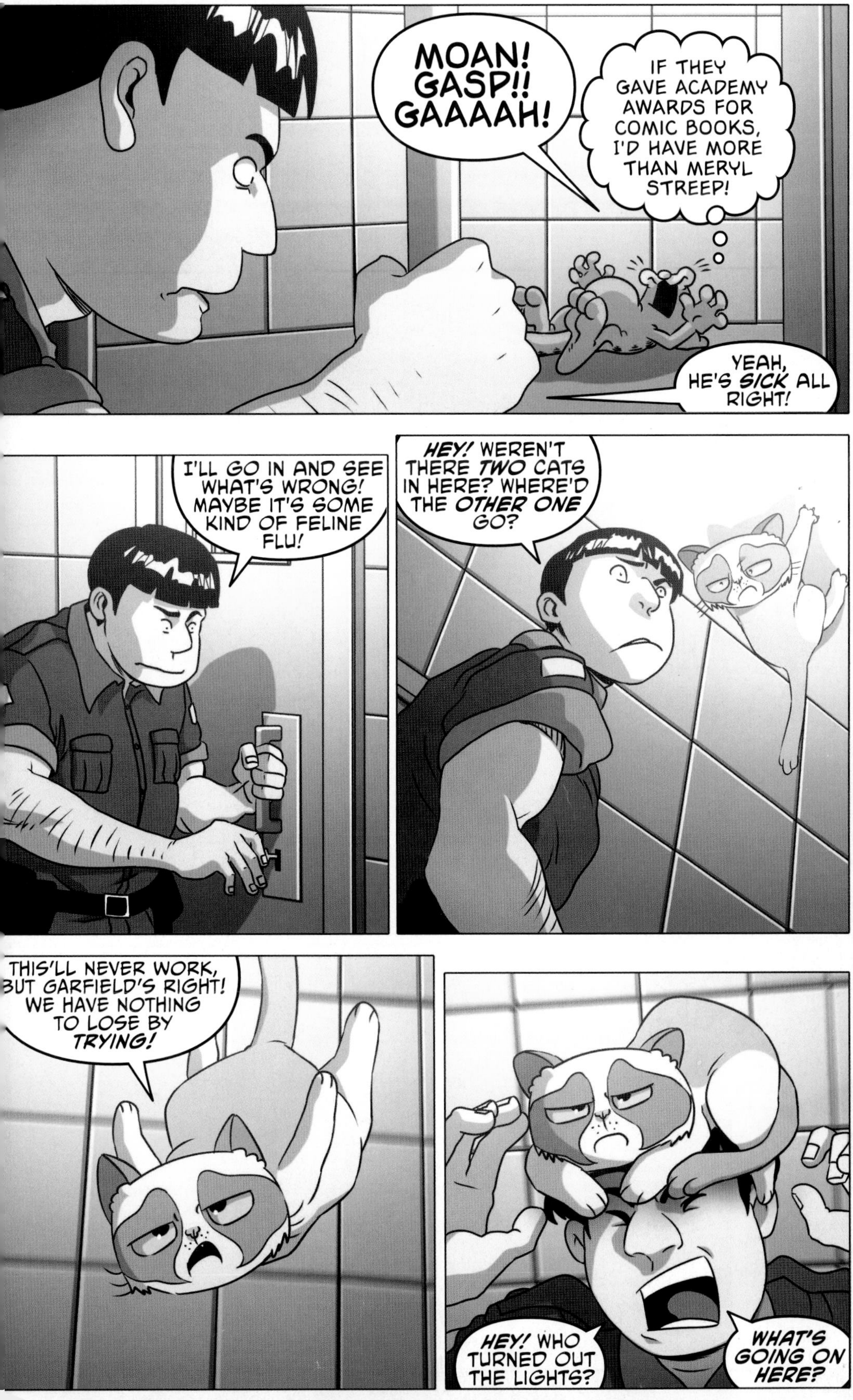

MOAN! GASP!! GAAAAH!
IF THEY GAVE ACADEMY AWARDS FOR COMIC BOOKS, I'D HAVE MORE THAN MERYL STREEP!
YEAH, HE'S SICK ALL RIGHT!
I'LL GO IN AND SEE WHAT'S WRONG! MAYBE IT'S SOME KIND OF FELINE FLU!
HEY! WEREN'T THERE TWO CATS IN HERE? WHERE'D THE OTHER ONE GO?
THIS'LL NEVER WORK, BUT GARFIELD'S RIGHT! WE HAVE NOTHING TO LOSE BY TRYING!
HEY! WHO TURNED OUT THE LIGHTS?
WHAT'S GOING ON HERE?

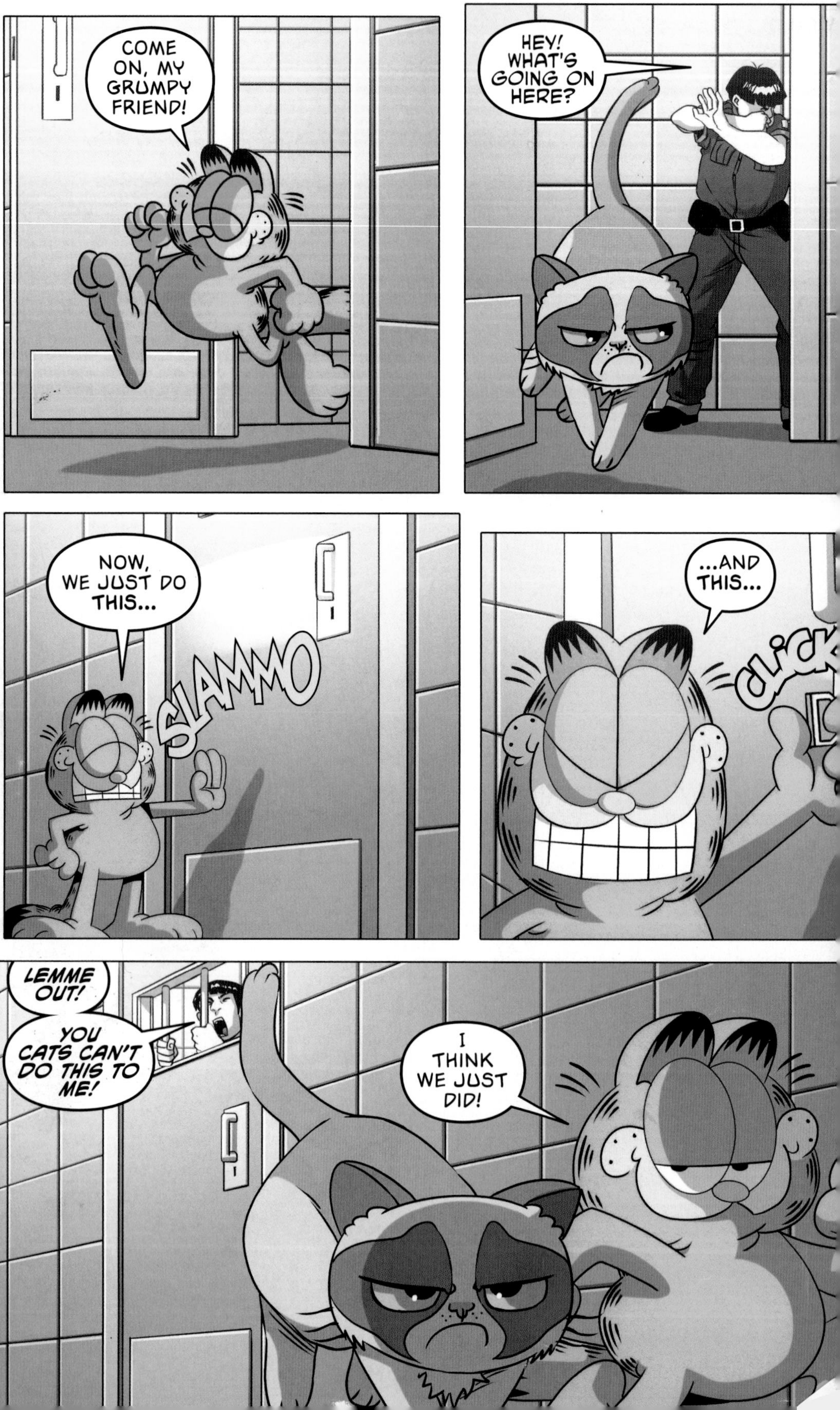

COME ON, MY GRUMPY FRIEND!
HEY! WHAT'S GOING ON HERE?
NOW, WE JUST DO THIS...
SLAMMO
...AND THIS...
LEMME OUT!
YOU CATS CAN'T DO THIS TO ME!
I THINK WE JUST DID!

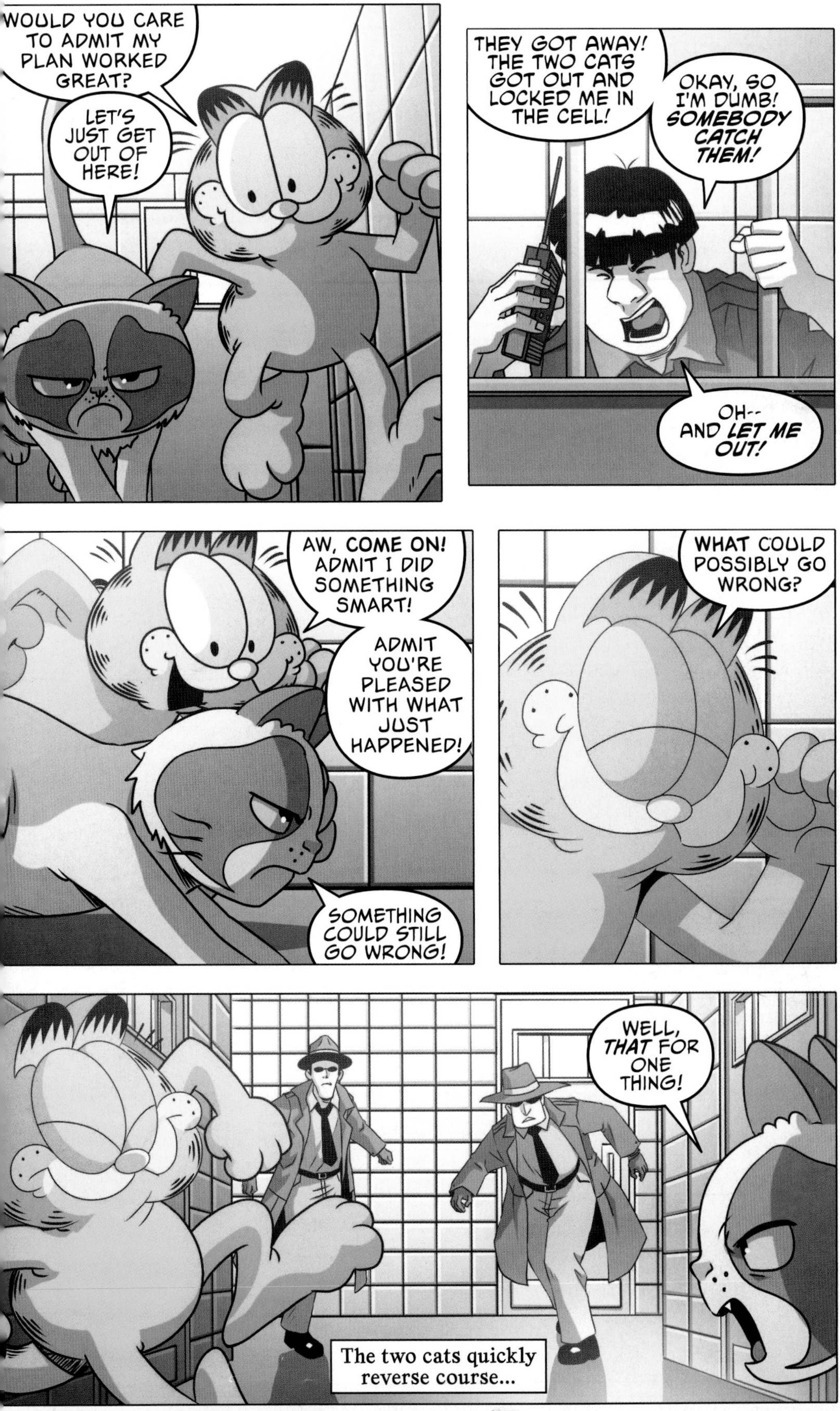
WOULD YOU CARE TO ADMIT MY PLAN WORKED GREAT?
LET'S JUST GET OUT OF HERE!
THEY GOT AWAY! THE TWO CATS GOT OUT AND LOCKED ME IN THE CELL!
OKAY, SO I'M DUMB! SOMEBODY CATCH THEM!
OH-- AND LET ME OUT!
AW, COME ON! ADMIT I DID SOMETHING SMART!
ADMIT YOU'RE PLEASED WITH WHAT JUST HAPPENED!
SOMETHING COULD STILL GO WRONG!
WHAT COULD POSSIBLY GO WRONG?
WELL, THAT FOR ONE THING!
The two cats quickly reverse course...

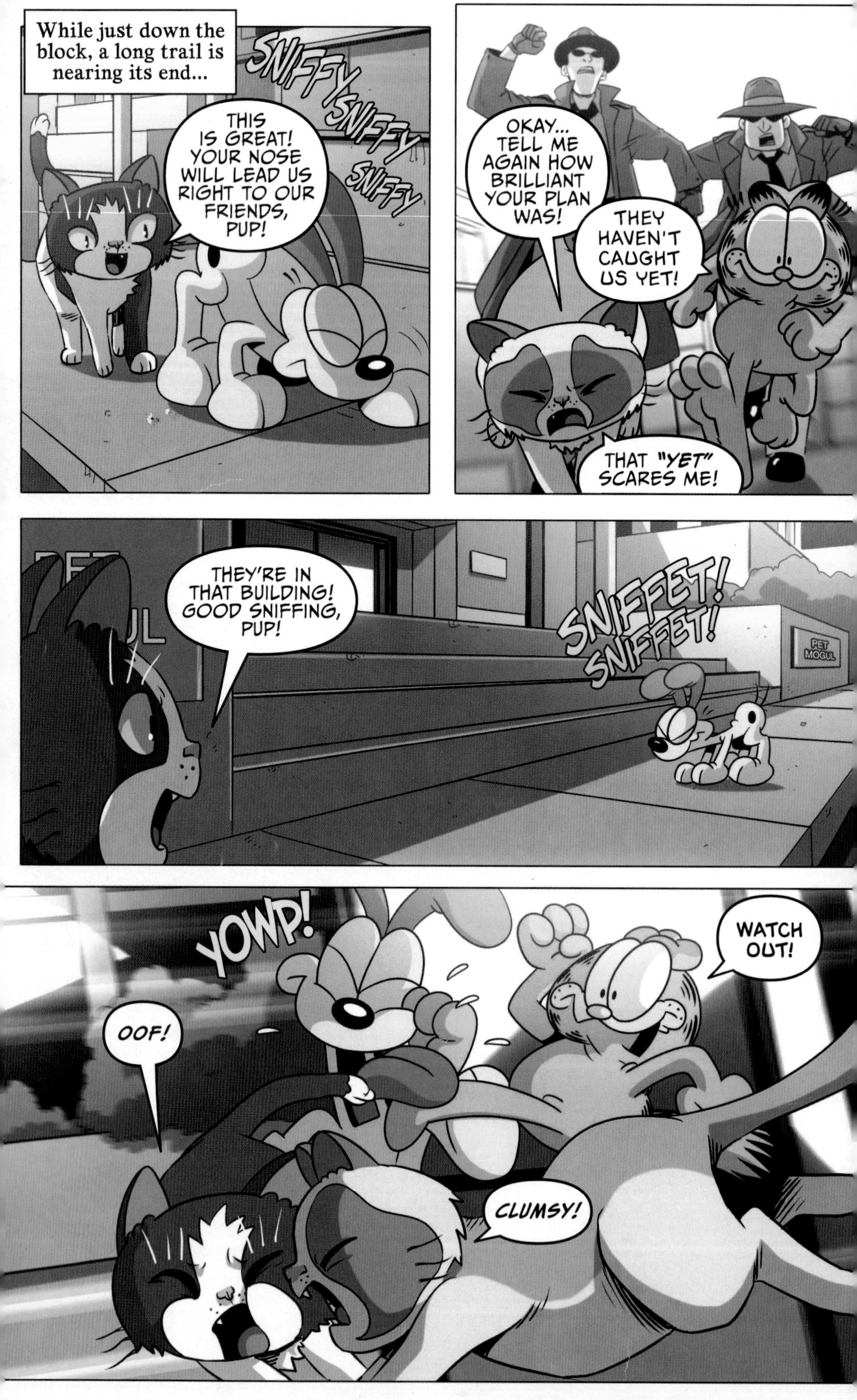
While just down the block, a long trail is nearing its end...
SNIFFY SNIFFY SNIFFY SNIFFY
THIS IS GREAT! YOUR NOSE WILL LEAD US RIGHT TO OUR FRIENDS, PUP!
OKAY... TELL ME AGAIN HOW BRILLIANT YOUR PLAN WAS!
THEY HAVEN'T CAUGHT US YET!
THAT "YET" SCARES ME!
THEY'RE IN THAT BUILDING! GOOD SNIFFING, PUP!
SNIFFET! SNIFFET!
PET MOGUL
YOWP!
WATCH OUT!
OOF!
CLUMSY!

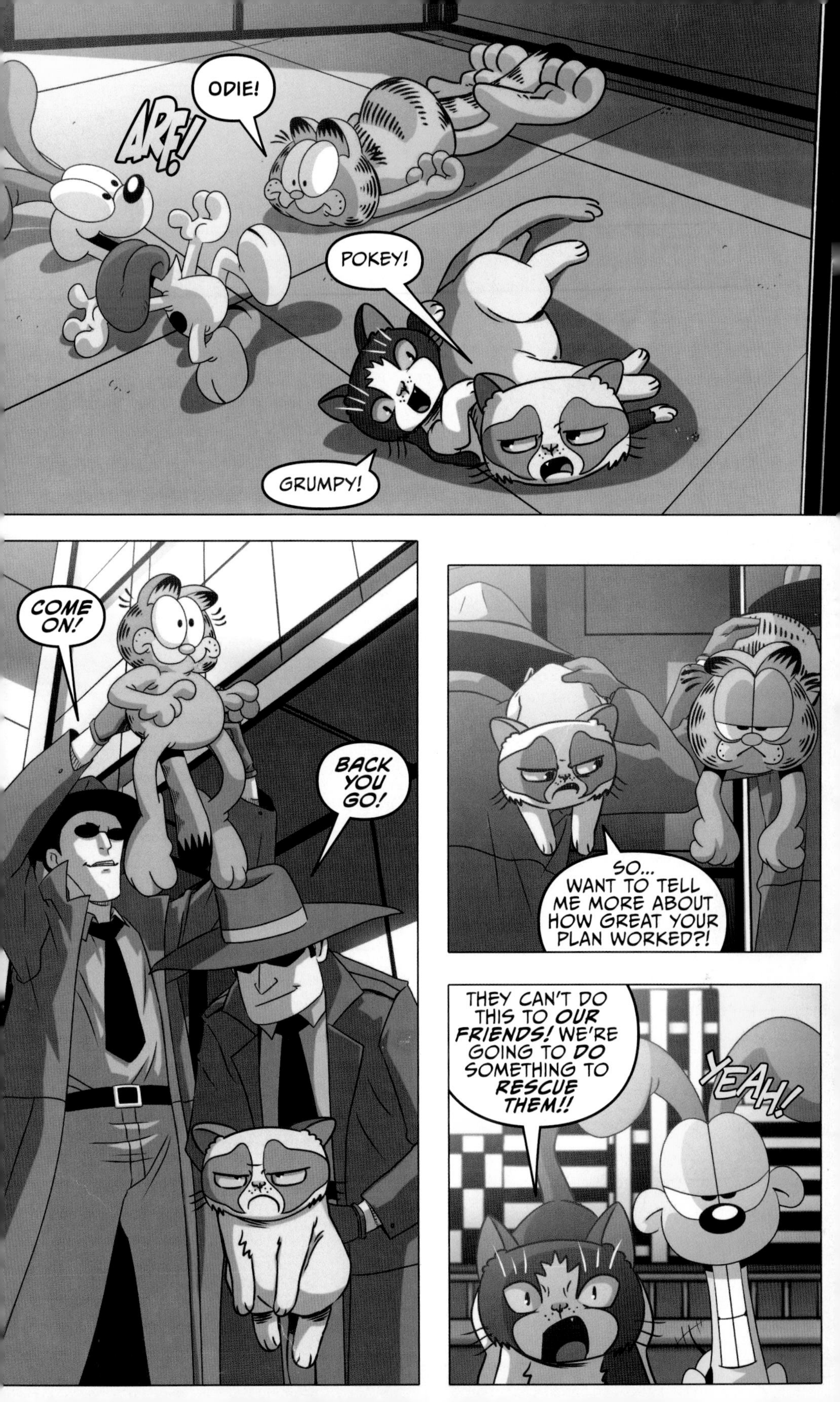
ODIE!
ARF!
POKEY!
GRUMPY!
COME ON!
BACK YOU GO!
SO... WANT TO TELL ME MORE ABOUT HOW GREAT YOUR PLAN WORKED?!
THEY CAN'T DO THIS TO OUR FRIENDS! WE'RE GOING TO DO SOMETHING TO RESCUE THEM!!
YEAH!

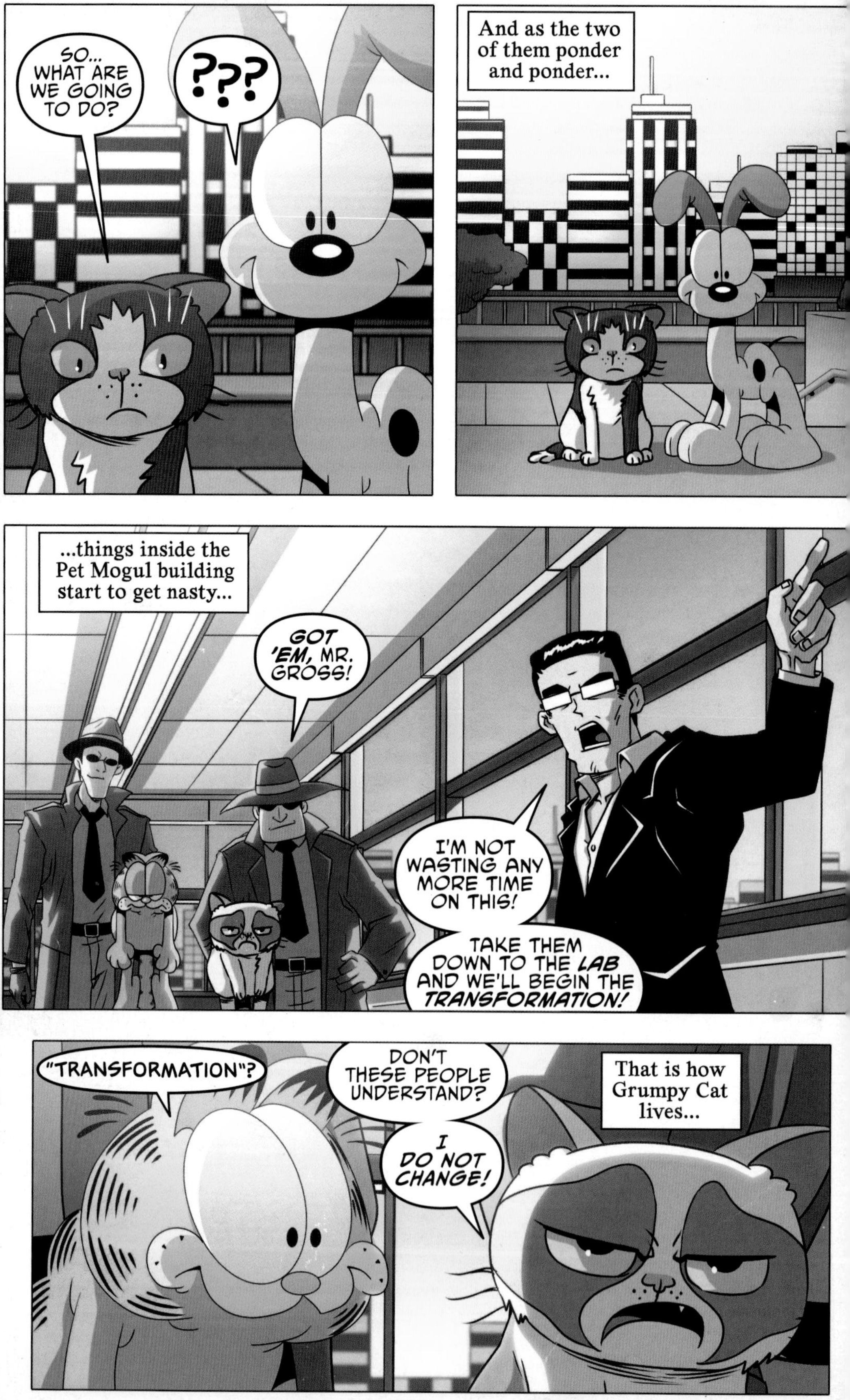
SO... WHAT ARE WE GOING TO DO?
???
And as the two of them ponder and ponder...
...things inside the Pet Mogul building start to get nasty...
GOT 'EM, MR. GROSS!
I'M NOT WASTING ANY MORE TIME ON THIS!
TAKE THEM DOWN TO THE LAB AND WE'LL BEGIN THE TRANSFORMATION!
"TRANSFORMATION"?
DON'T THESE PEOPLE UNDERSTAND?
I DO NOT CHANGE!
That is how Grumpy Cat lives...

...but in life, we do not always have that choice...

COULD I PERHAPS HAVE ANOTHER WEEK OR SO TO FINE-TUNE THE *CAT-CONVERSION PROGRAMMING DEVICE?*

I THOUGHT YOU SAID IT WAS FINISHED!

OH, IT IS, MR. GROSS! JUST AS YOU ORDERED!

IT'S JUST THAT... WELL, THIS IS THE FIRST TIME WE'VE TESTED IT ON REAL CATS, AND...

...I JUST THOUGHT SINCE IT COULD BE DANGEROUS...

YOU KNOW, I COULD GET ANOTHER HEAD OF RESEARCH AND DEVELOPMENT...

OH NO, MR. GROSS! NO NEED TO DO THAT! *I'LL GET THE TEST STARTED!*

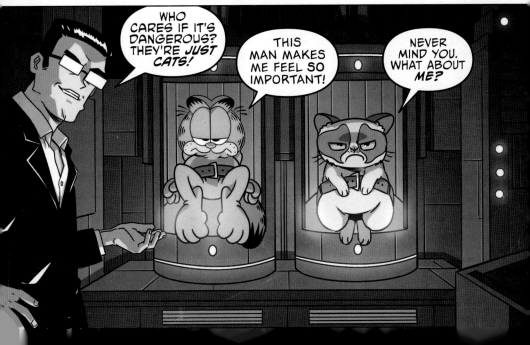

WHO CARES IF IT'S DANGEROUS? THEY'RE *JUST* CATS!

THIS MAN MAKES ME FEEL SO IMPORTANT!

NEVER MIND YOU. WHAT ABOUT *ME?*

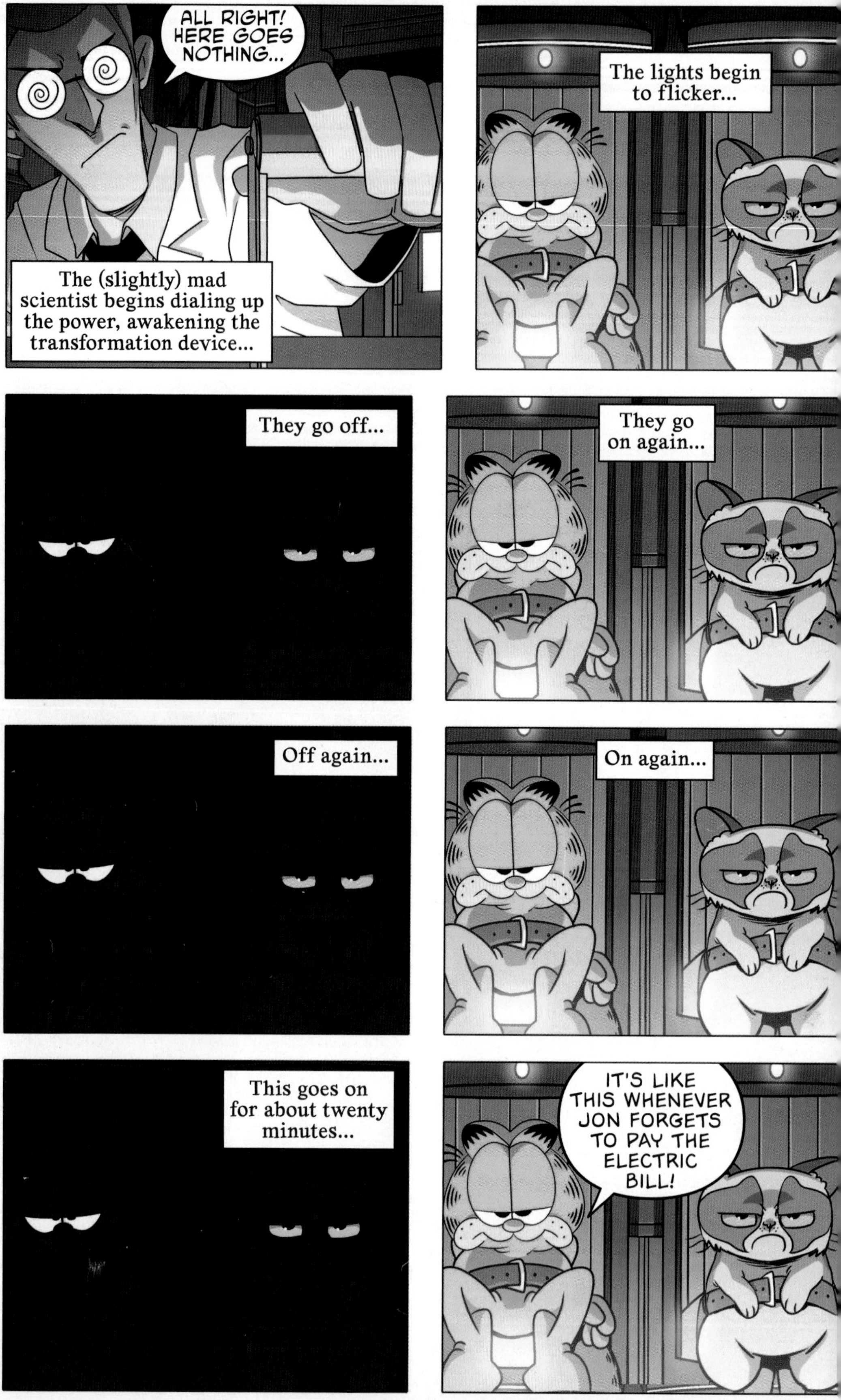

ALL RIGHT! HERE GOES NOTHING...
The (slightly) mad scientist begins dialing up the power, awakening the transformation device...
The lights begin to flicker...
They go off...
They go on again...
Off again...
On again...
This goes on for about twenty minutes...
IT'S LIKE THIS WHENEVER JON FORGETS TO PAY THE ELECTRIC BILL!

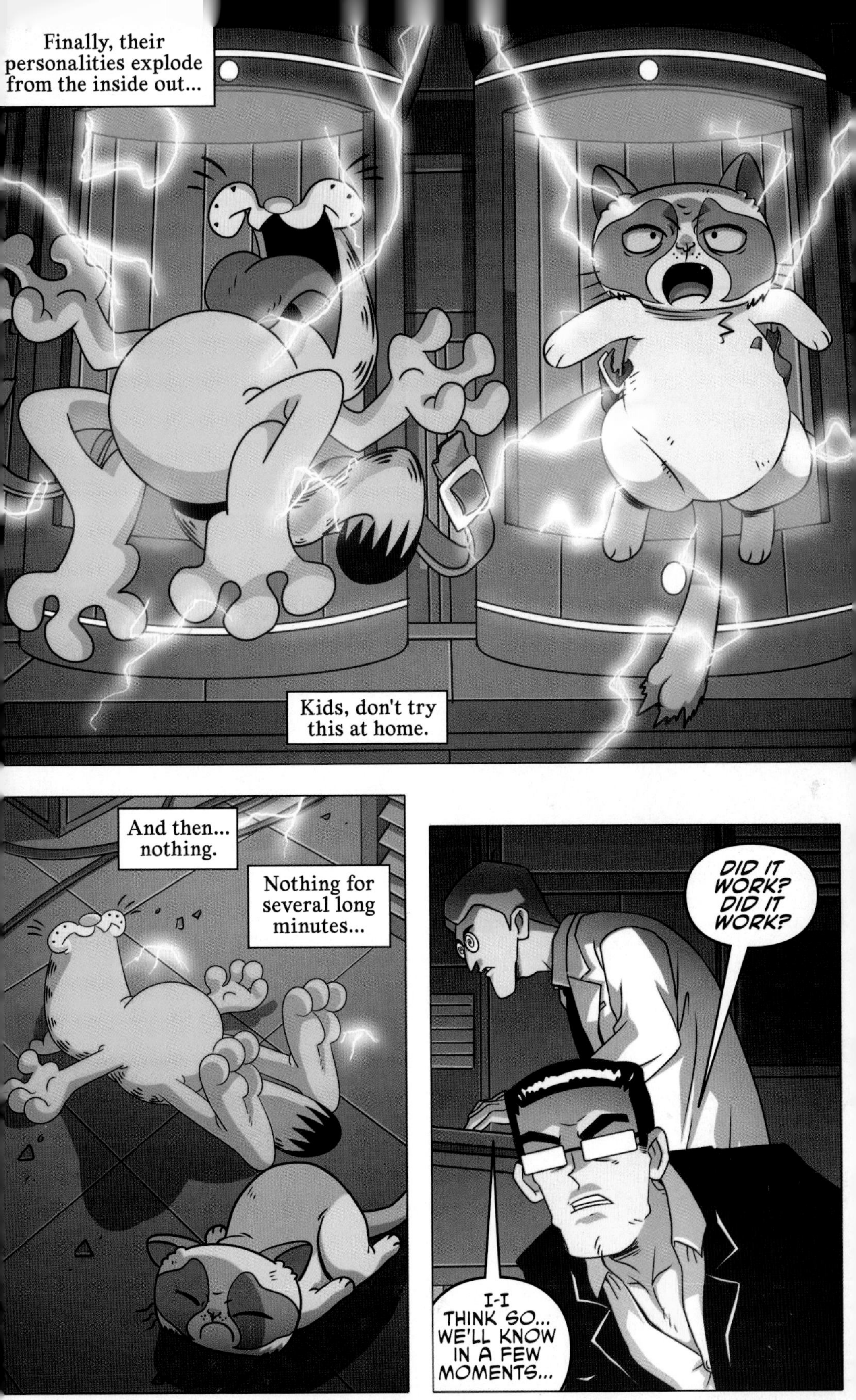
Finally, their personalities explode from the inside out...
Kids, don't try this at home.
And then... nothing.
Nothing for several long minutes...
DID IT WORK? DID IT WORK?
I-I THINK SO... WE'LL KNOW IN A FEW MOMENTS...

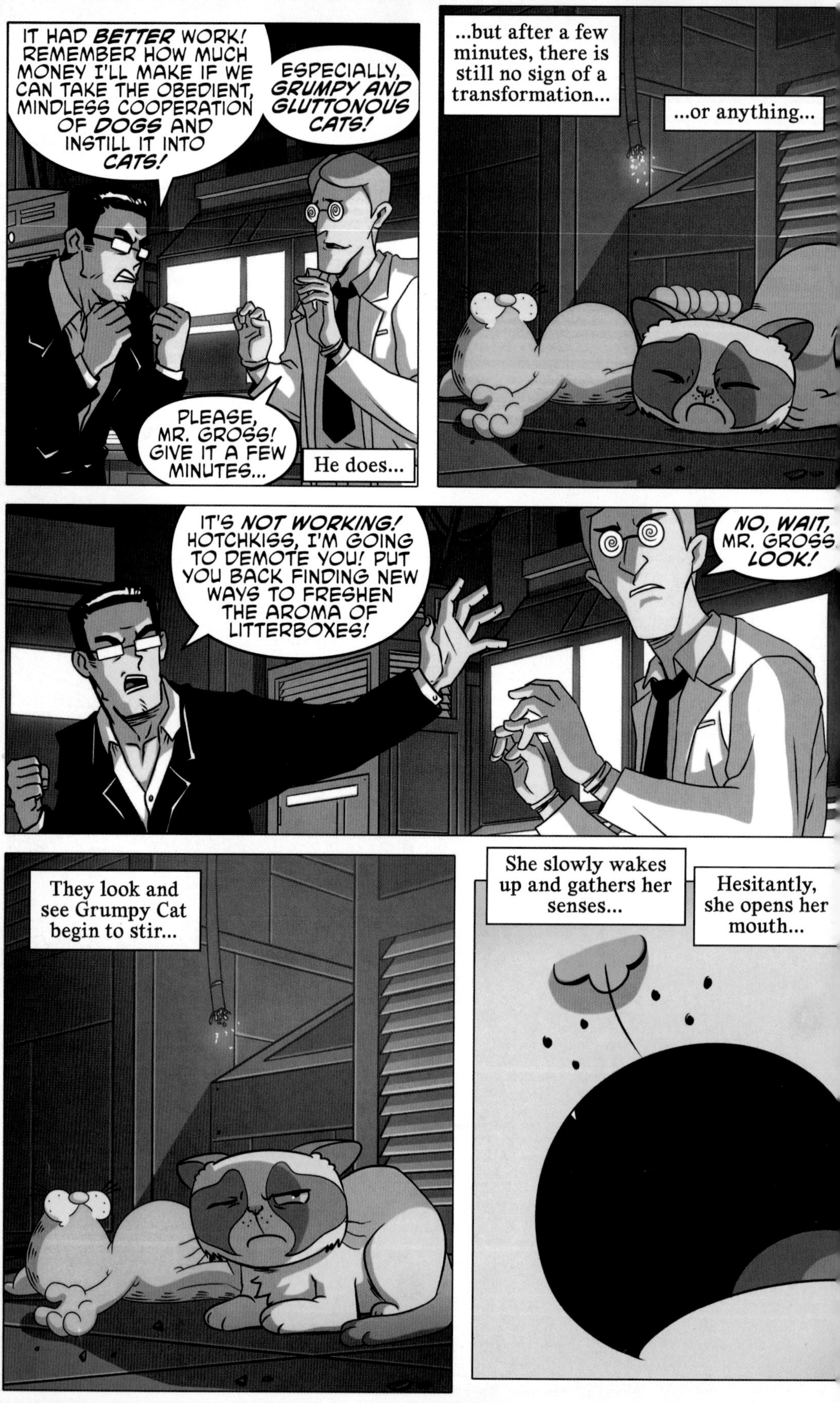
IT HAD BETTER WORK! REMEMBER HOW MUCH MONEY I'LL MAKE IF WE CAN TAKE THE OBEDIENT, MINDLESS COOPERATION OF DOGS AND INSTILL IT INTO CATS!
ESPECIALLY, GRUMPY AND GLUTTONOUS CATS!
PLEASE, MR. GROSS! GIVE IT A FEW MINUTES...
He does...
...but after a few minutes, there is still no sign of a transformation...
...or anything...
IT'S NOT WORKING! HOTCHKISS, I'M GOING TO DEMOTE YOU! PUT YOU BACK FINDING NEW WAYS TO FRESHEN THE AROMA OF LITTERBOXES!
NO, WAIT, MR. GROSS LOOK!
They look and see Grumpy Cat begin to stir...
She slowly wakes up and gathers her senses...
Hesitantly, she opens her mouth...

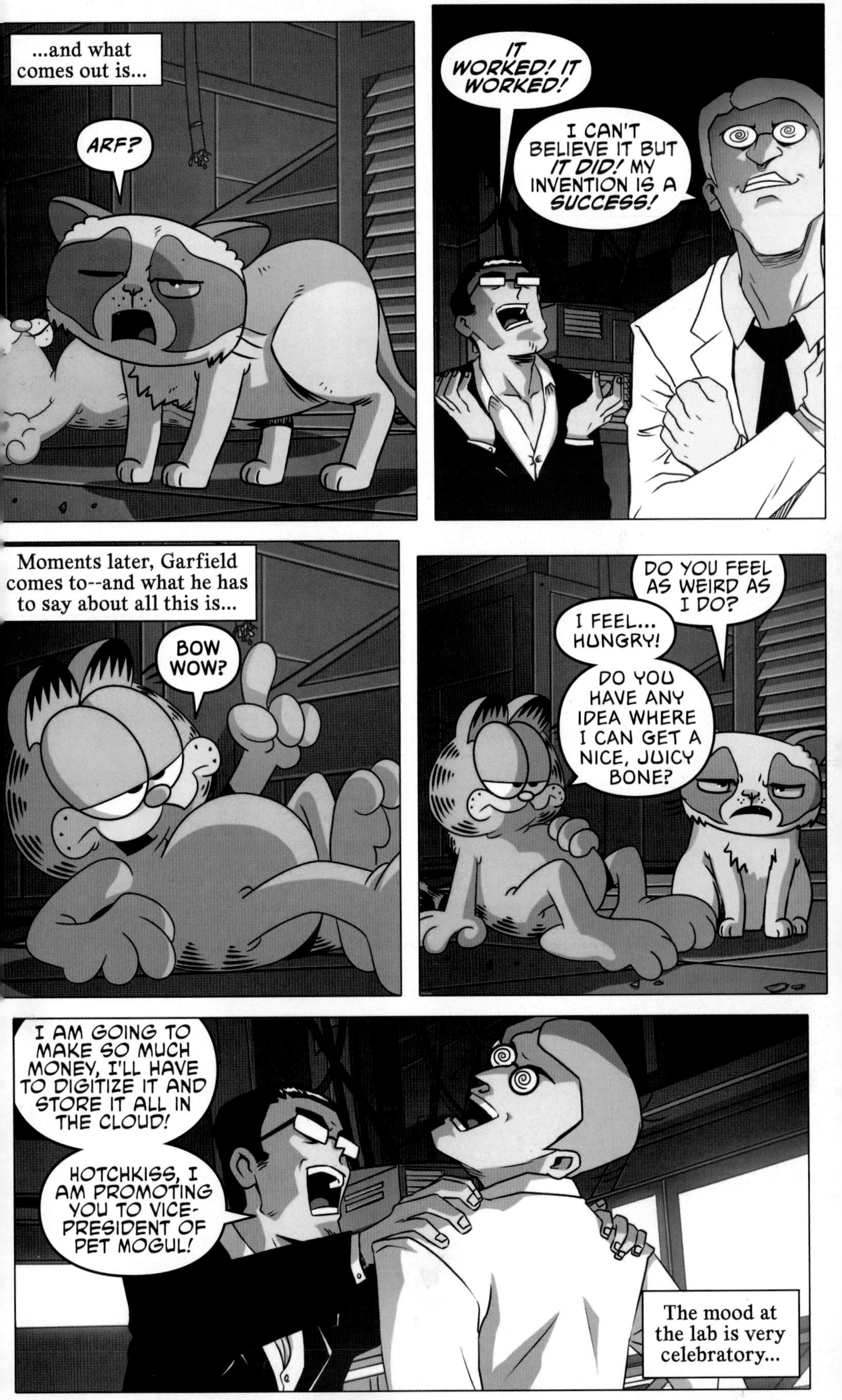
...and what comes out is...
ARF?
IT WORKED! IT WORKED!
I CAN'T BELIEVE IT BUT IT DID! MY INVENTION IS A SUCCESS!
Moments later, Garfield comes to--and what he has to say about all this is...
BOW WOW?
DO YOU FEEL AS WEIRD AS I DO?
I FEEL... HUNGRY!
DO YOU HAVE ANY IDEA WHERE I CAN GET A NICE, JUICY BONE?
I AM GOING TO MAKE SO MUCH MONEY, I'LL HAVE TO DIGITIZE IT AND STORE IT ALL IN THE CLOUD!
HOTCHKISS, I AM PROMOTING YOU TO VICE-PRESIDENT OF PET MOGUL!
The mood at the lab is very celebratory...

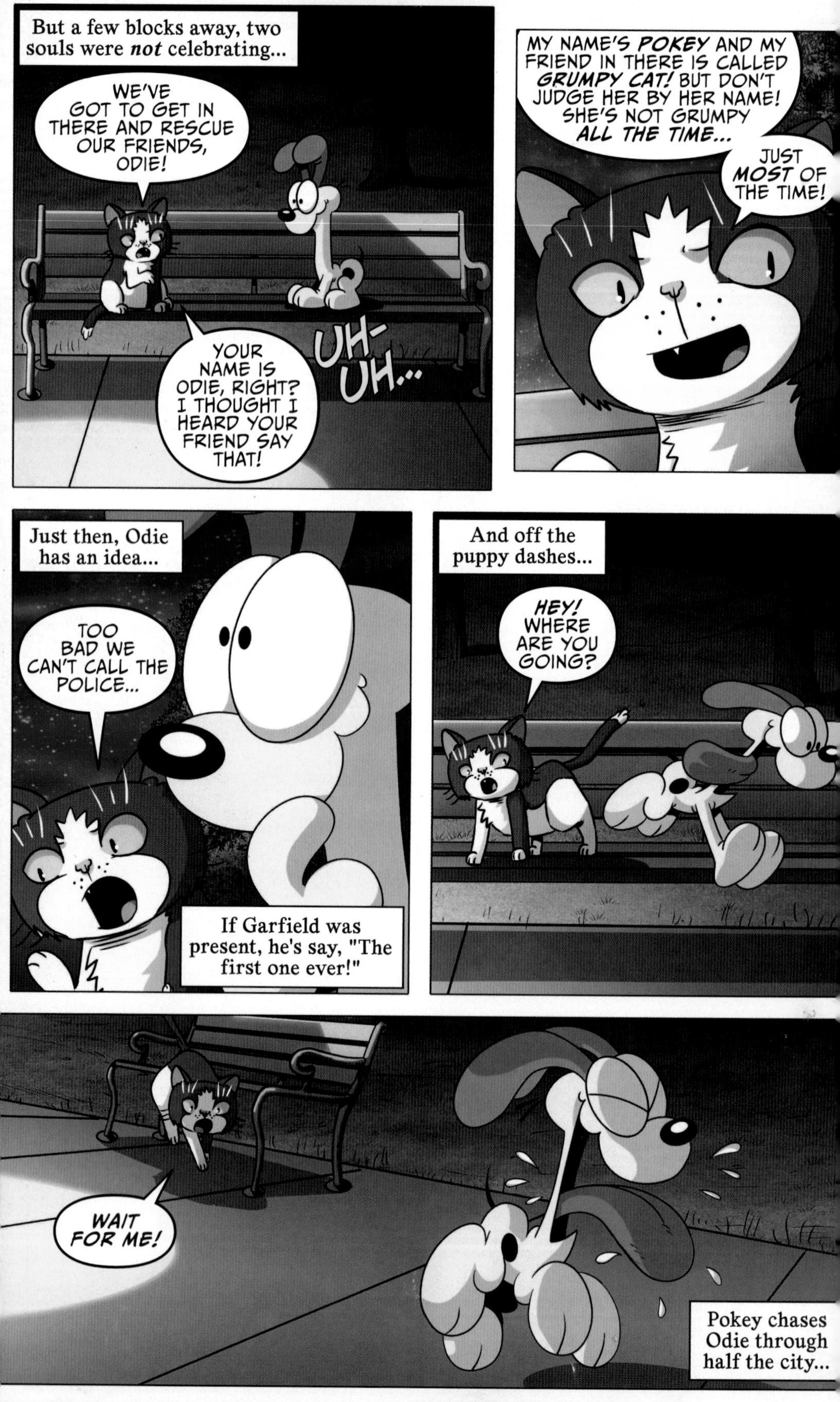
But a few blocks away, two souls were *not* celebrating...
WE'VE GOT TO GET IN THERE AND RESCUE OUR FRIENDS, ODIE!
YOUR NAME IS ODIE, RIGHT? I THOUGHT I HEARD YOUR FRIEND SAY THAT!
UH-UH...
MY NAME'S POKEY AND MY FRIEND IN THERE IS CALLED GRUMPY CAT! BUT DON'T JUDGE HER BY HER NAME! SHE'S NOT GRUMPY ALL THE TIME...
JUST MOST OF THE TIME!
Just then, Odie has an idea...
TOO BAD WE CAN'T CALL THE POLICE...
If Garfield was present, he's say, "The first one ever!"
And off the puppy dashes...
HEY! WHERE ARE YOU GOING?
WAIT FOR ME!
Pokey chases Odie through half the city...

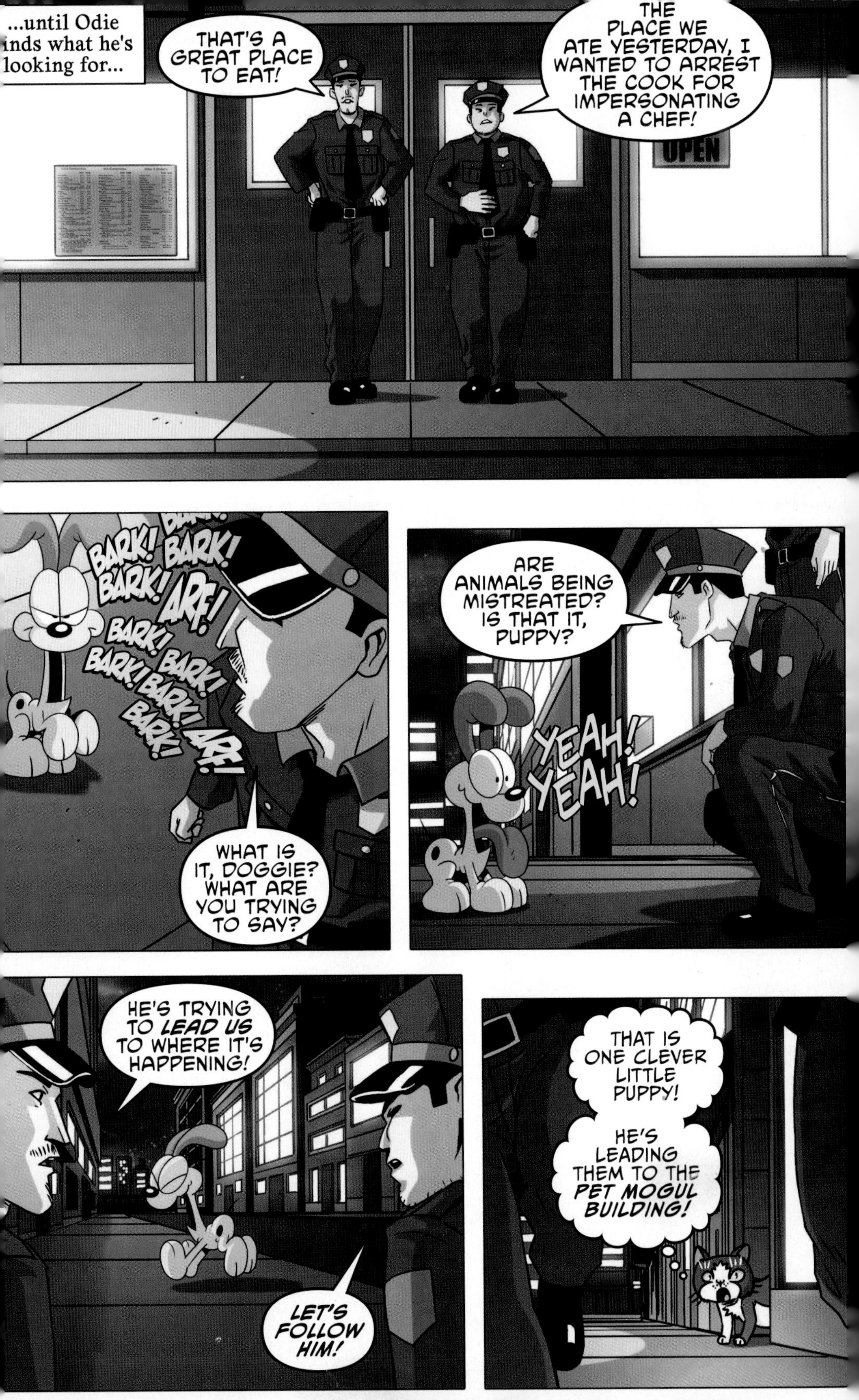
...until Odie
inds what he's
looking for...
THAT'S A GREAT PLACE TO EAT!
THE PLACE WE ATE YESTERDAY, I WANTED TO ARREST THE COOK FOR IMPERSONATING A CHEF!
OPEN
BARK! BARK! BARK! BARK! ARF! BARK! BARK! BARK! BARK! BARK! BARK! ARF!
WHAT IS IT, DOGGIE? WHAT ARE YOU TRYING TO SAY?
ARE ANIMALS BEING MISTREATED? IS THAT IT, PUPPY?
YEAH! YEAH!
HE'S TRYING TO *LEAD US* TO WHERE IT'S HAPPENING!
LET'S FOLLOW HIM!
THAT IS ONE CLEVER LITTLE PUPPY!
HE'S LEADING THEM TO THE *PET MOGUL BUILDING!*

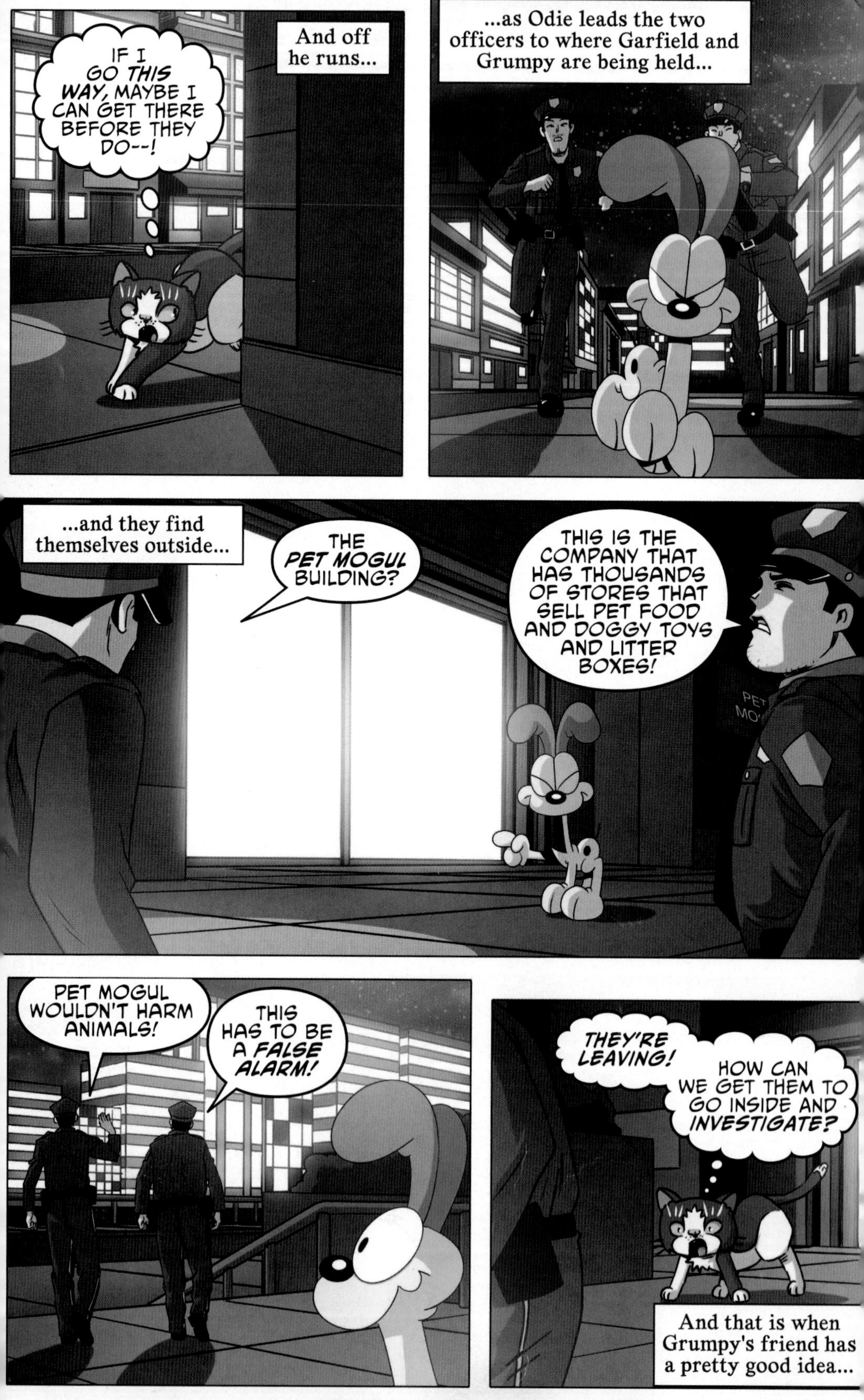
IF I GO THIS WAY, MAYBE I CAN GET THERE BEFORE THEY DO--!
And off he runs...
...as Odie leads the two officers to where Garfield and Grumpy are being held...
...and they find themselves outside...
THE PET MOGUL BUILDING?
THIS IS THE COMPANY THAT HAS THOUSANDS OF STORES THAT SELL PET FOOD AND DOGGY TOYS AND LITTER BOXES!
PET MOGUL WOULDN'T HARM ANIMALS!
THIS HAS TO BE A FALSE ALARM!
THEY'RE LEAVING!
HOW CAN WE GET THEM TO GO INSIDE AND INVESTIGATE?
And that is when Grumpy's friend has a pretty good idea...

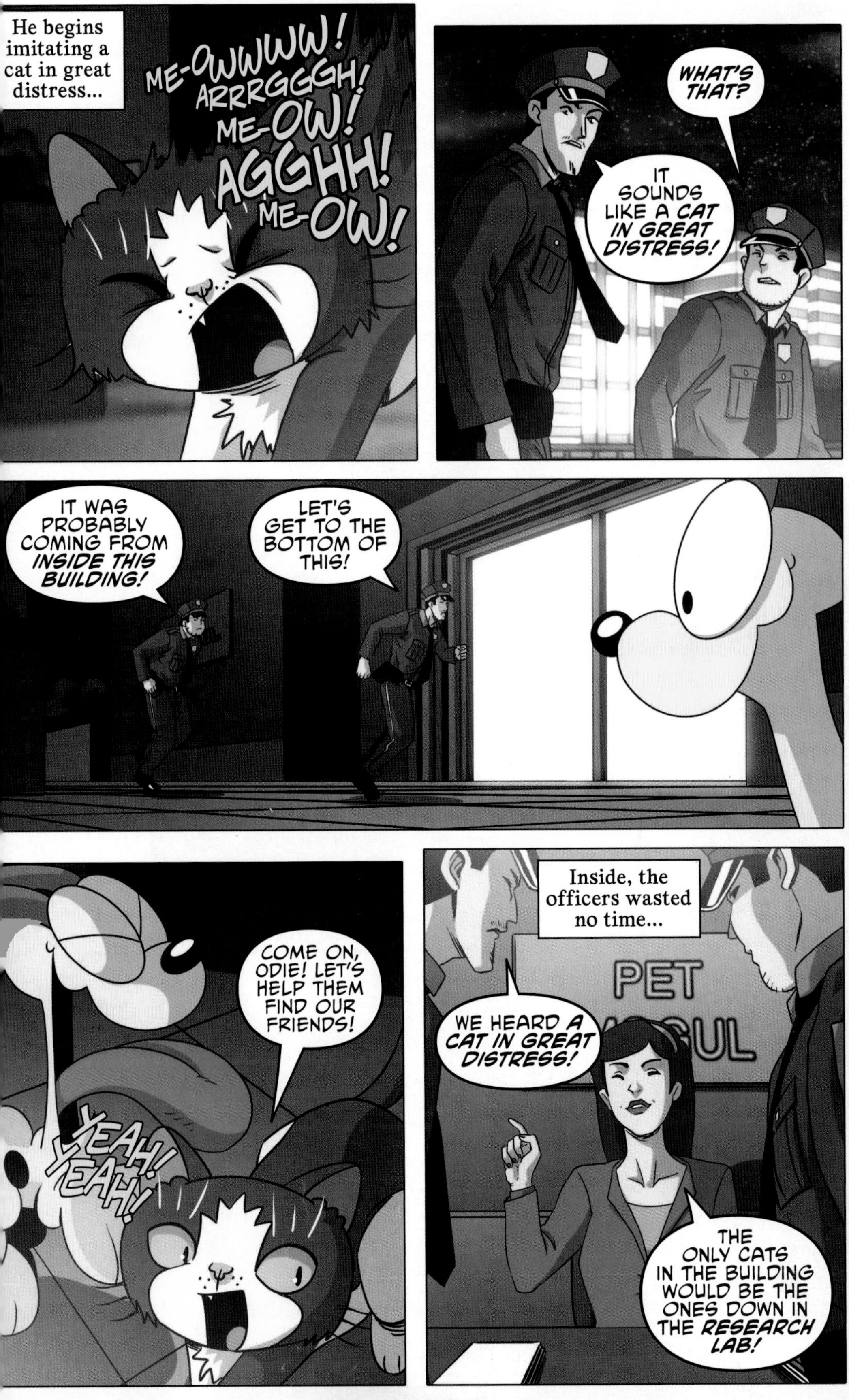
He begins imitating a cat in great distress...
ME-OWWWW! ARRRGGGH! ME-OW! AGGHH! ME-OW!
WHAT'S THAT?
IT SOUNDS LIKE A CAT IN GREAT DISTRESS!
IT WAS PROBABLY COMING FROM INSIDE THIS BUILDING!
LET'S GET TO THE BOTTOM OF THIS!
COME ON, ODIE! LET'S HELP THEM FIND OUR FRIENDS!
YEAH! YEAH!
Inside, the officers wasted no time...
PET
WE HEARD A CAT IN GREAT DISTRESS!
THE ONLY CATS IN THE BUILDING WOULD BE THE ONES DOWN IN THE RESEARCH LAB!

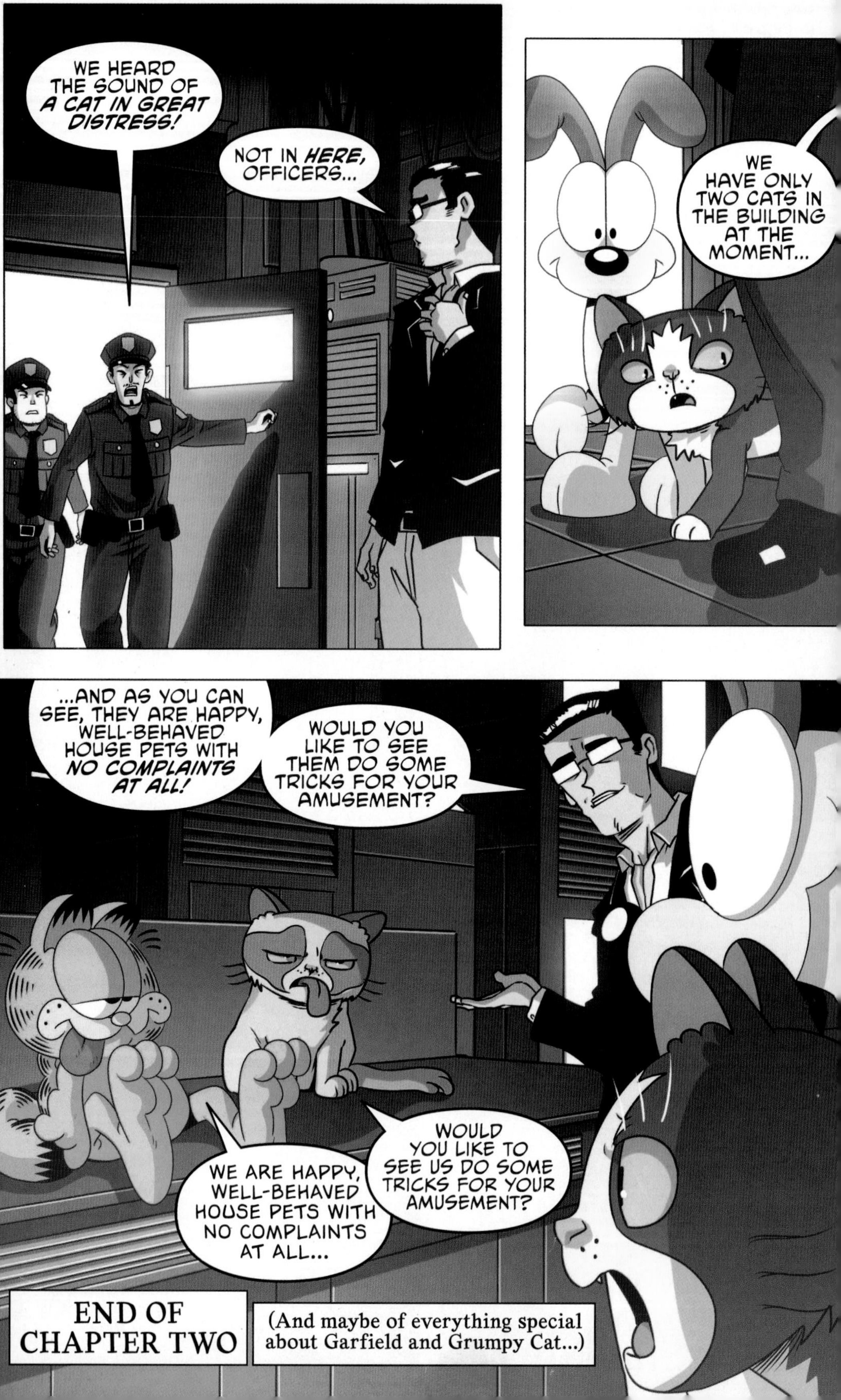
WE HEARD THE SOUND OF *A CAT IN GREAT DISTRESS!*
NOT IN *HERE*, OFFICERS...
WE HAVE ONLY TWO CATS IN THE BUILDING AT THE MOMENT...
...AND AS YOU CAN SEE, THEY ARE HAPPY, WELL-BEHAVED HOUSE PETS WITH *NO COMPLAINTS AT ALL!*
WOULD YOU LIKE TO SEE THEM DO SOME TRICKS FOR YOUR AMUSEMENT?
WE ARE HAPPY, WELL-BEHAVED HOUSE PETS WITH NO COMPLAINTS AT ALL...
WOULD YOU LIKE TO SEE US DO SOME TRICKS FOR YOUR AMUSEMENT?

END OF CHAPTER TWO

(And maybe of everything special about Garfield and Grumpy Cat...)

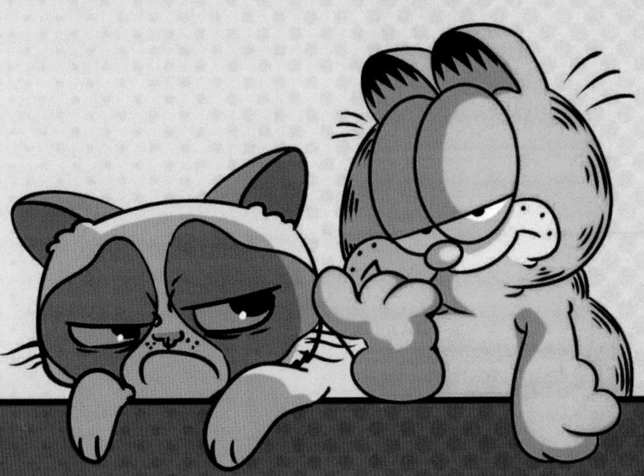

CHAPTER 3

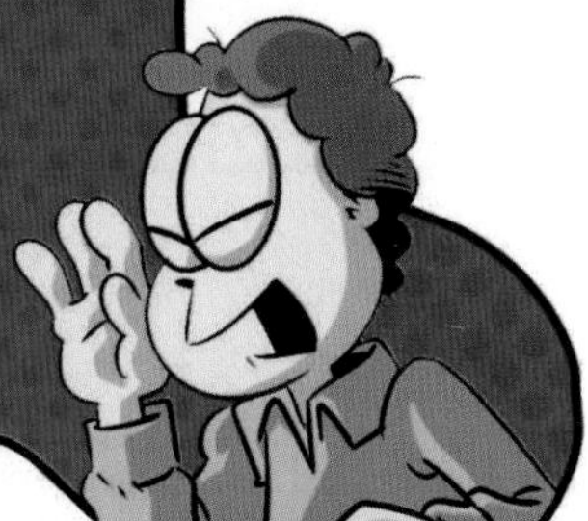

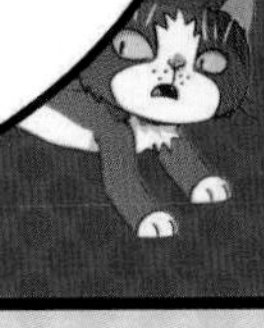

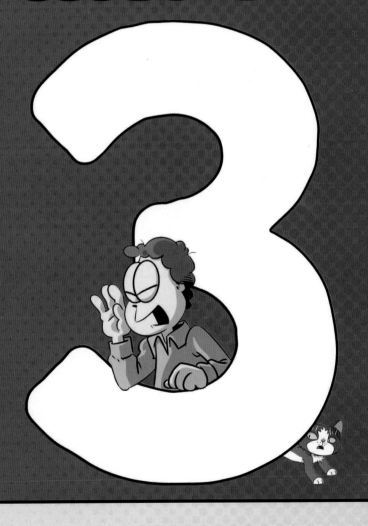

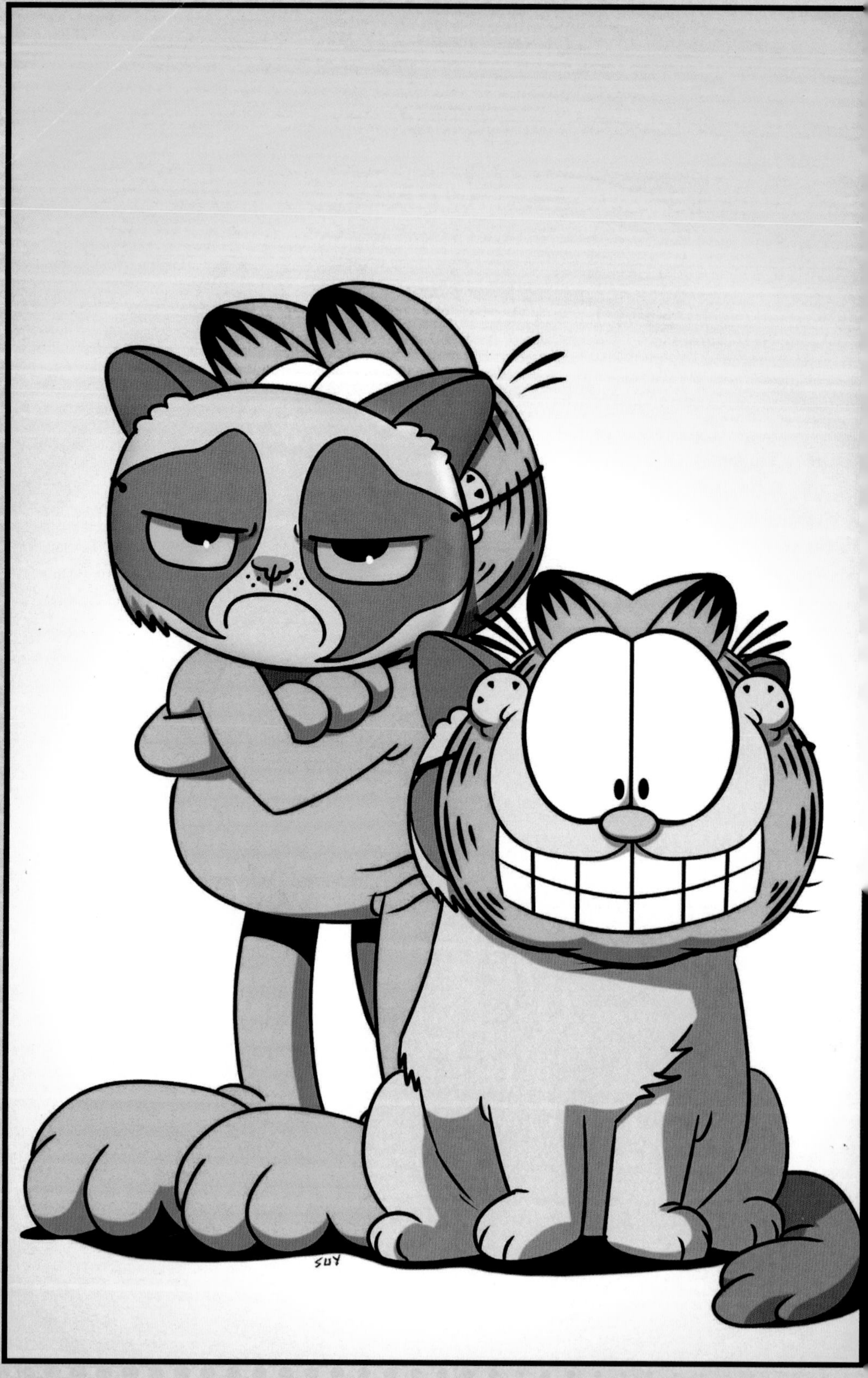
SUY

ISSUE 3 COVER BY: **STEVE UY**

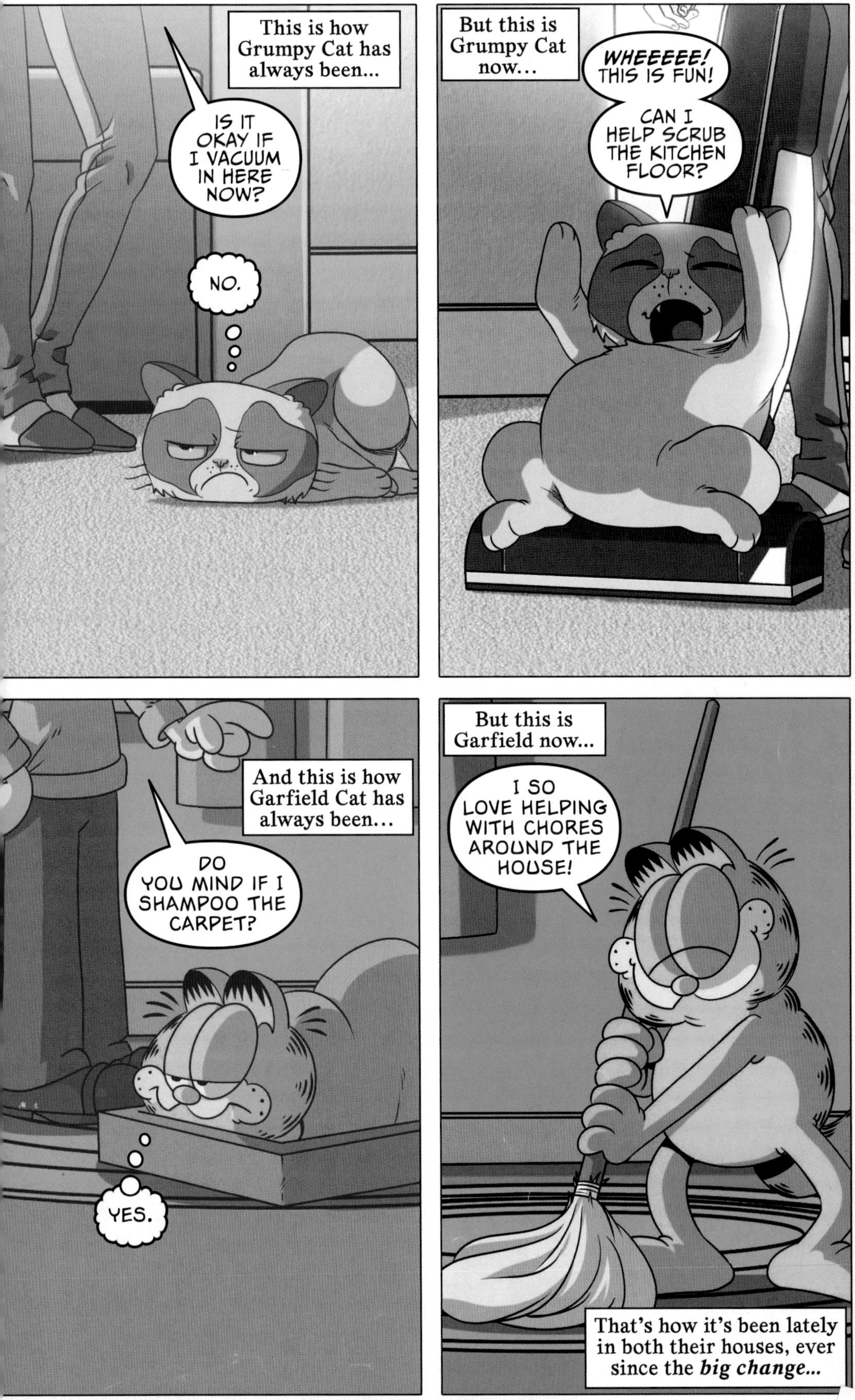
This is how Grumpy Cat has always been...
IS IT OKAY IF I VACUUM IN HERE NOW?
NO.
But this is Grumpy Cat now...
WHEEEEE! THIS IS FUN!
CAN I HELP SCRUB THE KITCHEN FLOOR?
And this is how Garfield Cat has always been...
DO YOU MIND IF I SHAMPOO THE CARPET?
YES.
But this is Garfield now...
I SO LOVE HELPING WITH CHORES AROUND THE HOUSE!
That's how it's been lately in both their houses, ever since the *big change...*

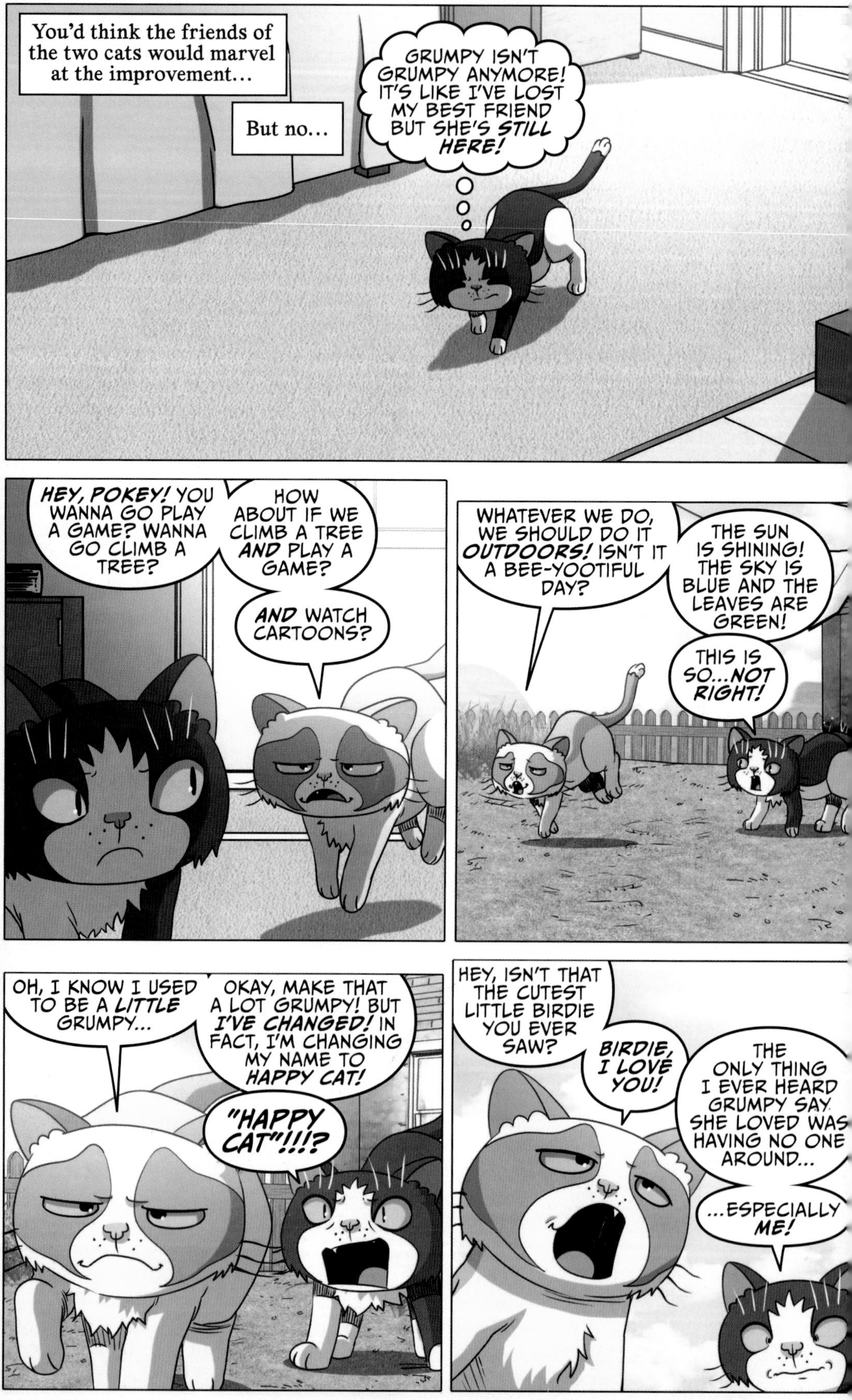
You'd think the friends of the two cats would marvel at the improvement…
But no…
GRUMPY ISN'T GRUMPY ANYMORE! IT'S LIKE I'VE LOST MY BEST FRIEND BUT SHE'S STILL HERE!
HEY, POKEY! YOU WANNA GO PLAY A GAME? WANNA GO CLIMB A TREE?
HOW ABOUT IF WE CLIMB A TREE AND PLAY A GAME?
AND WATCH CARTOONS?
WHATEVER WE DO, WE SHOULD DO IT OUTDOORS! ISN'T IT A BEE-YOOTIFUL DAY?
THE SUN IS SHINING! THE SKY IS BLUE AND THE LEAVES ARE GREEN!
THIS IS SO...NOT RIGHT!
OH, I KNOW I USED TO BE A LITTLE GRUMPY...
OKAY, MAKE THAT A LOT GRUMPY! BUT I'VE CHANGED! IN FACT, I'M CHANGING MY NAME TO HAPPY CAT!
"HAPPY CAT"!!!?
HEY, ISN'T THAT THE CUTEST LITTLE BIRDIE YOU EVER SAW?
BIRDIE, I LOVE YOU!
THE ONLY THING I EVER HEARD GRUMPY SAY SHE LOVED WAS HAVING NO ONE AROUND...
...ESPECIALLY ME!

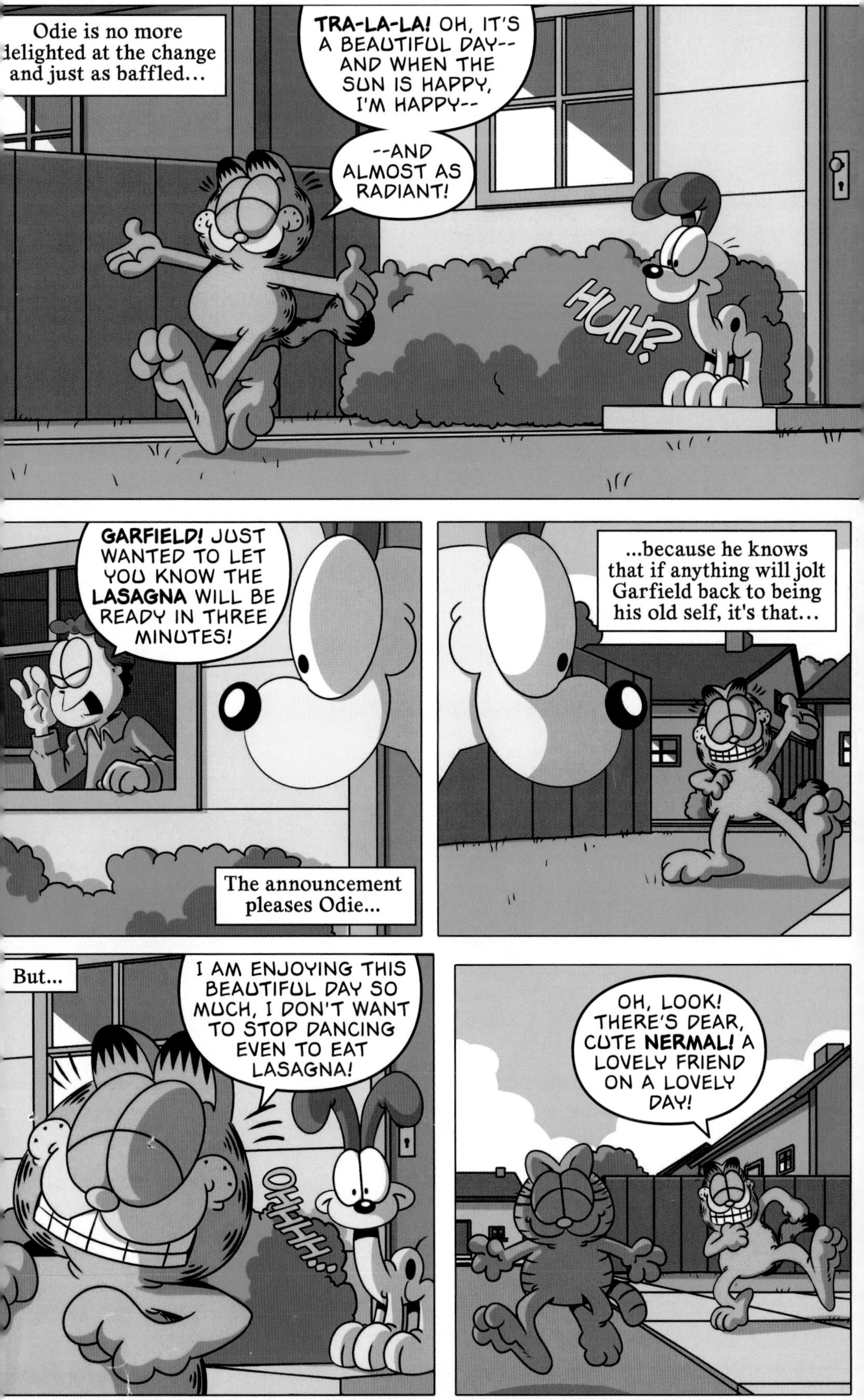

Odie is no more delighted at the change and just as baffled...
TRA-LA-LA! OH, IT'S A BEAUTIFUL DAY-- AND WHEN THE SUN IS HAPPY, I'M HAPPY--
--AND ALMOST AS RADIANT!
HUH?
GARFIELD! JUST WANTED TO LET YOU KNOW THE LASAGNA WILL BE READY IN THREE MINUTES!
The announcement pleases Odie...
...because he knows that if anything will jolt Garfield back to being his old self, it's that...
But...
I AM ENJOYING THIS BEAUTIFUL DAY SO MUCH, I DON'T WANT TO STOP DANCING EVEN TO EAT LASAGNA!
OHHHH...
OH, LOOK! THERE'S DEAR, CUTE NERMAL! A LOVELY FRIEND ON A LOVELY DAY!

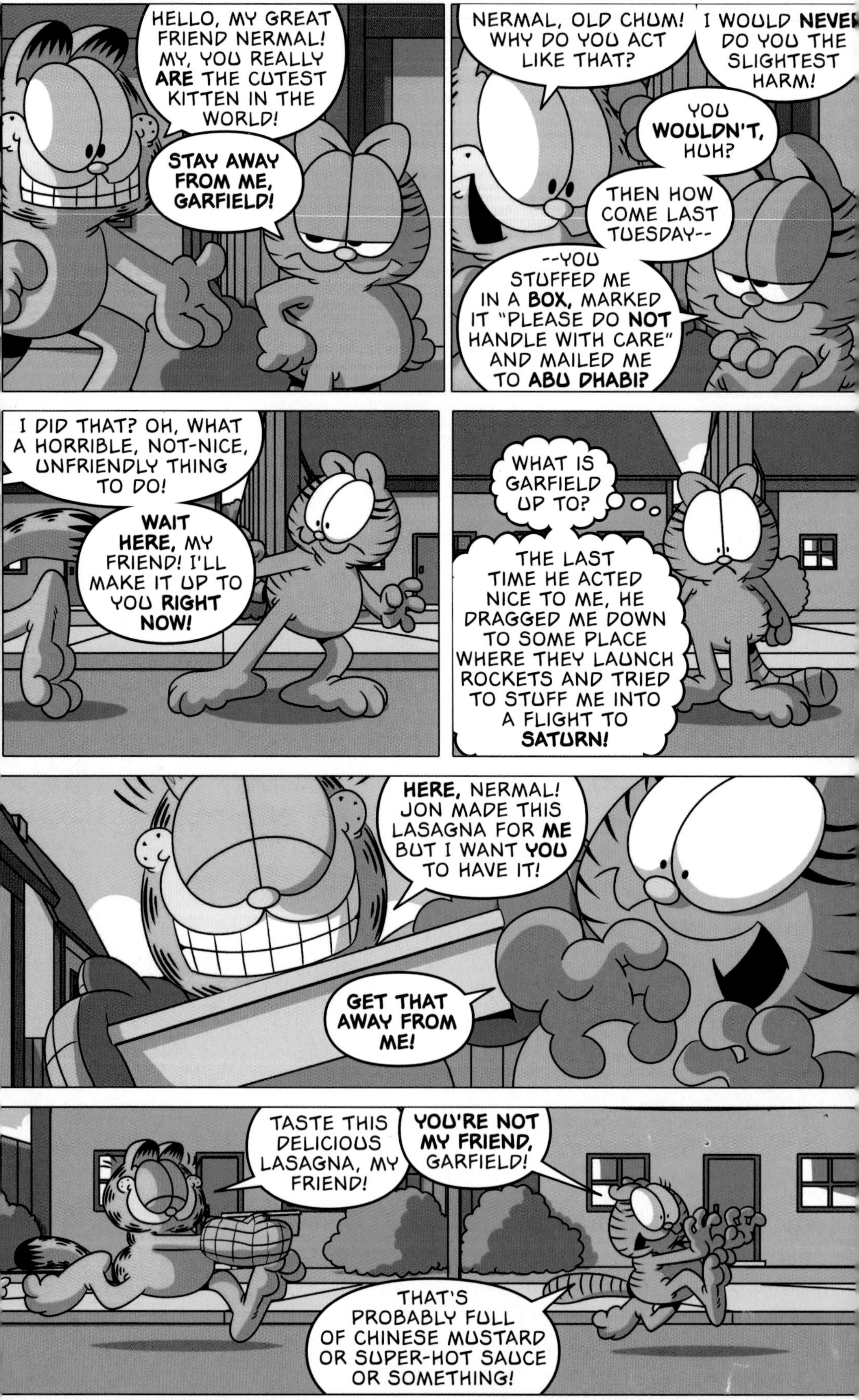
HELLO, MY GREAT FRIEND NERMAL! MY, YOU REALLY ARE THE CUTEST KITTEN IN THE WORLD!
STAY AWAY FROM ME, GARFIELD!
NERMAL, OLD CHUM! WHY DO YOU ACT LIKE THAT?
I WOULD NEVER DO YOU THE SLIGHTEST HARM!
YOU WOULDN'T, HUH?
THEN HOW COME LAST TUESDAY--
--YOU STUFFED ME IN A BOX, MARKED IT "PLEASE DO NOT HANDLE WITH CARE" AND MAILED ME TO ABU DHABI?
I DID THAT? OH, WHAT A HORRIBLE, NOT-NICE, UNFRIENDLY THING TO DO!
WAIT HERE, MY FRIEND! I'LL MAKE IT UP TO YOU RIGHT NOW!
WHAT IS GARFIELD UP TO?
THE LAST TIME HE ACTED NICE TO ME, HE DRAGGED ME DOWN TO SOME PLACE WHERE THEY LAUNCH ROCKETS AND TRIED TO STUFF ME INTO A FLIGHT TO SATURN!
HERE, NERMAL! JON MADE THIS LASAGNA FOR ME BUT I WANT YOU TO HAVE IT!
GET THAT AWAY FROM ME!
TASTE THIS DELICIOUS LASAGNA, MY FRIEND!
YOU'RE NOT MY FRIEND, GARFIELD!
THAT'S PROBABLY FULL OF CHINESE MUSTARD OR SUPER-HOT SAUCE OR SOMETHING!

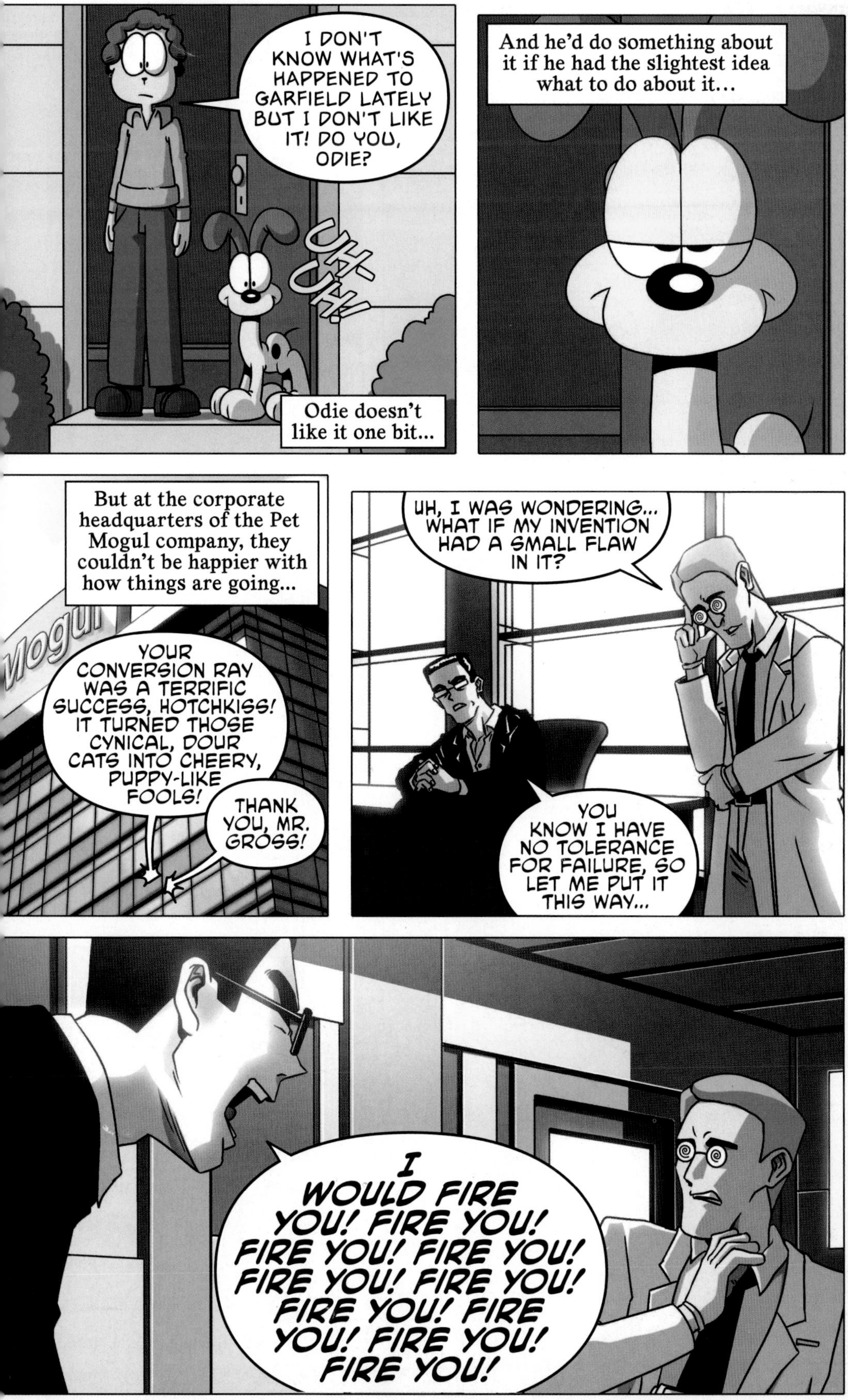
I DON'T KNOW WHAT'S HAPPENED TO GARFIELD LATELY BUT I DON'T LIKE IT! DO YOU, ODIE?
UH-UH!
Odie doesn't like it one bit...
And he'd do something about it if he had the slightest idea what to do about it…
But at the corporate headquarters of the Pet Mogul company, they couldn't be happier with how things are going...
Mogul
YOUR CONVERSION RAY WAS A TERRIFIC SUCCESS, HOTCHKISS! IT TURNED THOSE CYNICAL, DOUR CATS INTO CHEERY, PUPPY-LIKE FOOLS!
THANK YOU, MR. GROSS!
UH, I WAS WONDERING... WHAT IF MY INVENTION HAD A SMALL FLAW IN IT?
YOU KNOW I HAVE NO TOLERANCE FOR FAILURE, SO LET ME PUT IT THIS WAY...
I WOULD FIRE YOU! FIRE YOU! FIRE YOU! FIRE YOU! FIRE YOU! FIRE YOU! FIRE YOU! FIRE YOU! FIRE YOU! FIRE YOU!

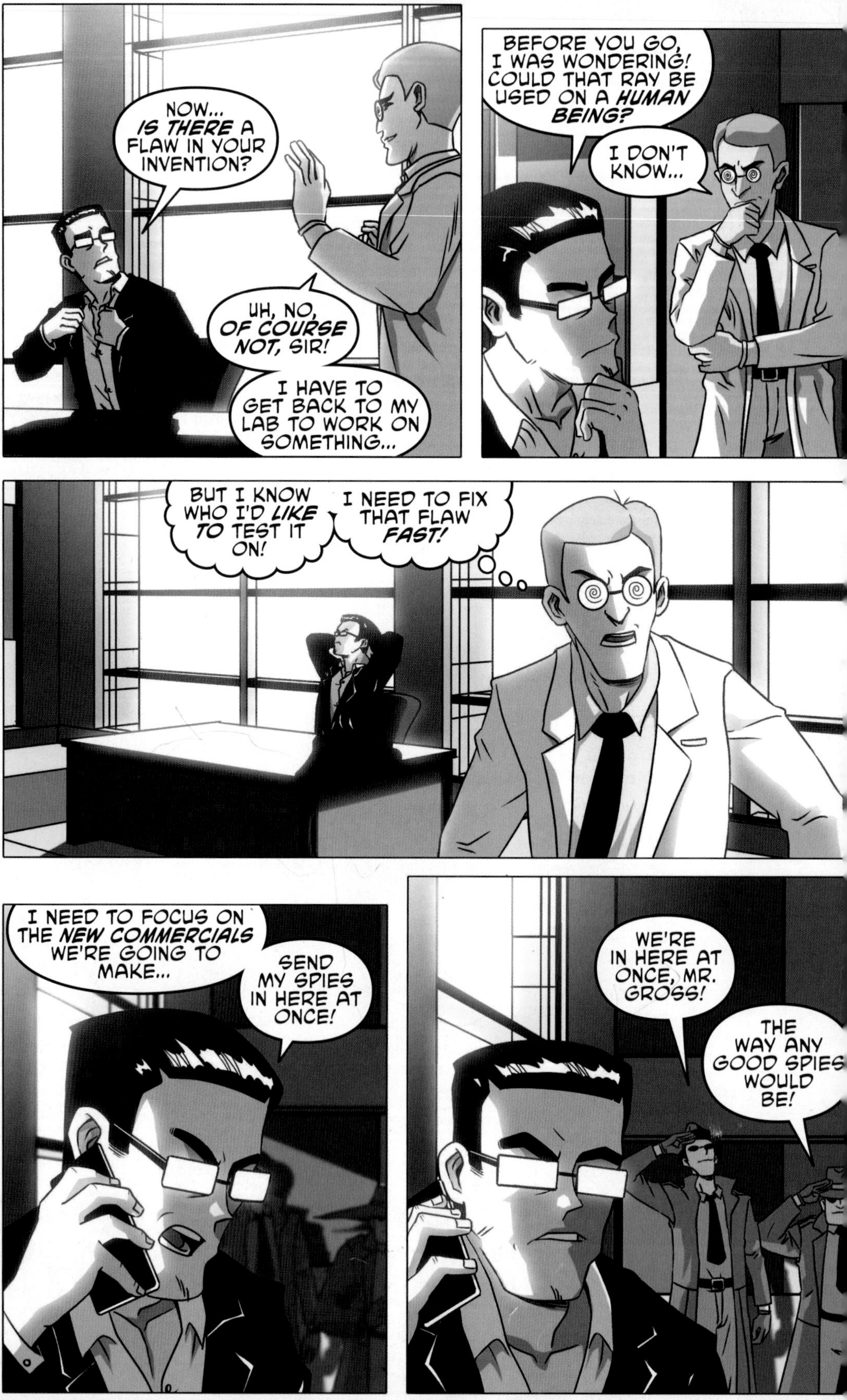
NOW... IS THERE A FLAW IN YOUR INVENTION?
UH, NO, OF COURSE NOT, SIR!
I HAVE TO GET BACK TO MY LAB TO WORK ON SOMETHING...
BEFORE YOU GO, I WAS WONDERING! COULD THAT RAY BE USED ON A HUMAN BEING?
I DON'T KNOW...
BUT I KNOW WHO I'D LIKE TO TEST IT ON!
I NEED TO FIX THAT FLAW FAST!
I NEED TO FOCUS ON THE NEW COMMERCIALS WE'RE GOING TO MAKE...
SEND MY SPIES IN HERE AT ONCE!
WE'RE IN HERE AT ONCE, MR. GROSS!
THE WAY ANY GOOD SPIES WOULD BE!

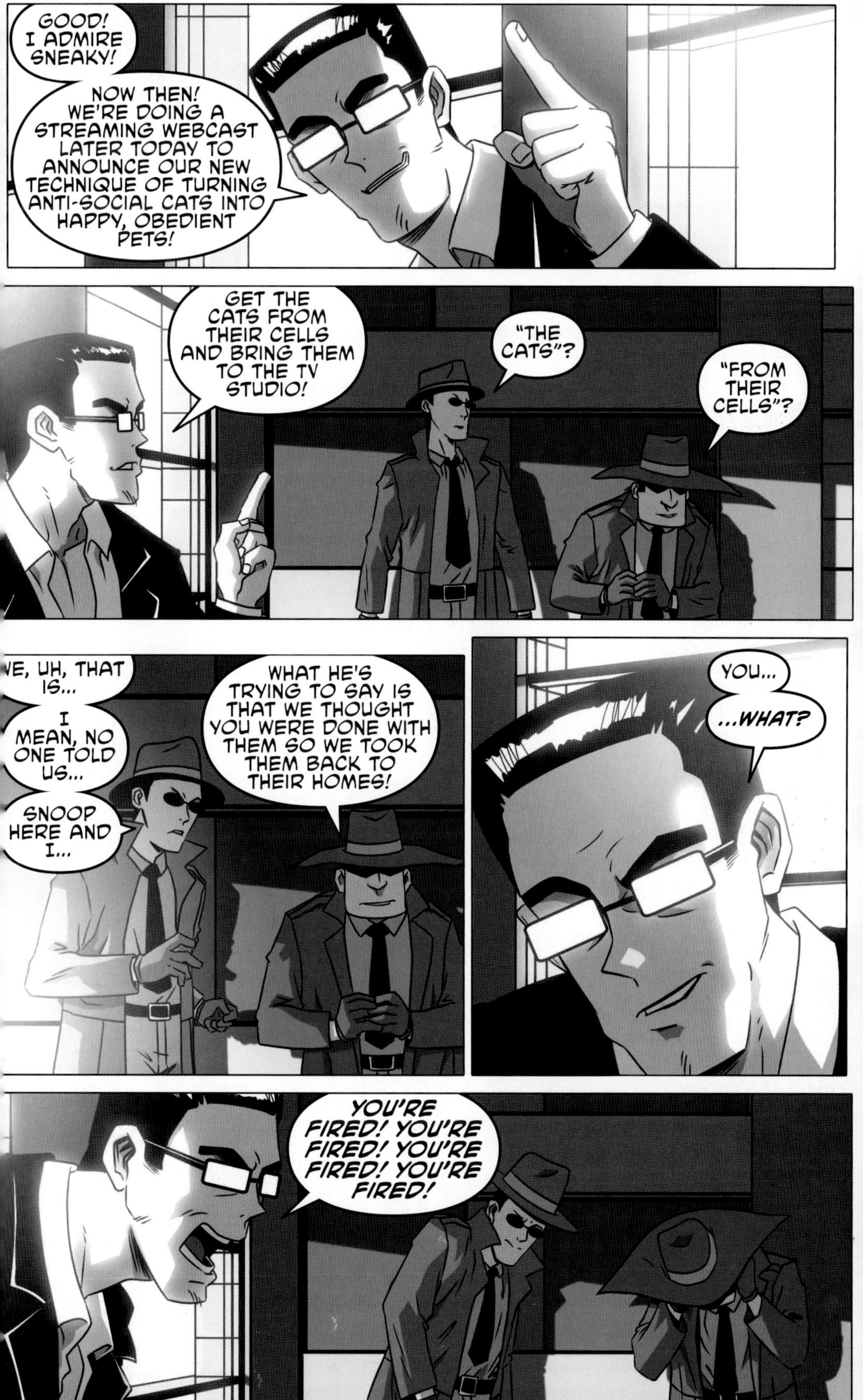
GOOD! I ADMIRE SNEAKY!
NOW THEN! WE'RE DOING A STREAMING WEBCAST LATER TODAY TO ANNOUNCE OUR NEW TECHNIQUE OF TURNING ANTI-SOCIAL CATS INTO HAPPY, OBEDIENT PETS!
GET THE CATS FROM THEIR CELLS AND BRING THEM TO THE TV STUDIO!
"THE CATS"?
"FROM THEIR CELLS"?
WE, UH, THAT IS...
I MEAN, NO ONE TOLD US...
SNOOP HERE AND I...
WHAT HE'S TRYING TO SAY IS THAT WE THOUGHT YOU WERE DONE WITH THEM SO WE TOOK THEM BACK TO THEIR HOMES!
YOU...
...WHAT?
YOU'RE FIRED! YOU'RE FIRED! YOU'RE FIRED! YOU'RE FIRED!

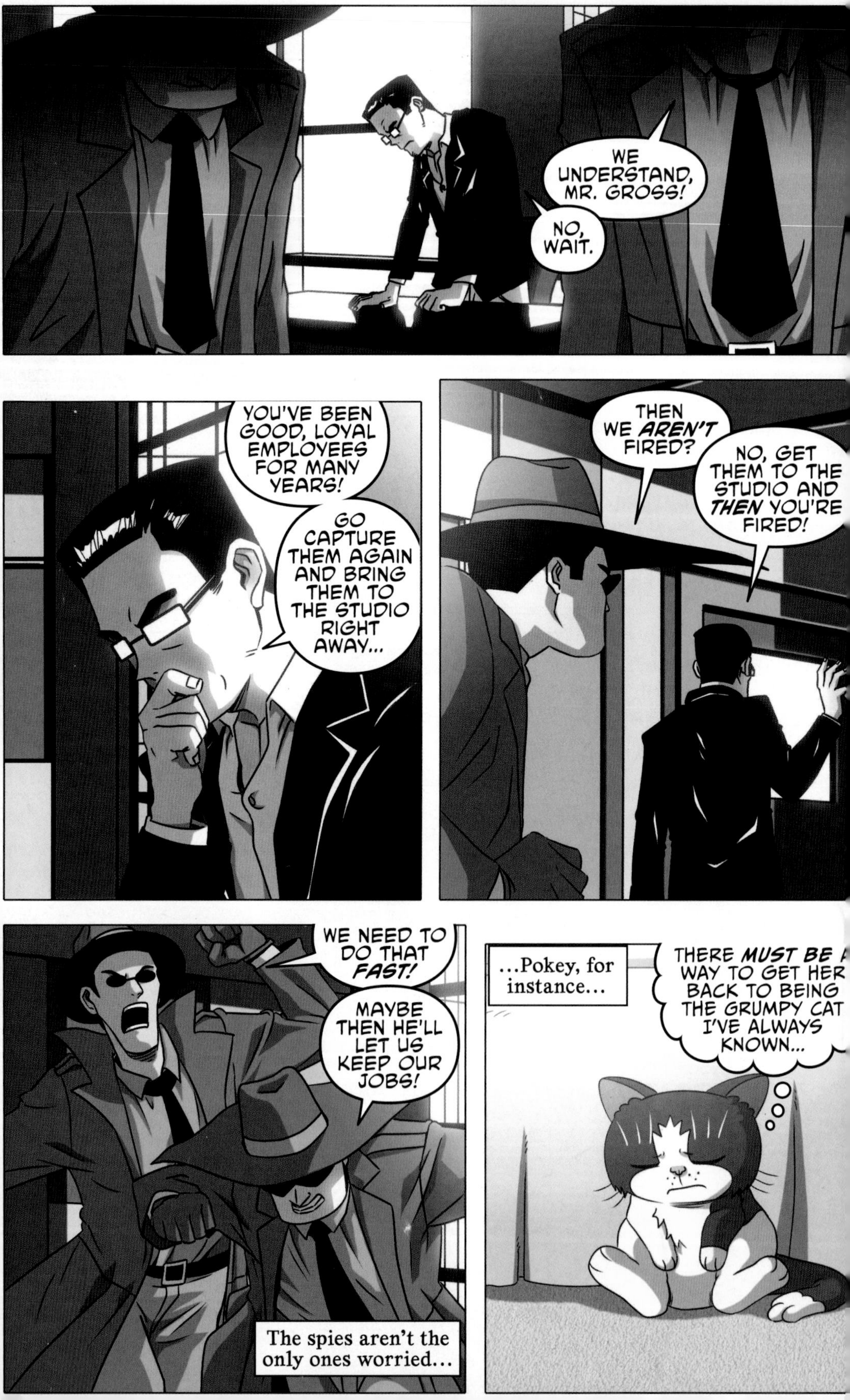
WE UNDERSTAND, MR. GROSS!
NO, WAIT.
YOU'VE BEEN GOOD, LOYAL EMPLOYEES FOR MANY YEARS!
GO CAPTURE THEM AGAIN AND BRING THEM TO THE STUDIO RIGHT AWAY...
THEN WE AREN'T FIRED?
NO, GET THEM TO THE STUDIO AND THEN YOU'RE FIRED!
WE NEED TO DO THAT FAST!
MAYBE THEN HE'LL LET US KEEP OUR JOBS!
The spies aren't the only ones worried...
...Pokey, for instance...
THERE MUST BE A WAY TO GET HER BACK TO BEING THE GRUMPY CAT I'VE ALWAYS KNOWN...

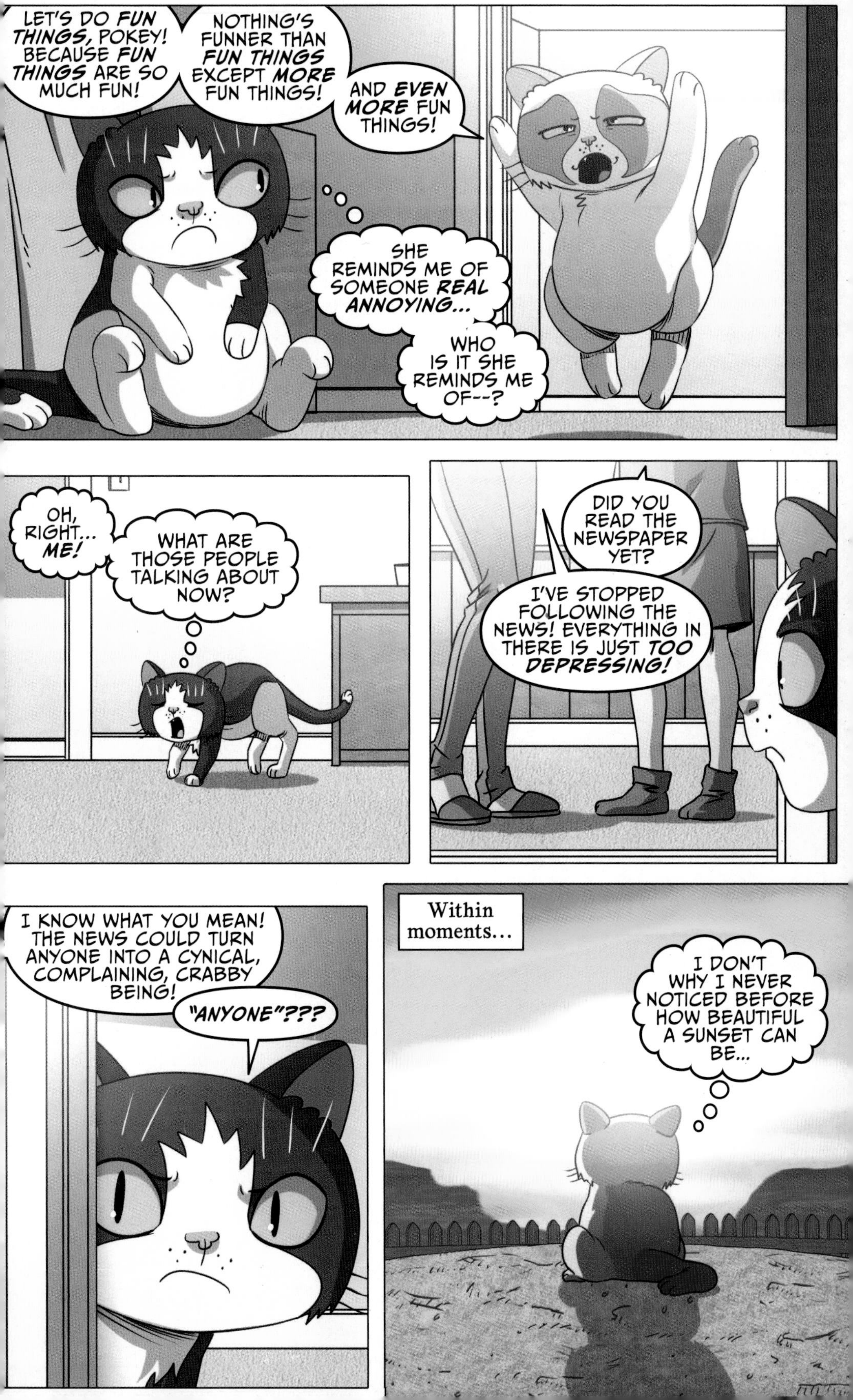
LET'S DO FUN THINGS, POKEY! BECAUSE FUN THINGS ARE SO MUCH FUN!
NOTHING'S FUNNER THAN FUN THINGS EXCEPT MORE FUN THINGS!
AND EVEN MORE FUN THINGS!
SHE REMINDS ME OF SOMEONE REAL ANNOYING...
WHO IS IT SHE REMINDS ME OF--?
OH, RIGHT... ME!
WHAT ARE THOSE PEOPLE TALKING ABOUT NOW?
DID YOU READ THE NEWSPAPER YET?
I'VE STOPPED FOLLOWING THE NEWS! EVERYTHING IN THERE IS JUST TOO DEPRESSING!
I KNOW WHAT YOU MEAN! THE NEWS COULD TURN ANYONE INTO A CYNICAL, COMPLAINING, CRABBY BEING!
"ANYONE"???
Within moments...
I DON'T WHY I NEVER NOTICED BEFORE HOW BEAUTIFUL A SUNSET CAN BE...

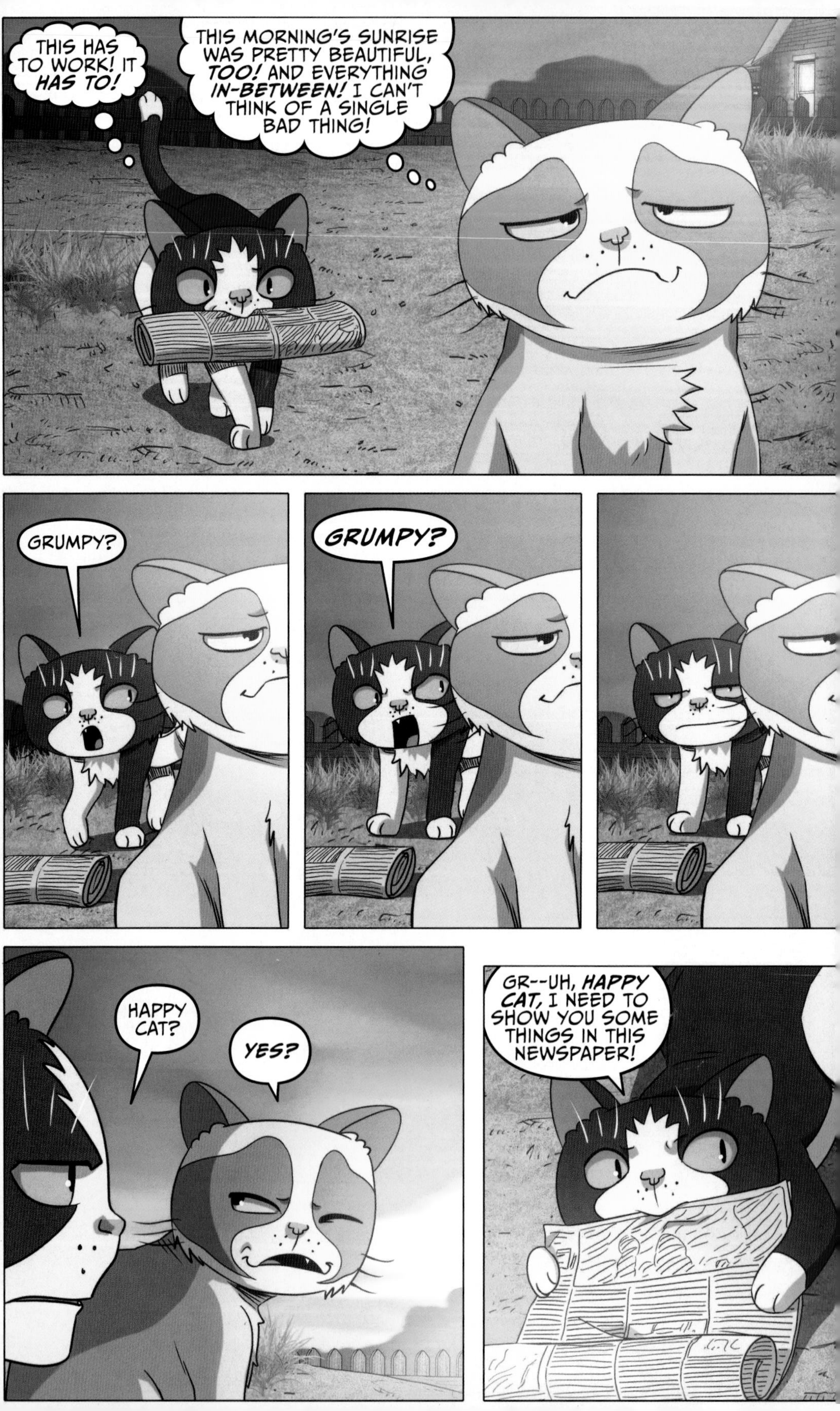
THIS HAS TO WORK! IT *HAS TO!*
THIS MORNING'S SUNRISE WAS PRETTY BEAUTIFUL, *TOO!* AND EVERYTHING *IN-BETWEEN!* I CAN'T THINK OF A SINGLE BAD THING!
GRUMPY?
GRUMPY?
HAPPY CAT?
YES?
GR--UH, *HAPPY CAT,* I NEED TO SHOW YOU SOME THINGS IN THIS NEWSPAPER!

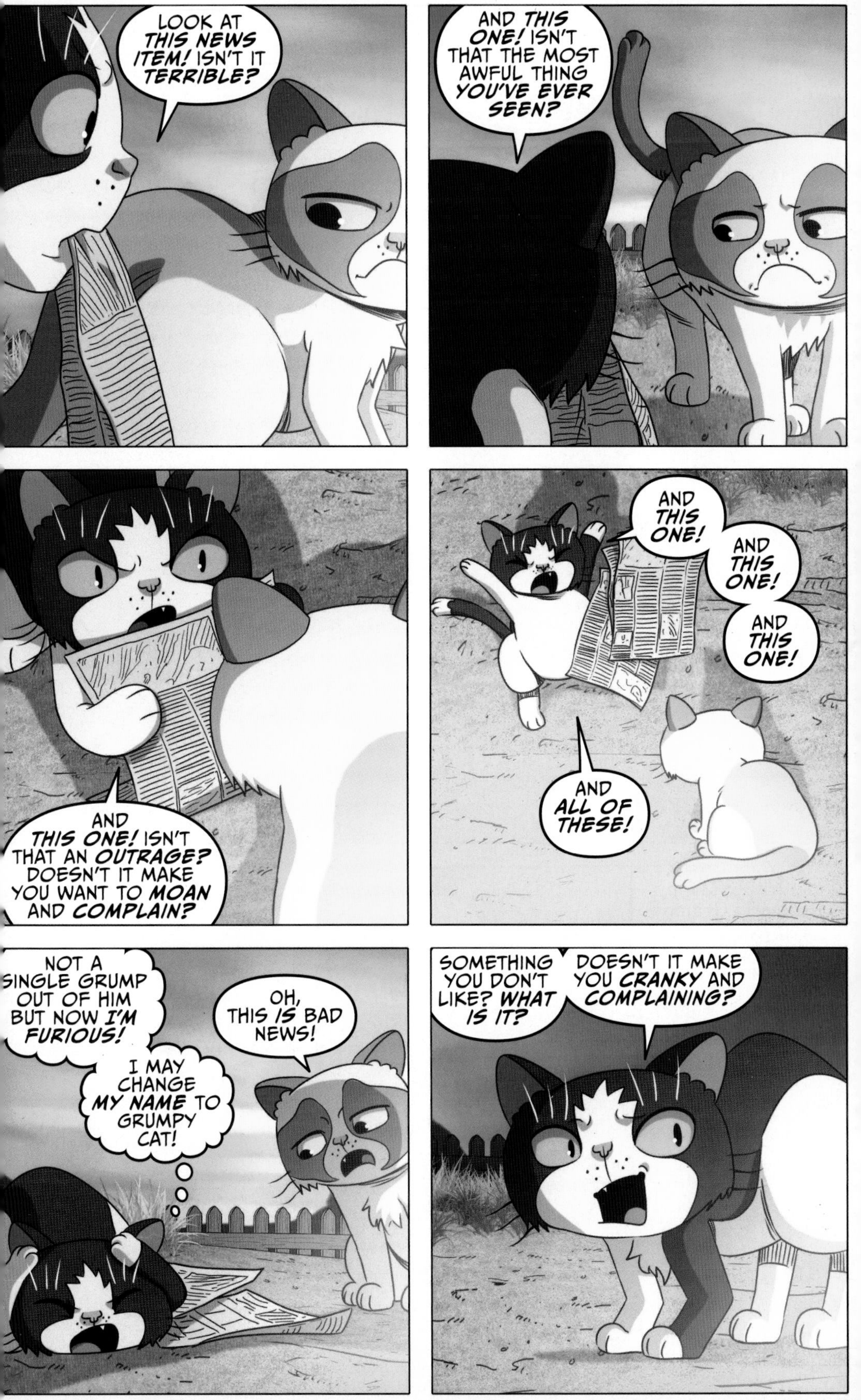
LOOK AT THIS NEWS ITEM! ISN'T IT TERRIBLE?
AND THIS ONE! ISN'T THAT THE MOST AWFUL THING YOU'VE EVER SEEN?
AND THIS ONE! ISN'T THAT AN OUTRAGE? DOESN'T IT MAKE YOU WANT TO MOAN AND COMPLAIN?
AND THIS ONE!
AND THIS ONE!
AND THIS ONE!
AND ALL OF THESE!
NOT A SINGLE GRUMP OUT OF HIM BUT NOW I'M FURIOUS!
I MAY CHANGE MY NAME TO GRUMPY CAT!
OH, THIS IS BAD NEWS!
SOMETHING YOU DON'T LIKE? WHAT IS IT?
DOESN'T IT MAKE YOU CRANKY AND COMPLAINING?

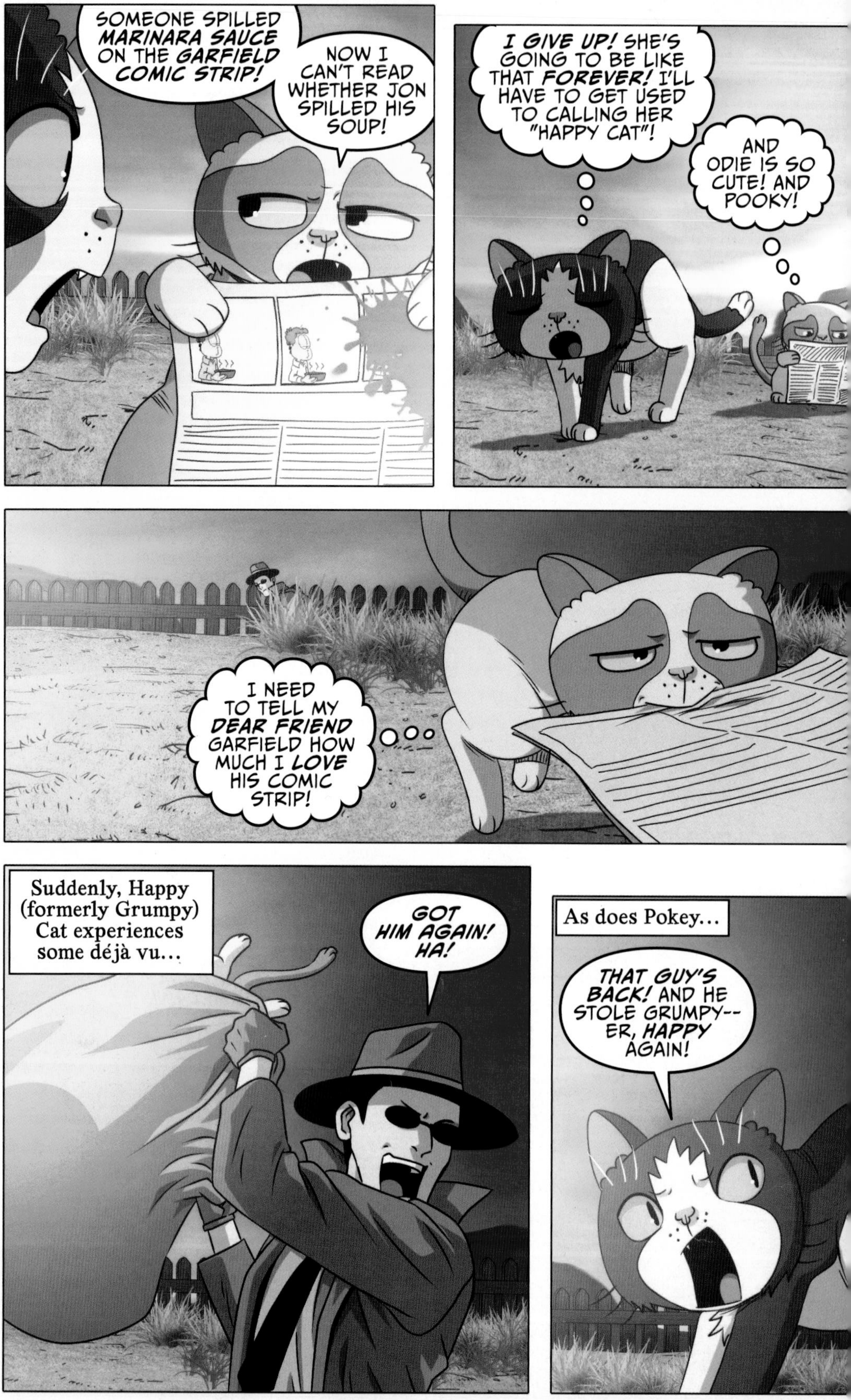
SOMEONE SPILLED MARINARA SAUCE ON THE GARFIELD COMIC STRIP!
NOW I CAN'T READ WHETHER JON SPILLED HIS SOUP!
I GIVE UP! SHE'S GOING TO BE LIKE THAT FOREVER! I'LL HAVE TO GET USED TO CALLING HER "HAPPY CAT"!
AND ODIE IS SO CUTE! AND POOKY!
I NEED TO TELL MY DEAR FRIEND GARFIELD HOW MUCH I LOVE HIS COMIC STRIP!
Suddenly, Happy (formerly Grumpy) Cat experiences some déjà vu…
GOT HIM AGAIN! HA!
As does Pokey…
THAT GUY'S BACK! AND HE STOLE GRUMPY-- ER, HAPPY AGAIN!

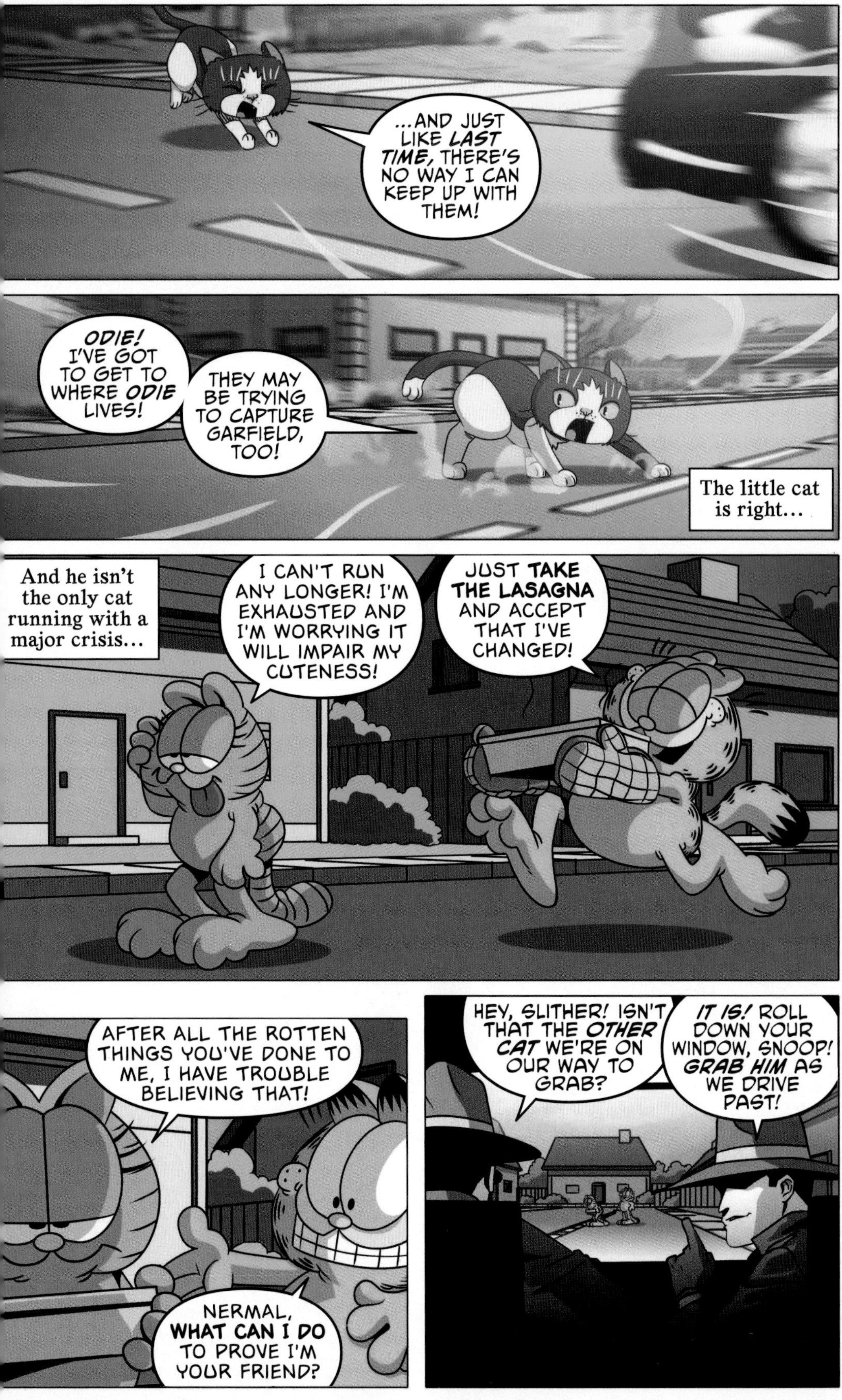

...AND JUST LIKE LAST TIME, THERE'S NO WAY I CAN KEEP UP WITH THEM!
ODIE! I'VE GOT TO GET TO WHERE ODIE LIVES!
THEY MAY BE TRYING TO CAPTURE GARFIELD, TOO!
The little cat is right...
And he isn't the only cat running with a major crisis...
I CAN'T RUN ANY LONGER! I'M EXHAUSTED AND I'M WORRYING IT WILL IMPAIR MY CUTENESS!
JUST TAKE THE LASAGNA AND ACCEPT THAT I'VE CHANGED!
AFTER ALL THE ROTTEN THINGS YOU'VE DONE TO ME, I HAVE TROUBLE BELIEVING THAT!
NERMAL, WHAT CAN I DO TO PROVE I'M YOUR FRIEND?
HEY, SLITHER! ISN'T THAT THE OTHER CAT WE'RE ON OUR WAY TO GRAB?
IT IS! ROLL DOWN YOUR WINDOW, SNOOP! GRAB HIM AS WE DRIVE PAST!

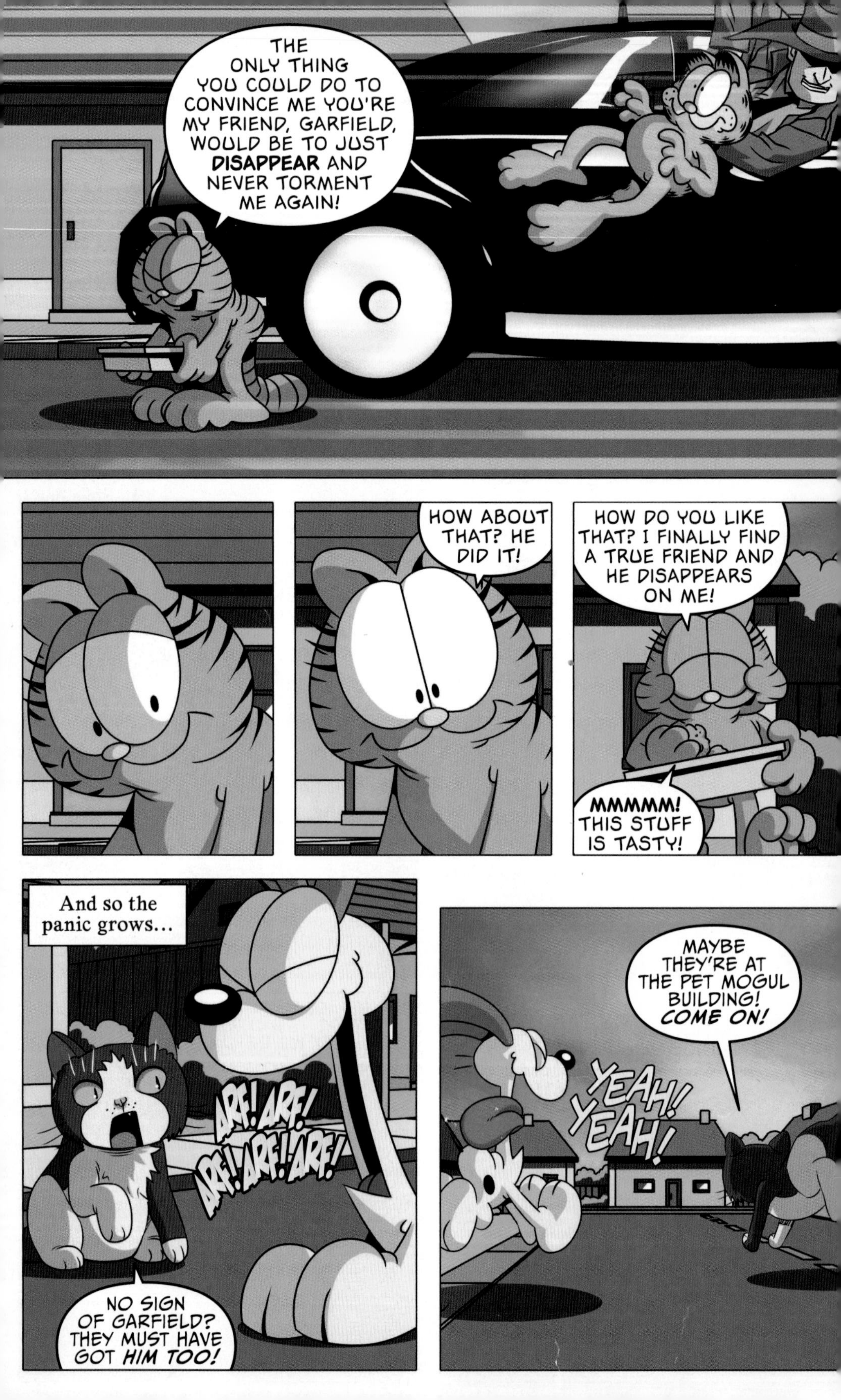

THE ONLY THING YOU COULD DO TO CONVINCE ME YOU'RE MY FRIEND, GARFIELD, WOULD BE TO JUST **DISAPPEAR** AND NEVER TORMENT ME AGAIN!
HOW ABOUT THAT? HE DID IT!
HOW DO YOU LIKE THAT? I FINALLY FIND A TRUE FRIEND AND HE DISAPPEARS ON ME!
MMMMM! THIS STUFF IS TASTY!
And so the panic grows…
ARF! ARF! ARF! ARF! ARF!
NO SIGN OF GARFIELD? THEY MUST HAVE GOT ***HIM TOO!***
MAYBE THEY'RE AT THE PET MOGUL BUILDING! ***COME ON!***
YEAH! YEAH!

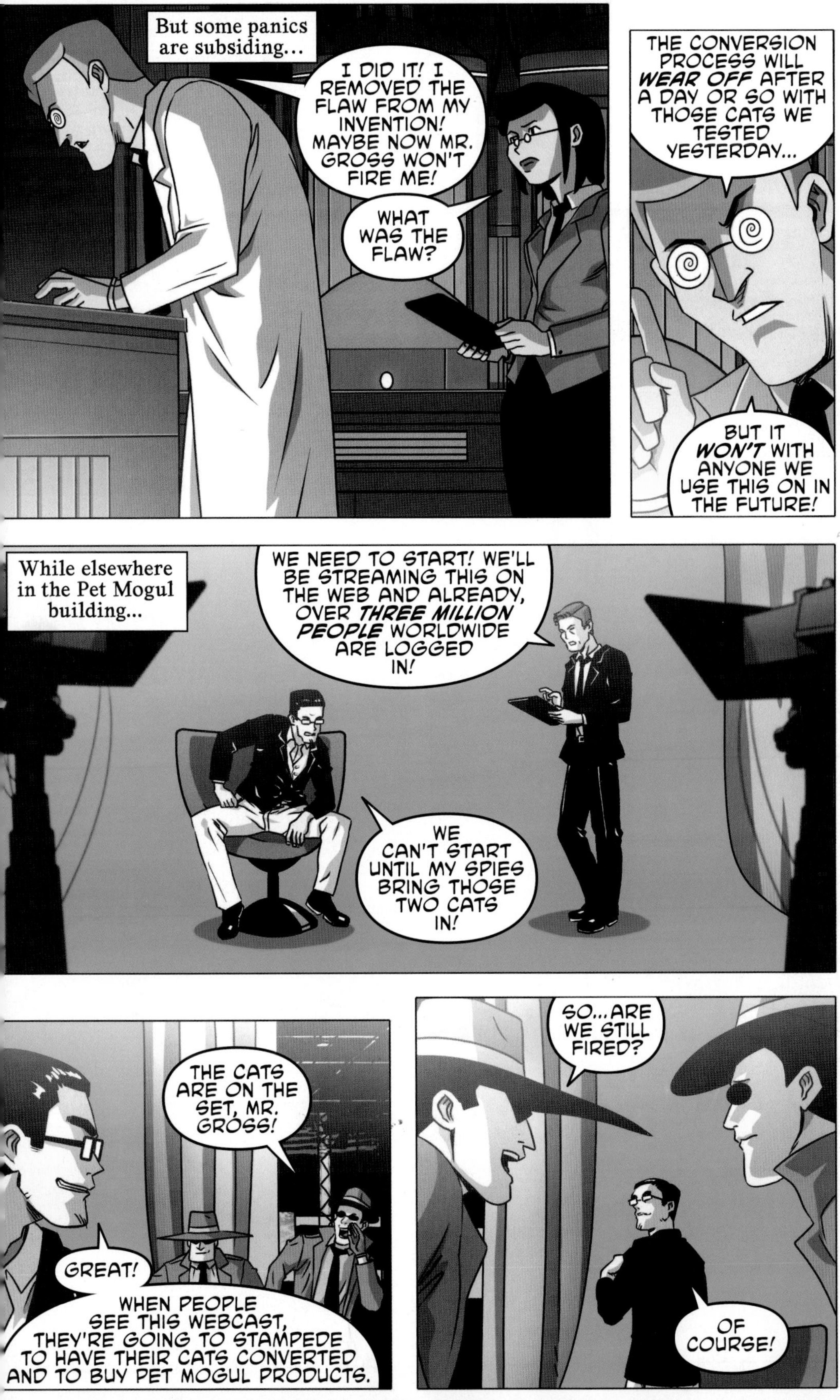
But some panics are subsiding…
I DID IT! I REMOVED THE FLAW FROM MY INVENTION! MAYBE NOW MR. GROSS WON'T FIRE ME!
WHAT WAS THE FLAW?
THE CONVERSION PROCESS WILL WEAR OFF AFTER A DAY OR SO WITH THOSE CATS WE TESTED YESTERDAY…
BUT IT WON'T WITH ANYONE WE USE THIS ON IN THE FUTURE!
While elsewhere in the Pet Mogul building...
WE NEED TO START! WE'LL BE STREAMING THIS ON THE WEB AND ALREADY, OVER THREE MILLION PEOPLE WORLDWIDE ARE LOGGED IN!
WE CAN'T START UNTIL MY SPIES BRING THOSE TWO CATS IN!
THE CATS ARE ON THE SET, MR. GROSS!
GREAT!
WHEN PEOPLE SEE THIS WEBCAST, THEY'RE GOING TO STAMPEDE TO HAVE THEIR CATS CONVERTED AND TO BUY PET MOGUL PRODUCTS.
SO...ARE WE STILL FIRED?
OF COURSE!

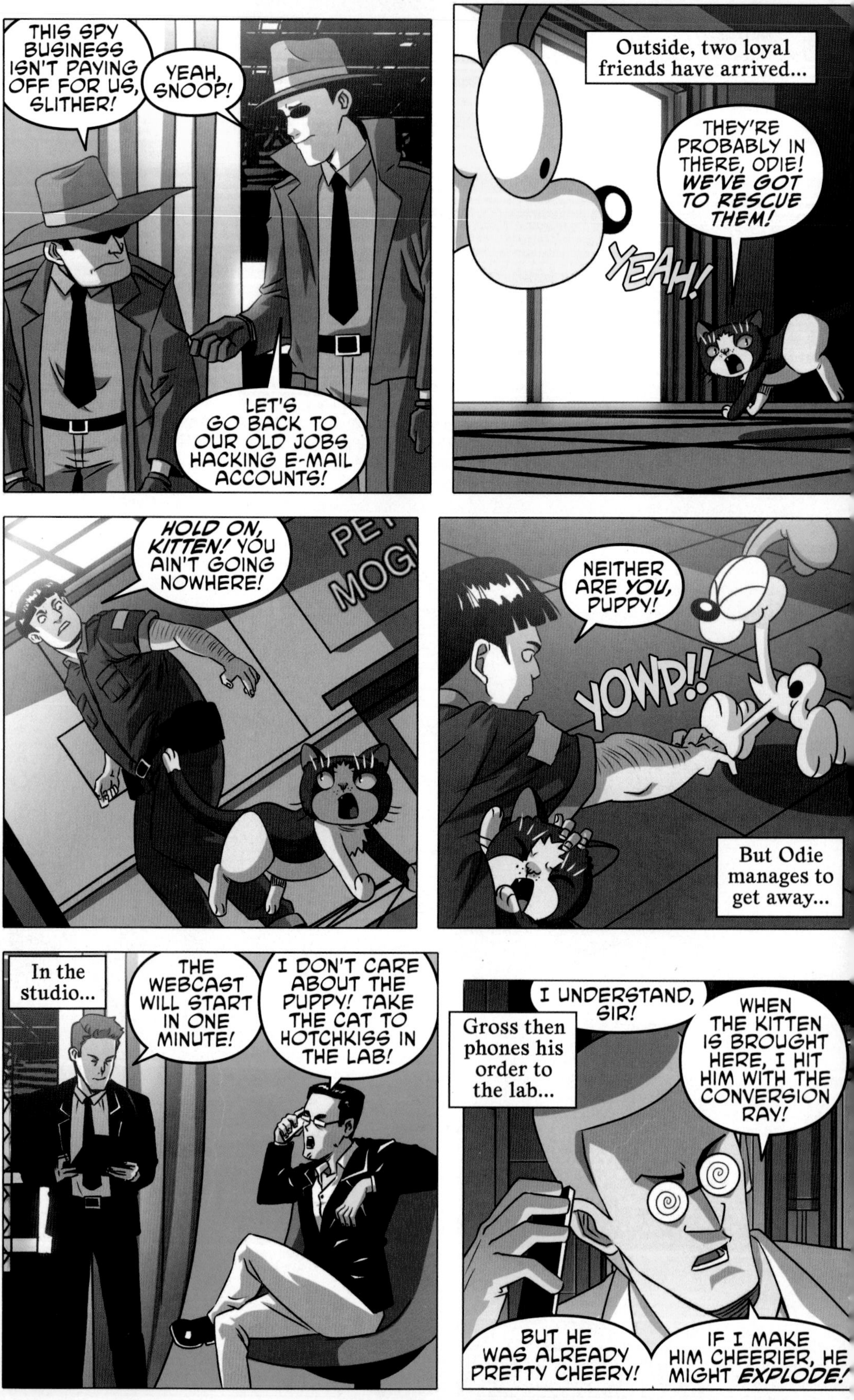
THIS SPY BUSINESS ISN'T PAYING OFF FOR US, SLITHER!
YEAH, SNOOP!
LET'S GO BACK TO OUR OLD JOBS HACKING E-MAIL ACCOUNTS!
Outside, two loyal friends have arrived...
THEY'RE PROBABLY IN THERE, ODIE! WE'VE GOT TO RESCUE THEM!
YEAH!
HOLD ON, KITTEN! YOU AIN'T GOING NOWHERE!
NEITHER ARE YOU, PUPPY!
YOWP!!
But Odie manages to get away...
In the studio...
THE WEBCAST WILL START IN ONE MINUTE!
I DON'T CARE ABOUT THE PUPPY! TAKE THE CAT TO HOTCHKISS IN THE LAB!
Gross then phones his order to the lab...
I UNDERSTAND, SIR!
WHEN THE KITTEN IS BROUGHT HERE, I HIT HIM WITH THE CONVERSION RAY!
BUT HE WAS ALREADY PRETTY CHEERY!
IF I MAKE HIM CHEERIER, HE MIGHT EXPLODE!

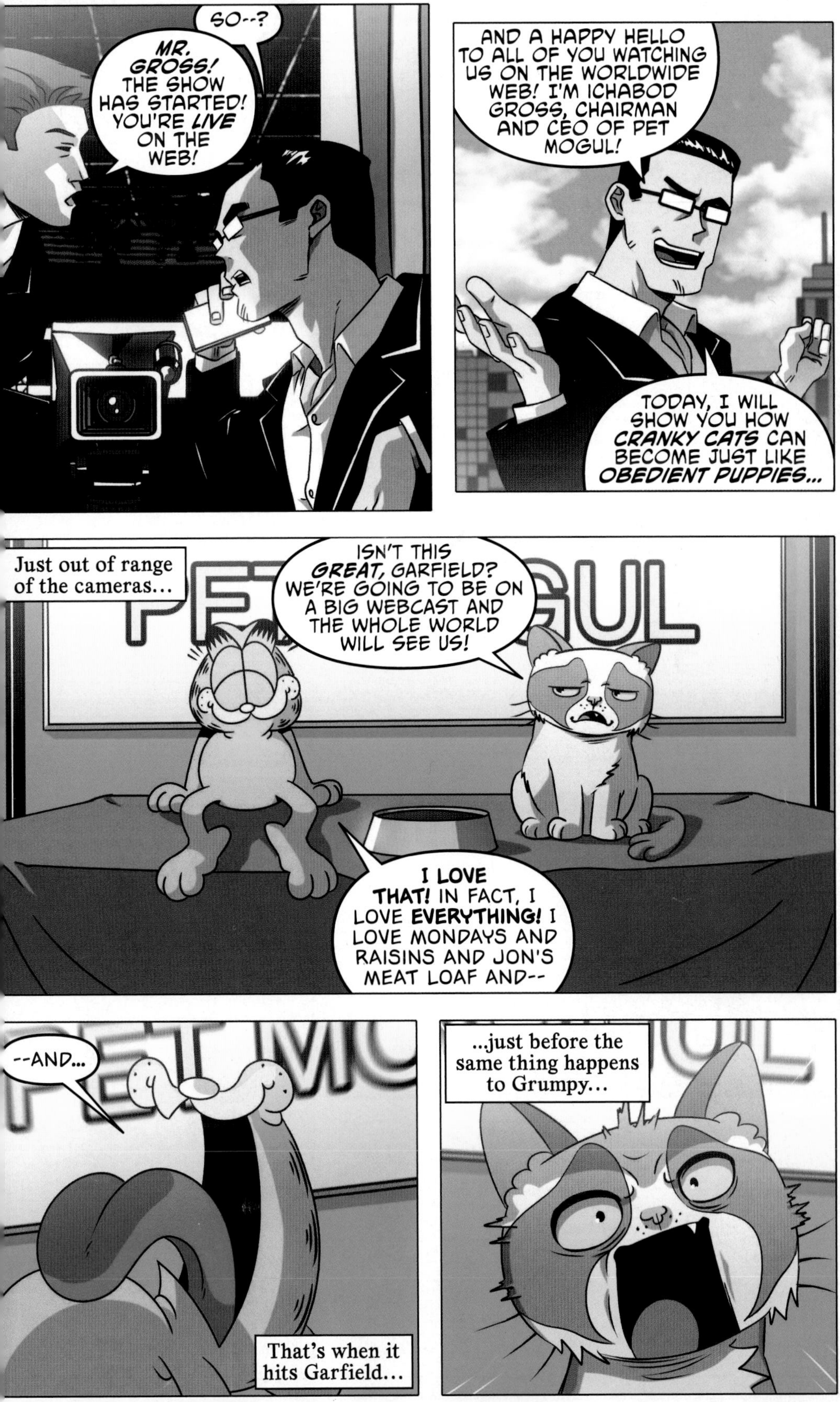
SO--?
MR. GROSS! THE SHOW HAS STARTED! YOU'RE LIVE ON THE WEB!
AND A HAPPY HELLO TO ALL OF YOU WATCHING US ON THE WORLDWIDE WEB! I'M ICHABOD GROSS, CHAIRMAN AND CEO OF PET MOGUL!
TODAY, I WILL SHOW YOU HOW CRANKY CATS CAN BECOME JUST LIKE OBEDIENT PUPPIES...
Just out of range of the cameras...
ISN'T THIS GREAT, GARFIELD? WE'RE GOING TO BE ON A BIG WEBCAST AND THE WHOLE WORLD WILL SEE US!
I LOVE THAT! IN FACT, I LOVE EVERYTHING! I LOVE MONDAYS AND RAISINS AND JON'S MEAT LOAF AND--
--AND...
That's when it hits Garfield...
...just before the same thing happens to Grumpy...

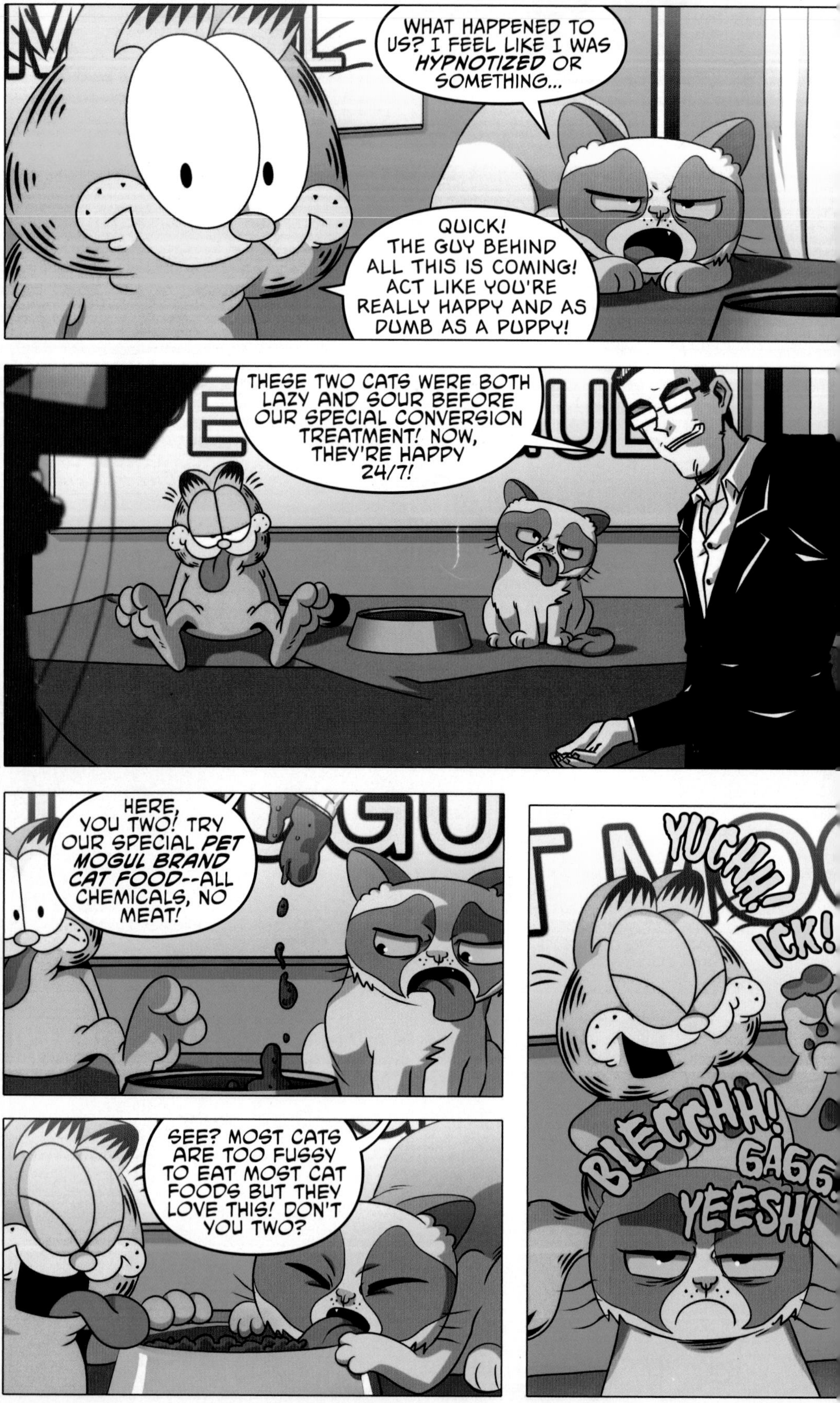
WHAT HAPPENED TO US? I FEEL LIKE I WAS *HYPNOTIZED* OR SOMETHING...
QUICK! THE GUY BEHIND ALL THIS IS COMING! ACT LIKE YOU'RE REALLY HAPPY AND AS DUMB AS A PUPPY!
THESE TWO CATS WERE BOTH LAZY AND SOUR BEFORE OUR SPECIAL CONVERSION TREATMENT! NOW, THEY'RE HAPPY 24/7!
HERE, YOU TWO! TRY OUR SPECIAL *PET MOGUL BRAND CAT FOOD*--ALL CHEMICALS, NO MEAT!
SEE? MOST CATS ARE TOO FUSSY TO EAT MOST CAT FOODS BUT THEY LOVE THIS! DON'T YOU TWO?
YUCHH!
ICK!
BLECCHH!
GAGG.
YEESH!

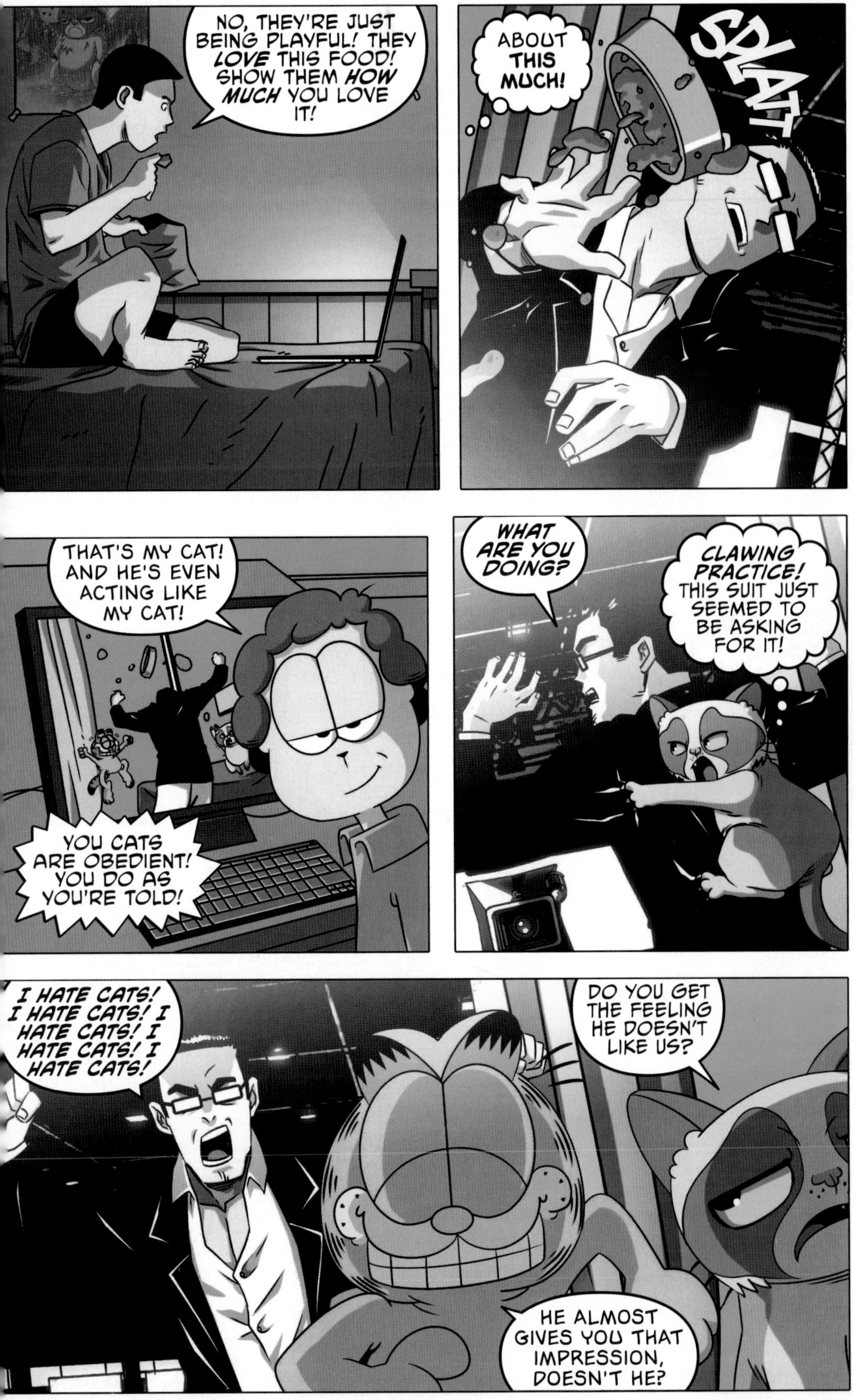
NO, THEY'RE JUST BEING PLAYFUL! THEY LOVE THIS FOOD! SHOW THEM HOW MUCH YOU LOVE IT!
ABOUT THIS MUCH!
SPLAT!
THAT'S MY CAT! AND HE'S EVEN ACTING LIKE MY CAT!
YOU CATS ARE OBEDIENT! YOU DO AS YOU'RE TOLD!
WHAT ARE YOU DOING?
CLAWING PRACTICE! THIS SUIT JUST SEEMED TO BE ASKING FOR IT!
I HATE CATS! I HATE CATS! I HATE CATS! I HATE CATS! I HATE CATS!
DO YOU GET THE FEELING HE DOESN'T LIKE US?
HE ALMOST GIVES YOU THAT IMPRESSION, DOESN'T HE?

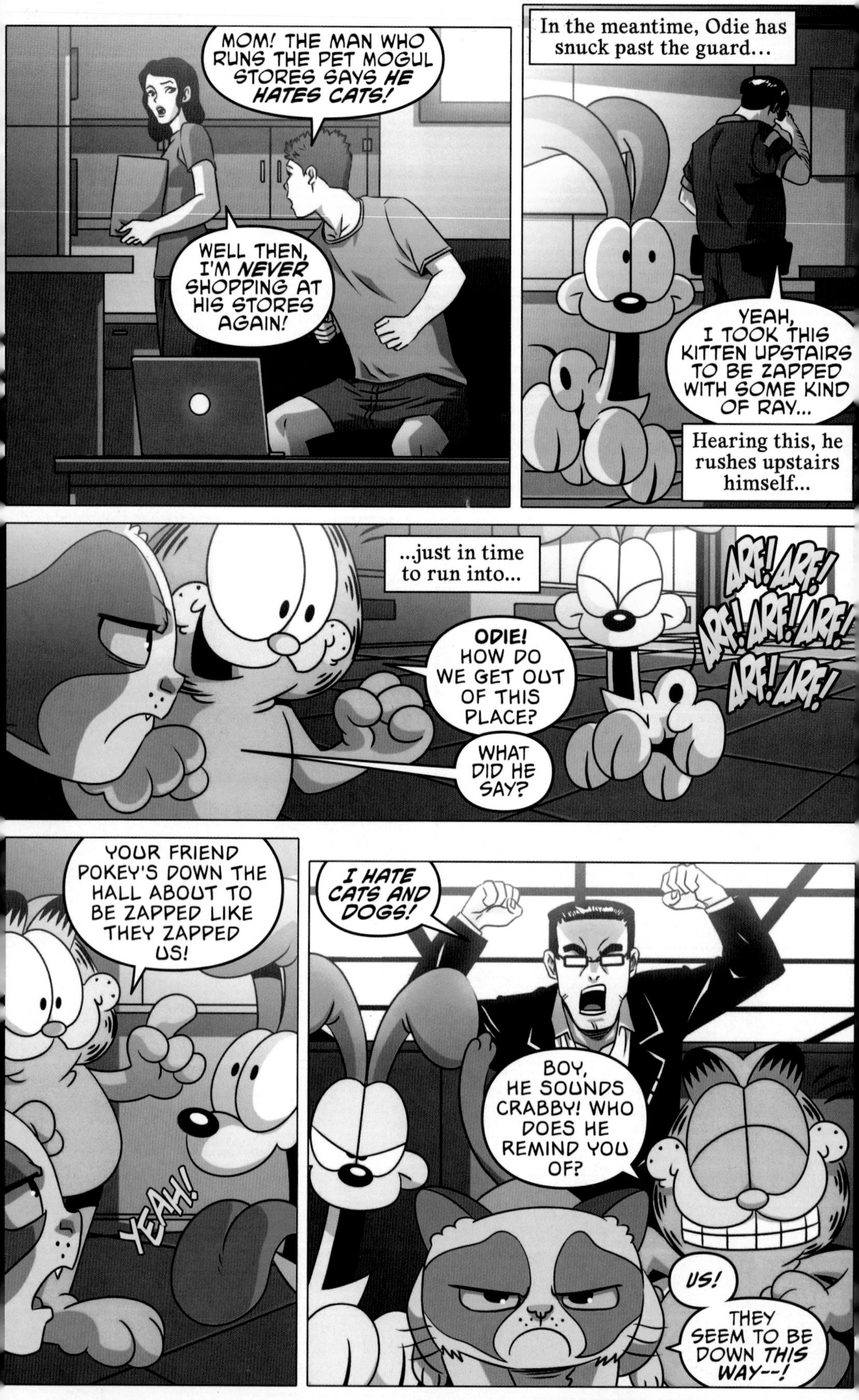
MOM! THE MAN WHO RUNS THE PET MOGUL STORES SAYS *HE HATES CATS!*
WELL THEN, I'M *NEVER* SHOPPING AT HIS STORES AGAIN!
In the meantime, Odie has snuck past the guard...
YEAH, I TOOK THIS KITTEN UPSTAIRS TO BE ZAPPED WITH SOME KIND OF RAY...
Hearing this, he rushes upstairs himself...
...just in time to run into...
ODIE! HOW DO WE GET OUT OF THIS PLACE?
ARF! ARF! ARF! ARF! ARF! ARF! ARF!
WHAT DID HE SAY?
YOUR FRIEND POKEY'S DOWN THE HALL ABOUT TO BE ZAPPED LIKE THEY ZAPPED US!
YEAH!
I HATE CATS AND DOGS!
BOY, HE SOUNDS CRABBY! WHO DOES HE REMIND YOU OF?
US!
THEY SEEM TO BE DOWN *THIS WAY*--!

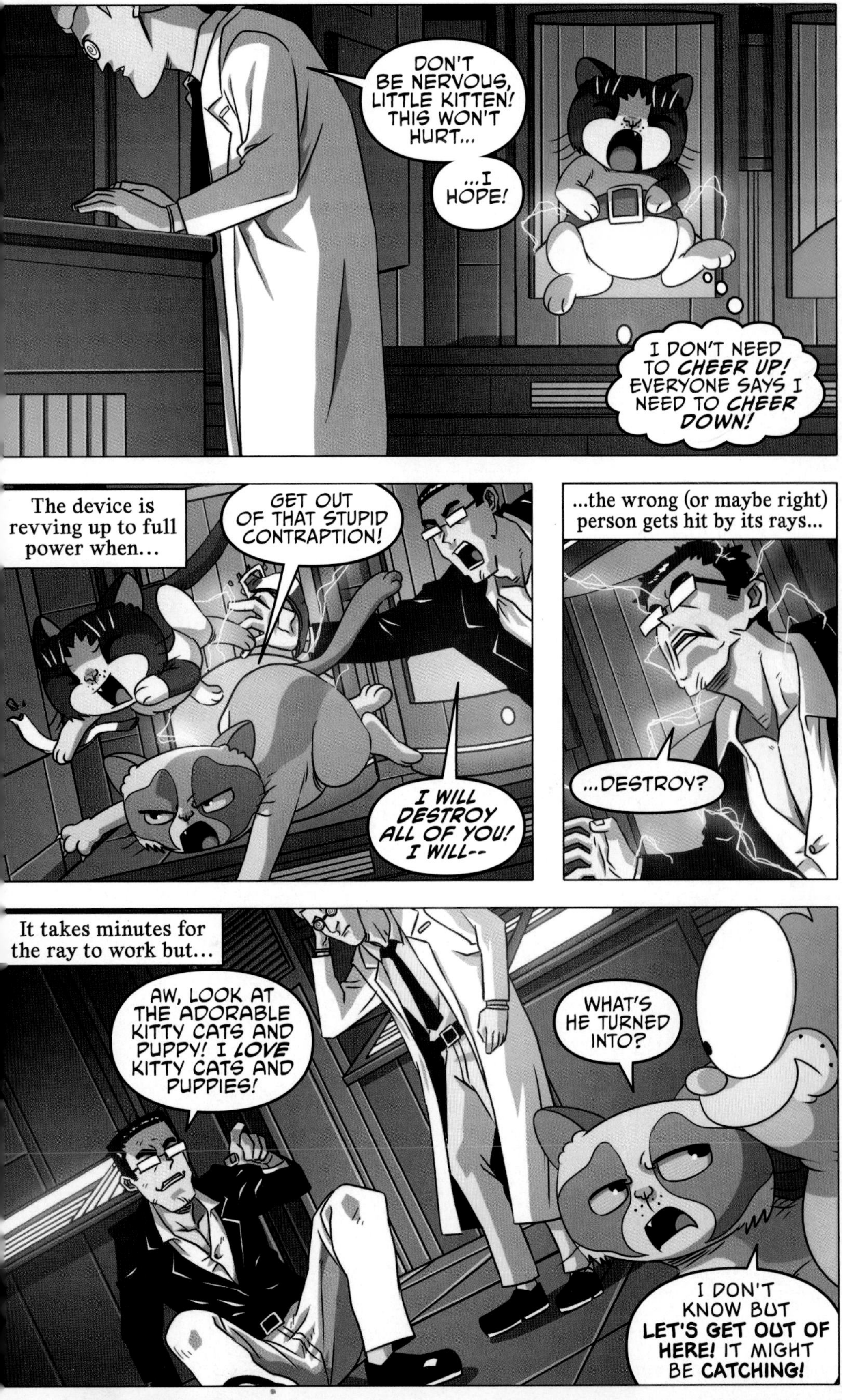
DON'T BE NERVOUS, LITTLE KITTEN! THIS WON'T HURT...
...I HOPE!
I DON'T NEED TO CHEER UP! EVERYONE SAYS I NEED TO CHEER DOWN!
The device is revving up to full power when...
GET OUT OF THAT STUPID CONTRAPTION!
I WILL DESTROY ALL OF YOU! I WILL--
...the wrong (or maybe right) person gets hit by its rays...
...DESTROY?
It takes minutes for the ray to work but...
AW, LOOK AT THE ADORABLE KITTY CATS AND PUPPY! I LOVE KITTY CATS AND PUPPIES!
WHAT'S HE TURNED INTO?
I DON'T KNOW BUT LET'S GET OUT OF HERE! IT MIGHT BE CATCHING!

And so...

I'D SAY WE GET ALONG WELL, GARFIELD, BUT I DON'T SAY THAT ABOUT ANYONE!

I ONLY SAY THAT ABOUT CHEFS WHO MAKE GREAT LASAGNA!

HEY, GARFIELD!

I FINALLY DECIDED THAT YOU'RE REALLY A GOOD FRIEND AND THAT YOU DO LIKE ME! **EVERYONE DOES!**

I'LL BET YOUR FRIENDS WOULD LIKE TO MEET **ME**, THE CUTEST AND MOST ADORABLE KITTEN IN **THE WHOLE WIDE WORLD...**

NO... MAKE THAT THE **ENTIRE UNIVERSE!**

WHAT DO YOU THINK?

I'M THINKING **OVERNIGHT EXPRESS** TO ABU DHABI!

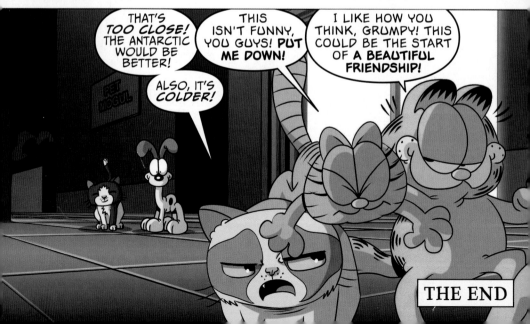

THAT'S **TOO CLOSE!** THE ANTARCTIC WOULD BE BETTER!

ALSO, IT'S **COLDER!**

THIS ISN'T FUNNY, YOU GUYS! **PUT ME DOWN!**

I LIKE HOW YOU THINK, GRUMPY! THIS COULD BE THE START OF **A BEAUTIFUL FRIENDSHIP!**

THE END

BONUS CONTENT

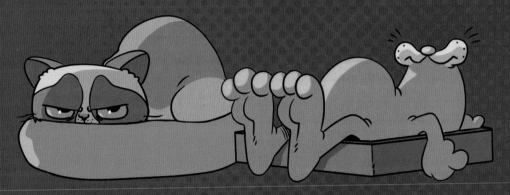

Grumpy Cat® COMIC STRIPS
ORIGINALLY AVAILABLE ON DYNAMITE.COM

TUMBLE DRY

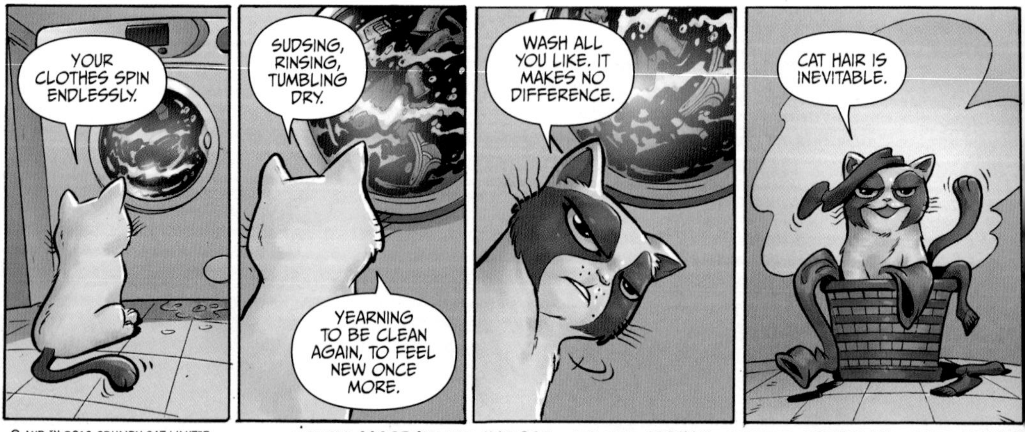
YOUR CLOTHES SPIN ENDLESSLY.
SUDSING, RINSING, TUMBLING DRY.
YEARNING TO BE CLEAN AGAIN, TO FEEL NEW ONCE MORE.
WASH ALL YOU LIKE. IT MAKES NO DIFFERENCE.
CAT HAIR IS INEVITABLE.

SCRIPT: ***MCGRAW*** ART: ***VARGAS*** COLORS: ***MOHAN*** LETTERS: ***TORTOLINI*** EDITS: ***YOUNG***

TREATS

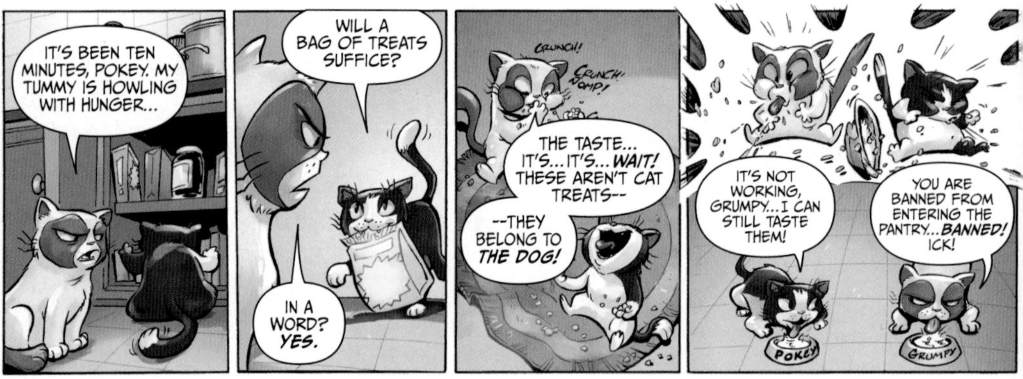
IT'S BEEN TEN MINUTES, POKEY. MY TUMMY IS HOWLING WITH HUNGER...
WILL A BAG OF TREATS SUFFICE?
IN A WORD? ***YES.***
CRUNCH!
CRUNCH! NOMP!
THE TASTE... IT'S... IT'S... ***WAIT!*** THESE AREN'T CAT TREATS--
--THEY BELONG TO ***THE DOG!***
IT'S NOT WORKING, GRUMPY... I CAN STILL TASTE THEM!
YOU ARE BANNED FROM ENTERING THE PANTRY... ***BANNED!*** ICK!
POKEY
GRUMPY

SCRIPT: ***MCCOOL*** ART: ***VARGAS*** COLORS: ***MOHAN*** LETTERS: ***TORTOLINI*** EDITS: ***YOUNG***

THE LIST

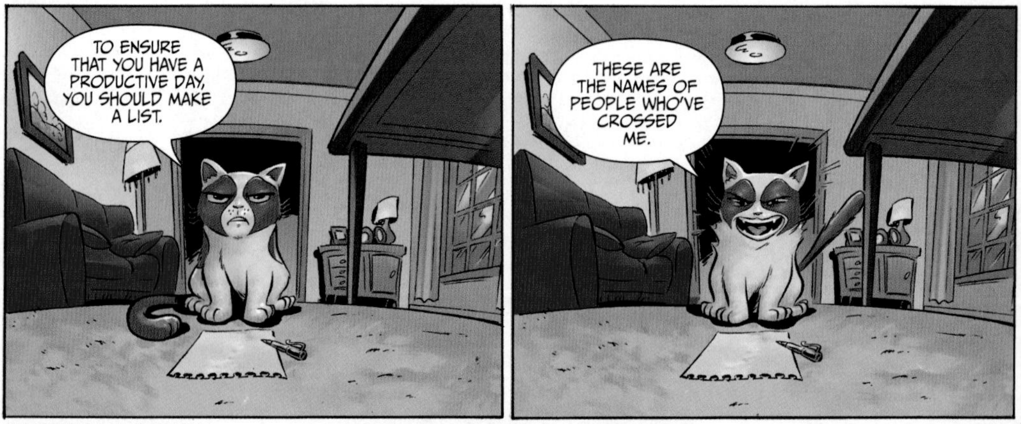
TO ENSURE THAT YOU HAVE A PRODUCTIVE DAY, YOU SHOULD MAKE A LIST.
THESE ARE THE NAMES OF PEOPLE WHO'VE CROSSED ME.

SCRIPT: ***MCGRAW*** ART: ***VARGAS*** COLORS: ***MOHAN*** LETTERS: ***TORTOLINI*** EDITS: ***YOUNG***

RIDING THE DOG

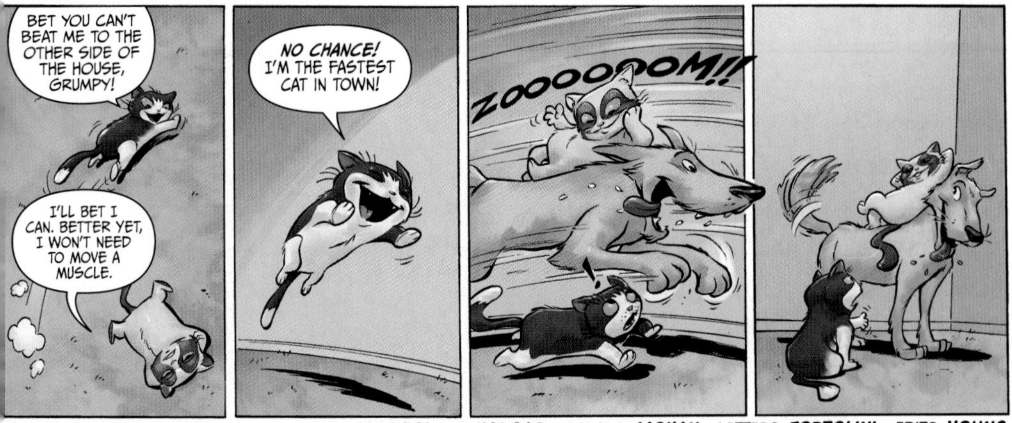
BET YOU CAN'T BEAT ME TO THE OTHER SIDE OF THE HOUSE, GRUMPY!
I'LL BET I CAN. BETTER YET, I WON'T NEED TO MOVE A MUSCLE.
NO CHANCE! I'M THE FASTEST CAT IN TOWN!
ZOOOOOOOM!!
!

SCRIPT: **MCCOOL** ART: **VARGAS** COLORS: **MOHAN** LETTERS: **TORTOLINI** EDITS: **YOUNG**

THE MISSING TOY

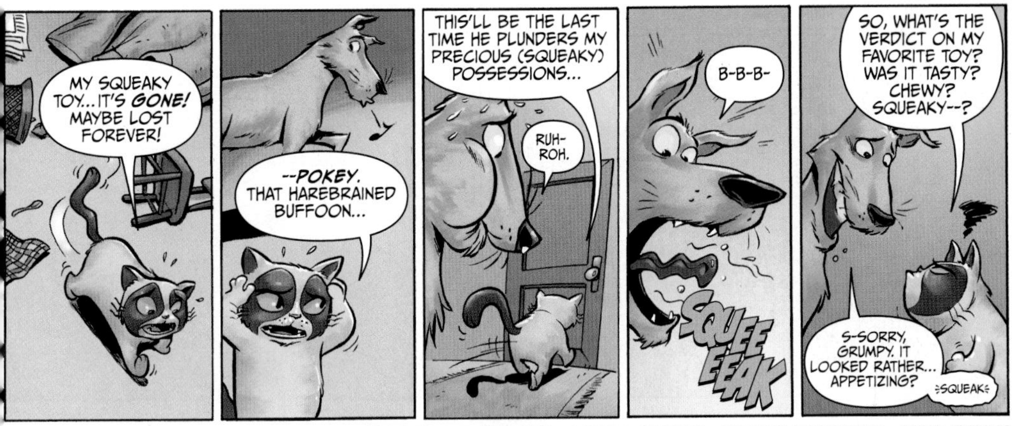
MY SQUEAKY TOY... IT'S GONE! MAYBE LOST FOREVER!
--POKEY. THAT HAREBRAINED BUFFOON...
THIS'LL BE THE LAST TIME HE PLUNDERS MY PRECIOUS (SQUEAKY) POSSESSIONS...
RUH-ROH.
B-B-B-
SQUEEEEAK
SO, WHAT'S THE VERDICT ON MY FAVORITE TOY? WAS IT TASTY? CHEWY? SQUEAKY--?
S-SORRY, GRUMPY. IT LOOKED RATHER... APPETIZING?
SQUEAK

SCRIPT: **MCCOOL** ART: **VARGAS** COLORS: **MOHAN** LETTERS: **TORTOLINI** EDITS: **YOUNG**

LASER FOCUS

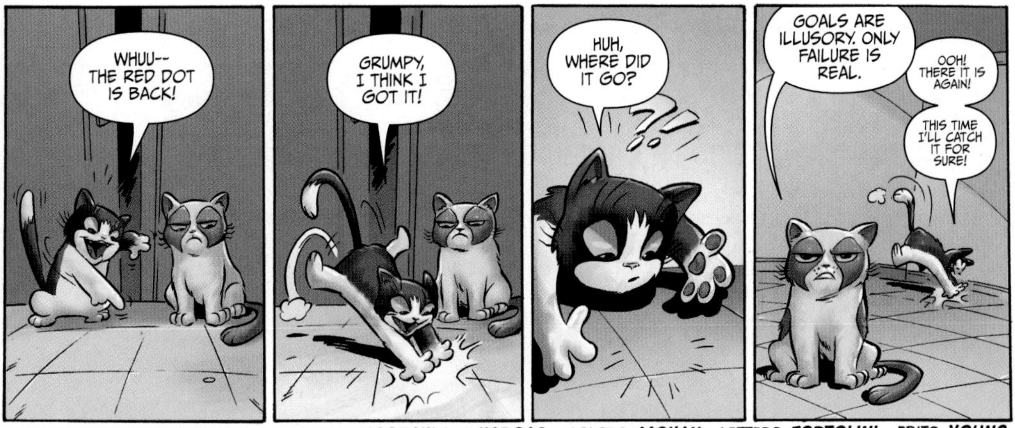
WHUU-- THE RED DOT IS BACK!
GRUMPY, I THINK I GOT IT!
HUH, WHERE DID IT GO?
?!
GOALS ARE ILLUSORY. ONLY FAILURE IS REAL.
OOH! THERE IT IS AGAIN!
THIS TIME I'LL CATCH IT FOR SURE!

SCRIPT: **MCGRAW** ART: **VARGAS** COLORS: **MOHAN** LETTERS: **TORTOLINI** EDITS: **YOUNG**

Grumpy Cat® COMIC STRIPS
ORIGINALLY AVAILABLE ON DYNAMITE.COM

KNOW YOUR AUDIENCE

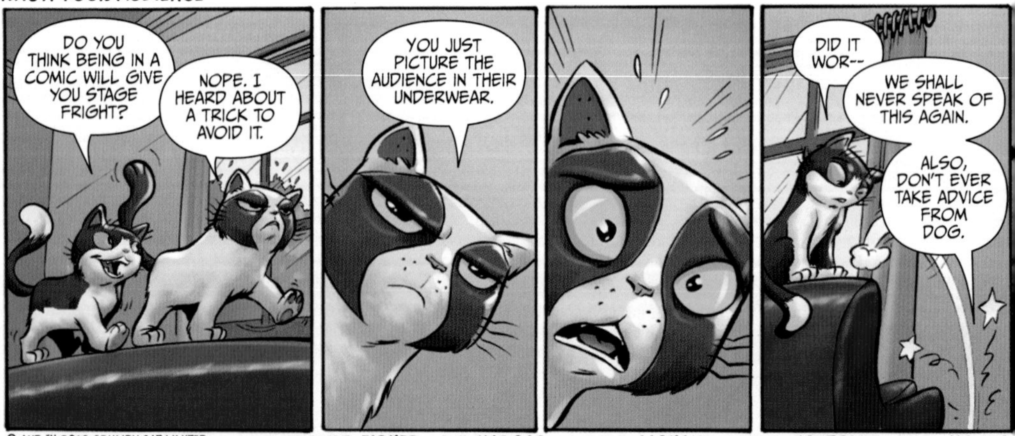
DO YOU THINK BEING IN A COMIC WILL GIVE YOU STAGE FRIGHT?
NOPE. I HEARD ABOUT A TRICK TO AVOID IT.
YOU JUST PICTURE THE AUDIENCE IN THEIR UNDERWEAR.
DID IT WOR--
WE SHALL NEVER SPEAK OF THIS AGAIN.
ALSO, DON'T EVER TAKE ADVICE FROM DOG.

SCRIPT: **FISHER** ART: **VARGAS** COLORS: **MOHAN** LETTERS: **TORTOLINI** EDITS: **YOUNG**

INSOMNIA

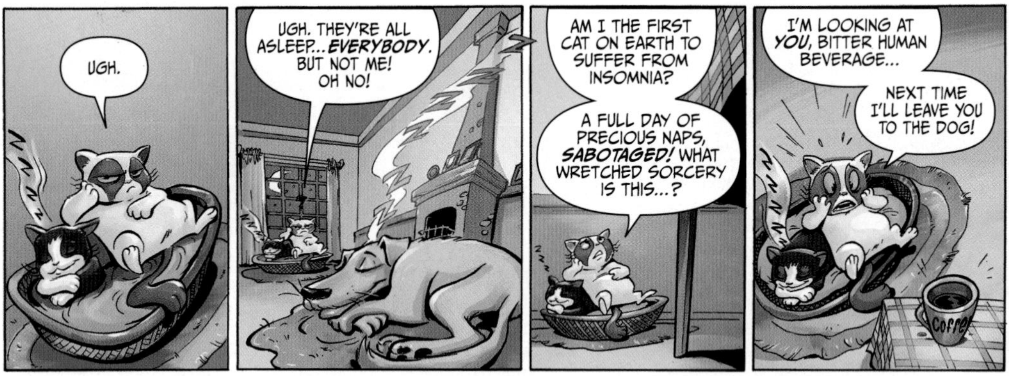
UGH.
UGH. THEY'RE ALL ASLEEP... *EVERYBODY*. BUT NOT ME! OH NO!
AM I THE FIRST CAT ON EARTH TO SUFFER FROM INSOMNIA?
A FULL DAY OF PRECIOUS NAPS, *SABOTAGED!* WHAT WRETCHED SORCERY IS THIS...?
I'M LOOKING AT *YOU*, BITTER HUMAN BEVERAGE...
NEXT TIME I'LL LEAVE YOU TO THE DOG!
COFFEE

SCRIPT: **MCCOOL**ART: **VARGAS** COLORS: **MOHAN** LETTERS: **TORTOLINI** EDITS: **YOUNG**

GRUMPY ON INFINITE EARTHS

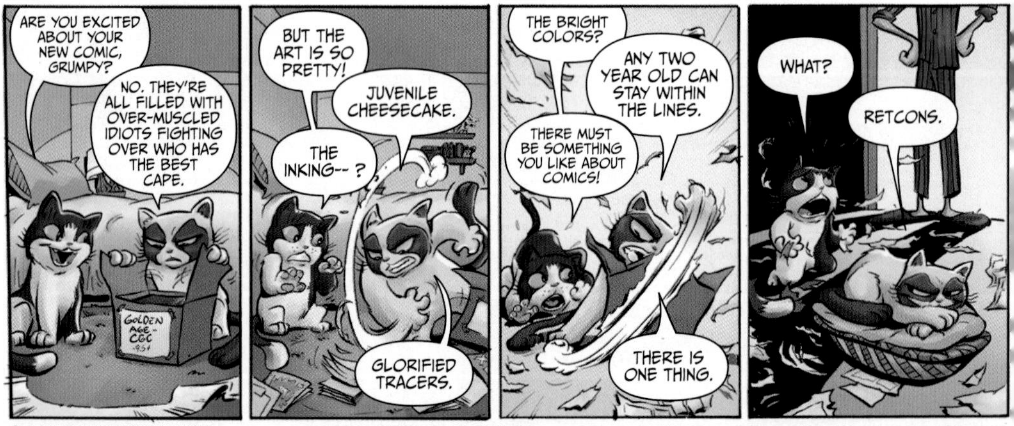
ARE YOU EXCITED ABOUT YOUR NEW COMIC, GRUMPY?
NO. THEY'RE ALL FILLED WITH OVER-MUSCLED IDIOTS FIGHTING OVER WHO HAS THE BEST CAPE.
GOLDEN AGE CGC
BUT THE ART IS SO PRETTY!
JUVENILE CHEESECAKE.
THE INKING-- ?
GLORIFIED TRACERS.
THE BRIGHT COLORS?
ANY TWO YEAR OLD CAN STAY WITHIN THE LINES.
THERE MUST BE SOMETHING YOU LIKE ABOUT COMICS!
THERE IS ONE THING.
WHAT?
RETCONS.

SCRIPT: **FISHER** ART: **VARGAS** COLORS: **MOHAN** LETTERS: **TORTOLINI** EDITS: **YOUNG**

Garfield BY JIM DAVIS

Mondays Bite!

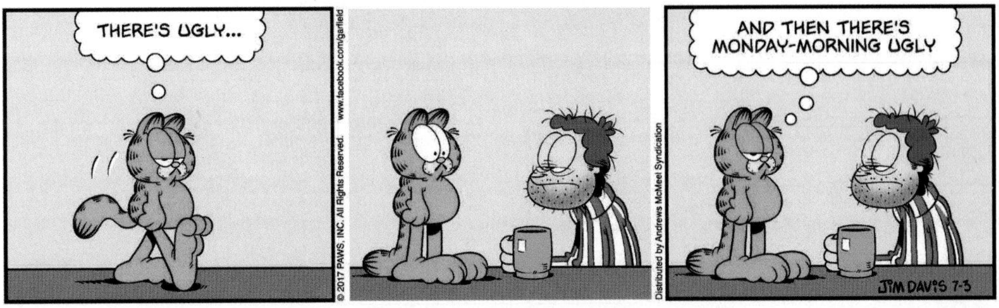

THERE'S UGLY...
AND THEN THERE'S MONDAY-MORNING UGLY
JIM DAVIS 7-3
© 2017 PAWS, INC. All Rights Reserved. www.facebook.com/garfield
Distributed by Andrews McMeel Syndication

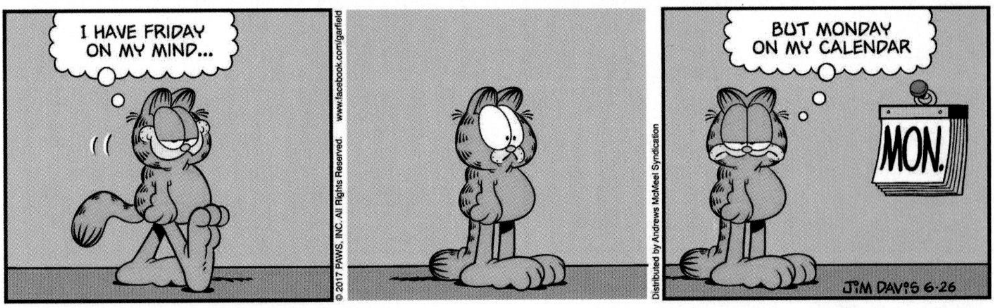

I HAVE FRIDAY ON MY MIND...
BUT MONDAY ON MY CALENDAR
MON.
JIM DAVIS 6-26
© 2017 PAWS, INC. All Rights Reserved. www.facebook.com/garfield
Distributed by Andrews McMeel Syndication

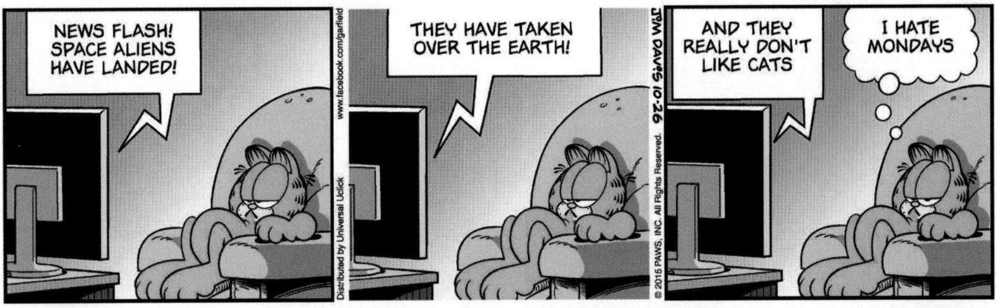

NEWS FLASH! SPACE ALIENS HAVE LANDED!
THEY HAVE TAKEN OVER THE EARTH!
AND THEY REALLY DON'T LIKE CATS
I HATE MONDAYS
JIM DAVIS 10-26
Distributed by Universal Uclick www.facebook.com/garfield
© 2015 PAWS, INC. All Rights Reserved.

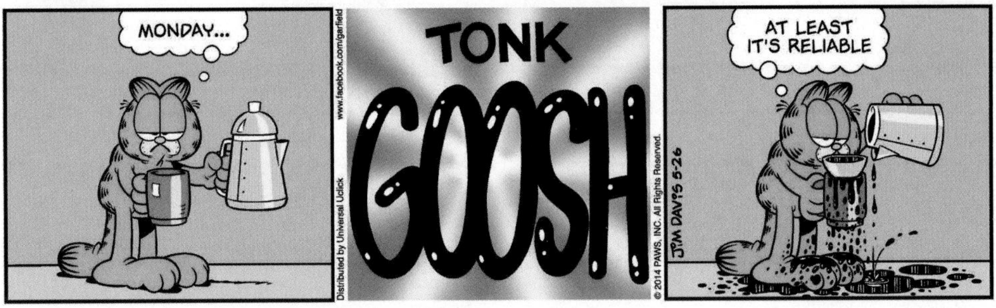

MONDAY...
TONK
GOOSH
AT LEAST IT'S RELIABLE
JIM DAVIS 5-26
Distributed by Universal Uclick www.facebook.com/garfield
© 2014 PAWS, INC. All Rights Reserved.

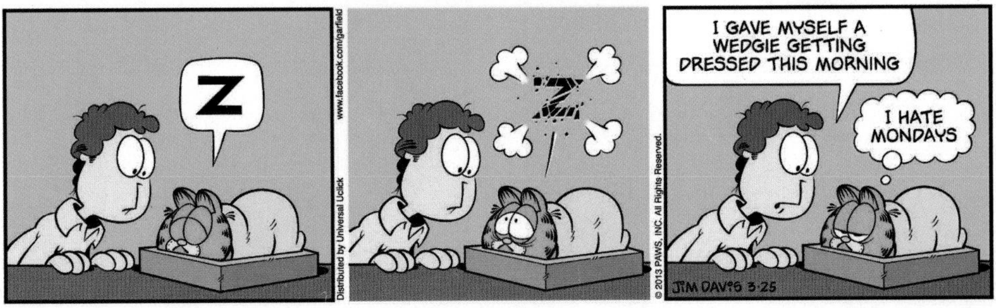

Z
I GAVE MYSELF A WEDGIE GETTING DRESSED THIS MORNING
I HATE MONDAYS
JIM DAVIS 3-25
Distributed by Universal Uclick www.facebook.com/garfield
© 2013 PAWS, INC. All Rights Reserved.

The Many Moods of Garfield

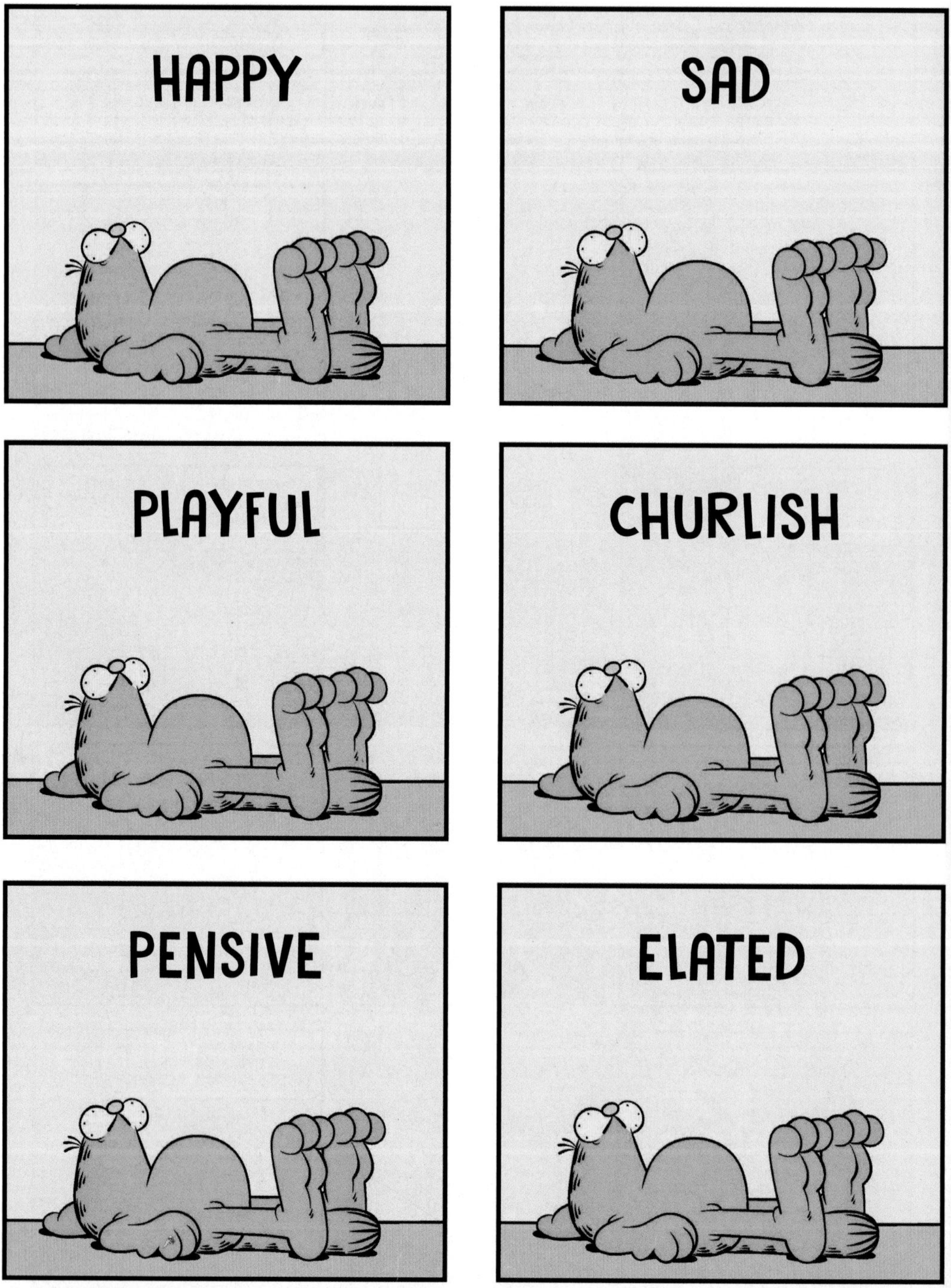
HAPPY
SAD
PLAYFUL
CHURLISH
PENSIVE
ELATED

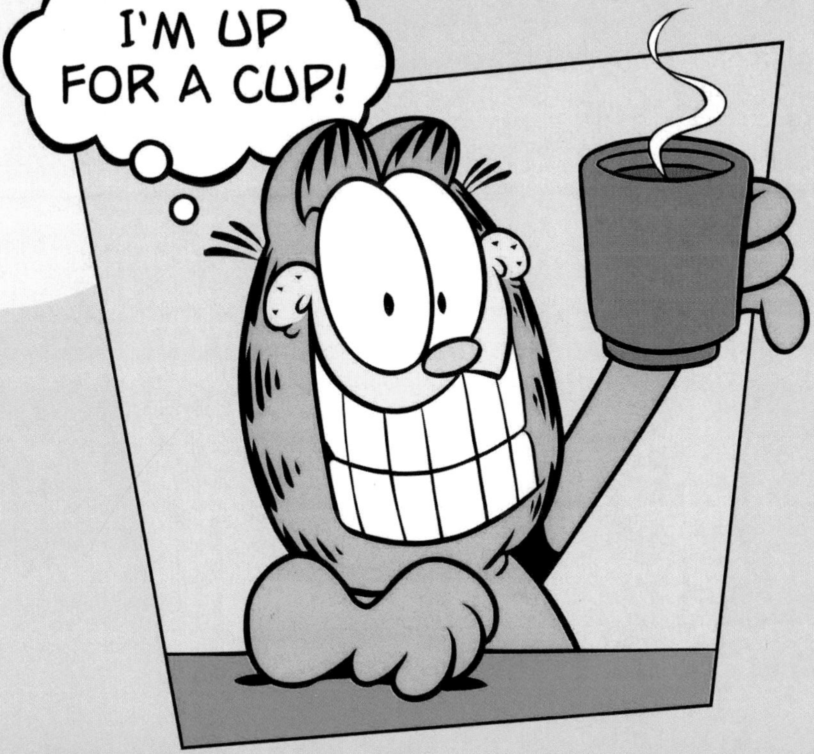
I'M UP
FOR A CUP!

GARFIELD'S FAVORITE COFFEE FLAVORS

- French Toast Roast
- Irish Cream of Potato
- Hickory Smochaccino
- Peruvian Pig Roast
- Cherry Canary
- Hazelnut-Pepperoni
- Lava Java
- Turkish Tuna Toffee
- Kona Bologna
- Jamaican Bacon
- Costa Rican Corndog
- Turkey Jerky Supremo

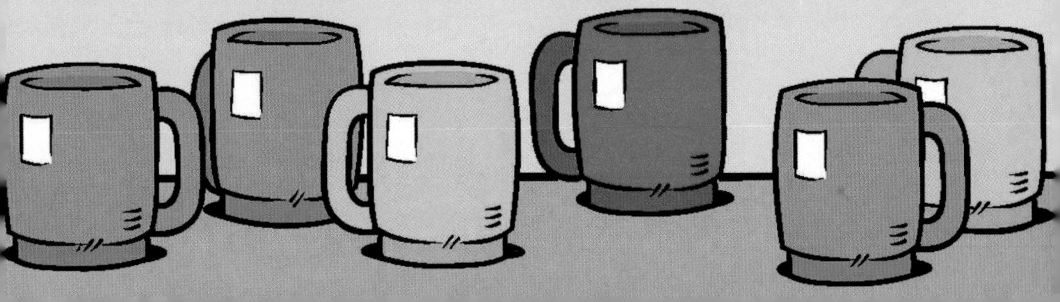

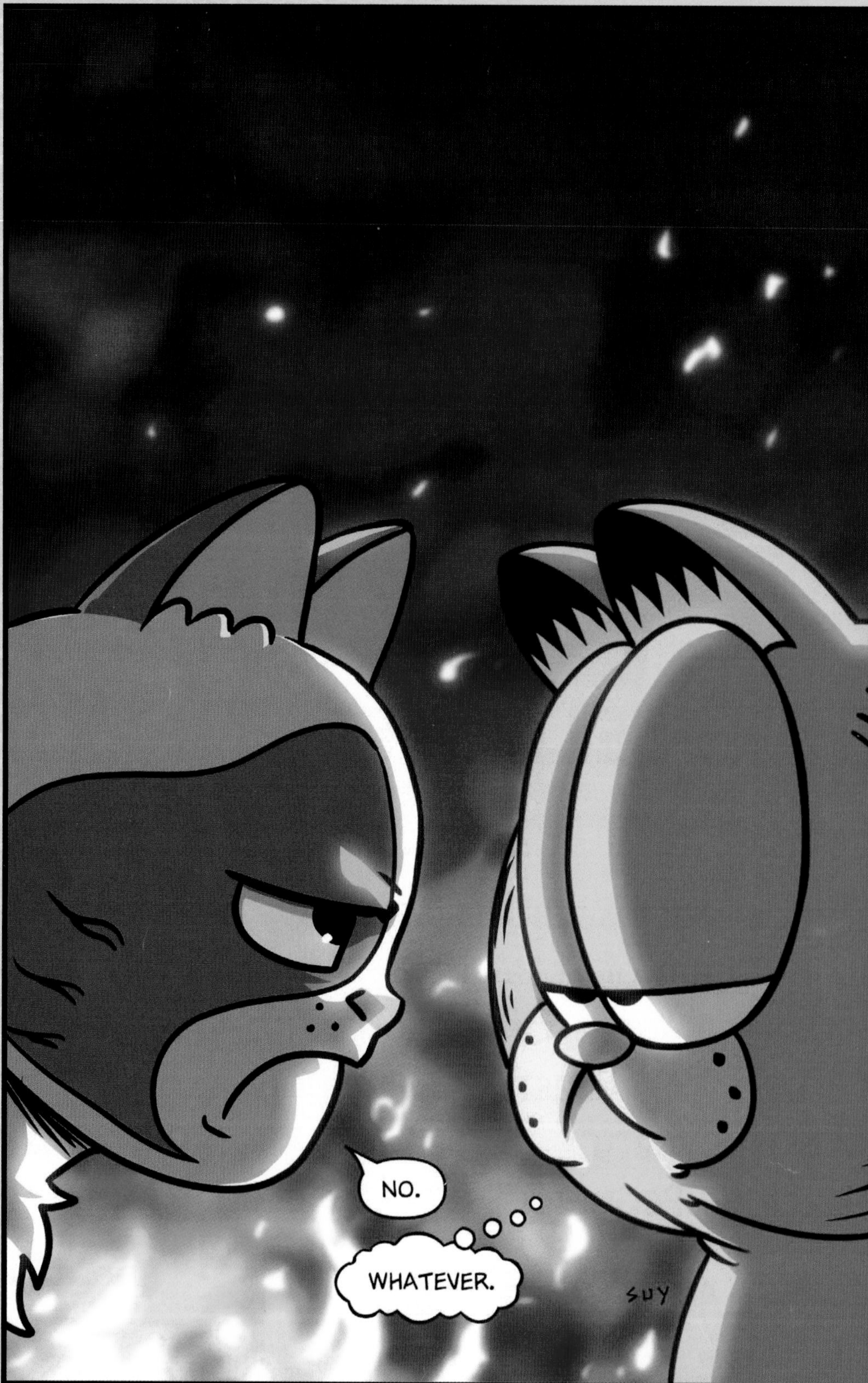
NO.
WHATEVER.
SUY

PROMOTIONAL ART BY: **STEVE UY**

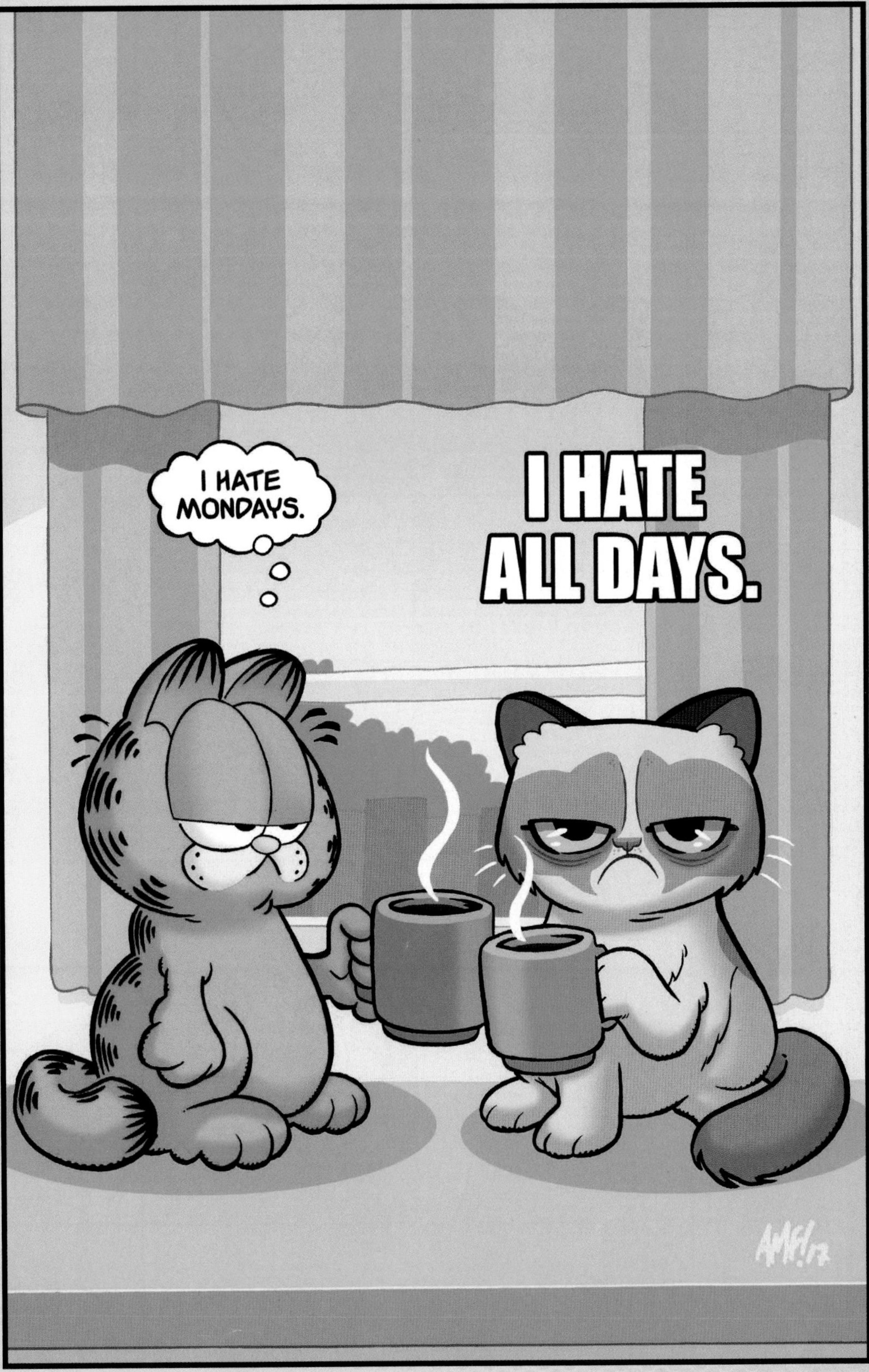
I HATE MONDAYS.
I HATE ALL DAYS.
AMF!'17

ISSUE 1 COVER BY: **TONY FLEECS**

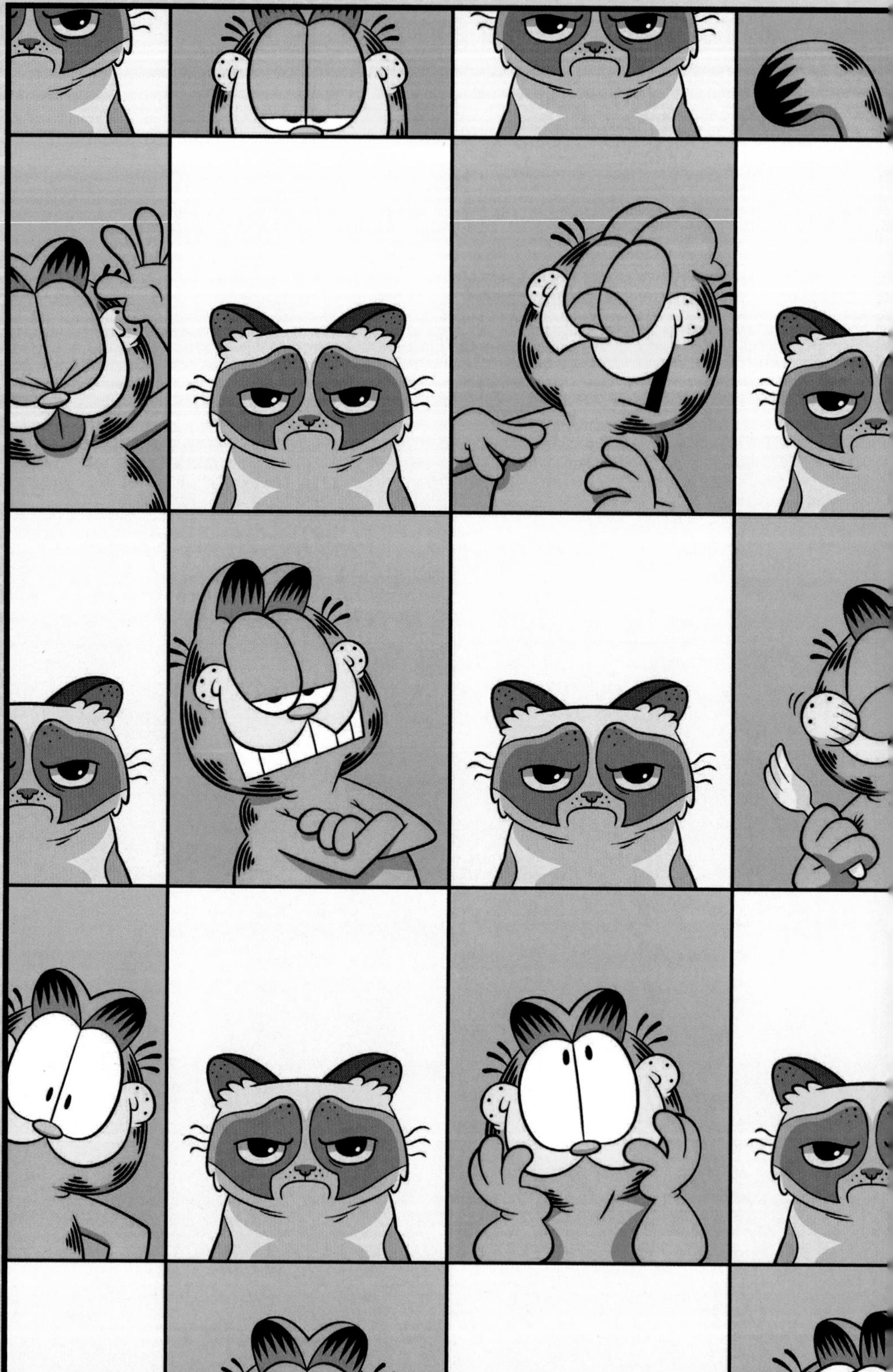

ISSUE 1 COVER BY: **ANDY HIRSCH**

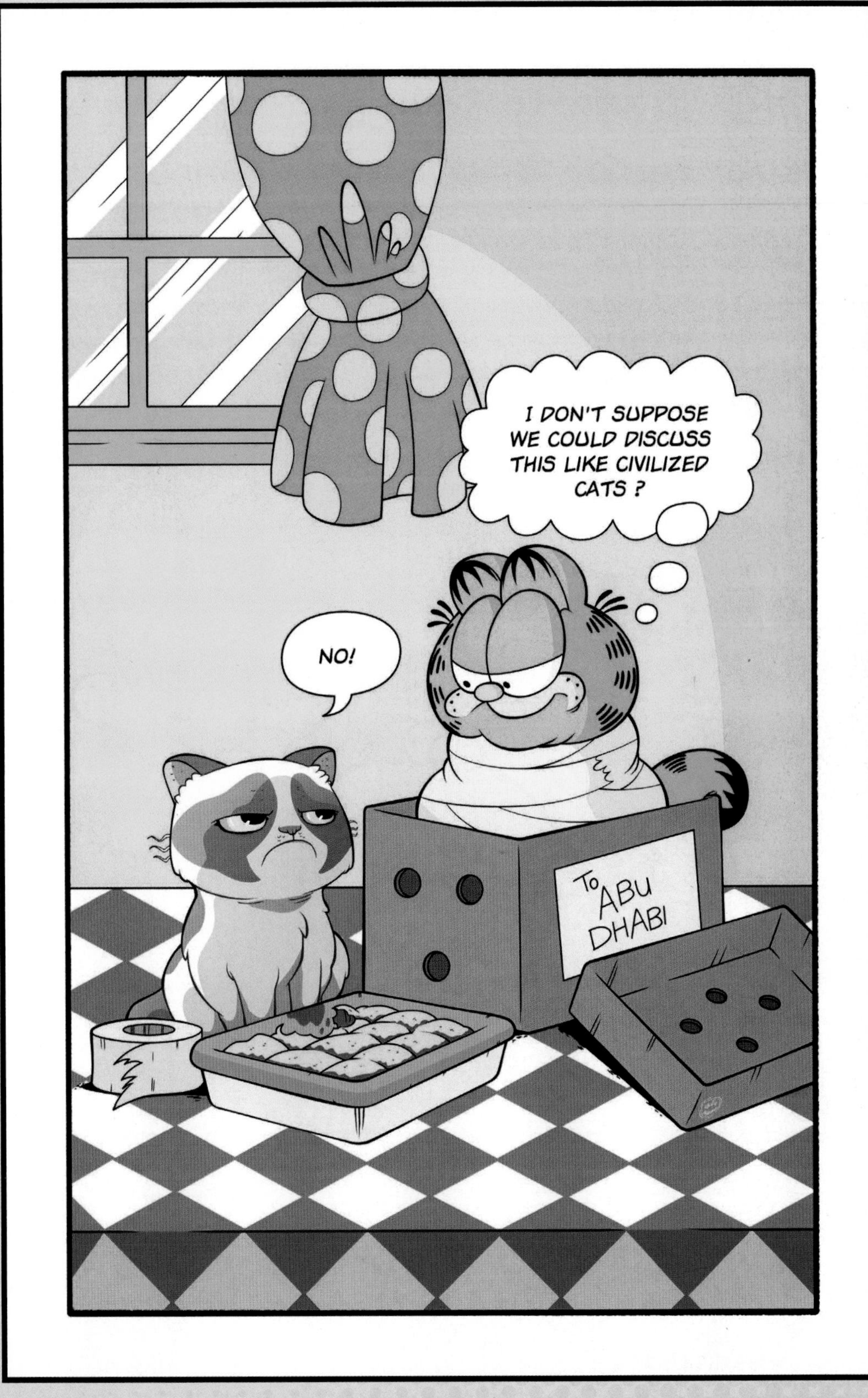
I DON'T SUPPOSE WE COULD DISCUSS THIS LIKE CIVILIZED CATS ?
NO!
To ABU DHABI

ISSUE 1 COVER BY: **PHIL MURPHY**

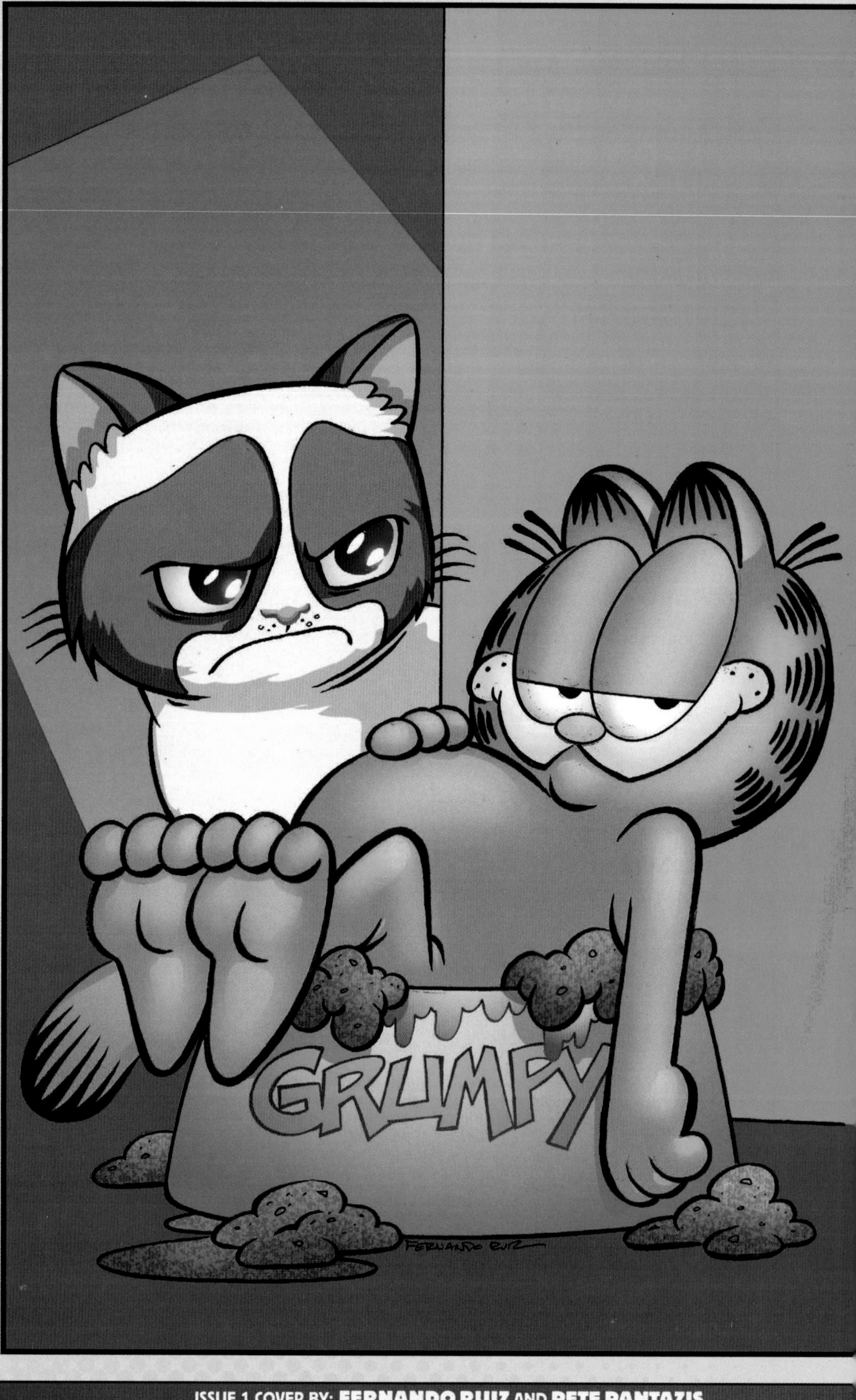
GRUMPY
FERNANDO RUIZ

ISSUE 1 COVER BY: **FERNANDO RUIZ** AND **PETE PANTAZIS**

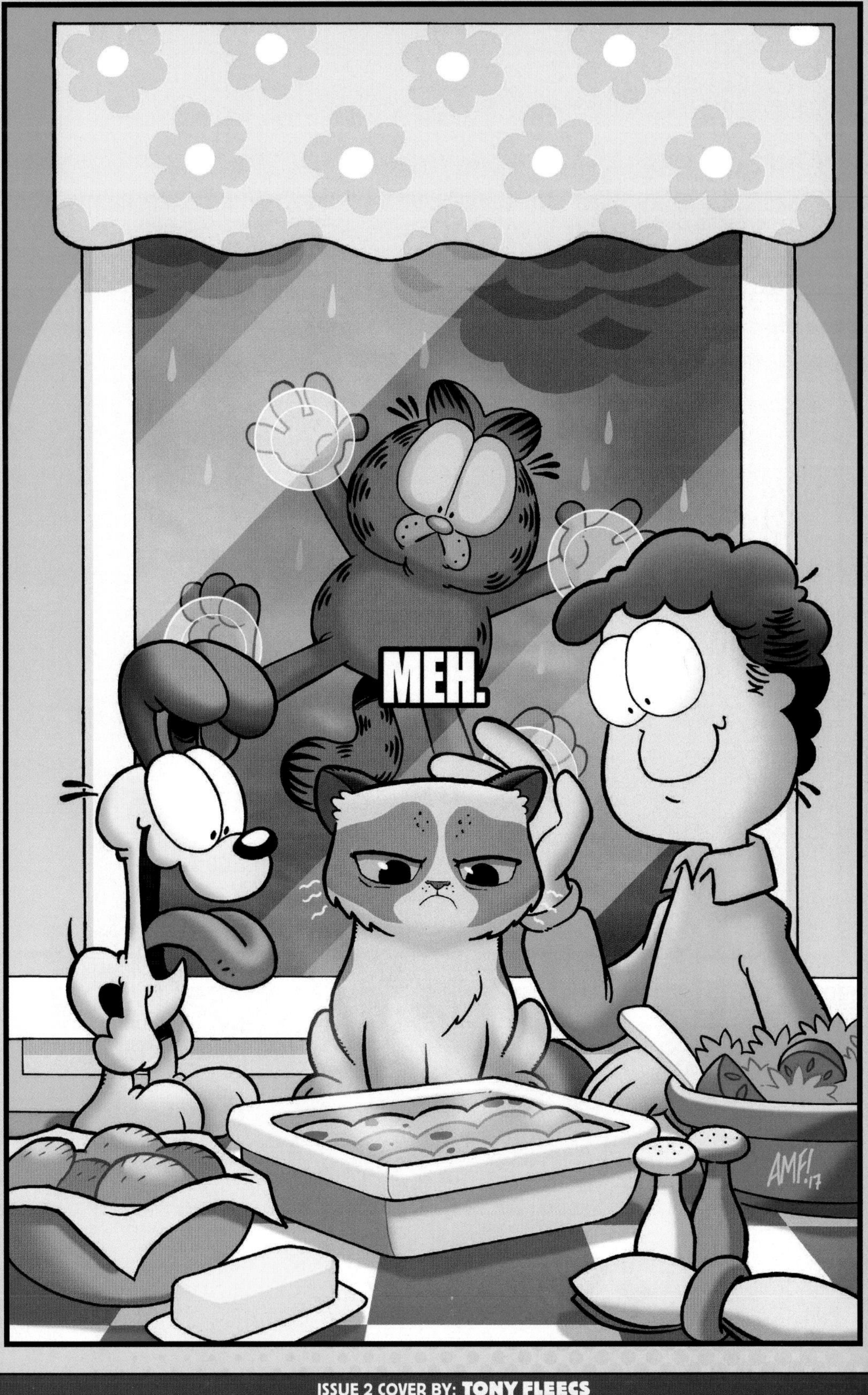
MEH.
AMF! '17

ISSUE 2 COVER BY: **TONY FLEECS**

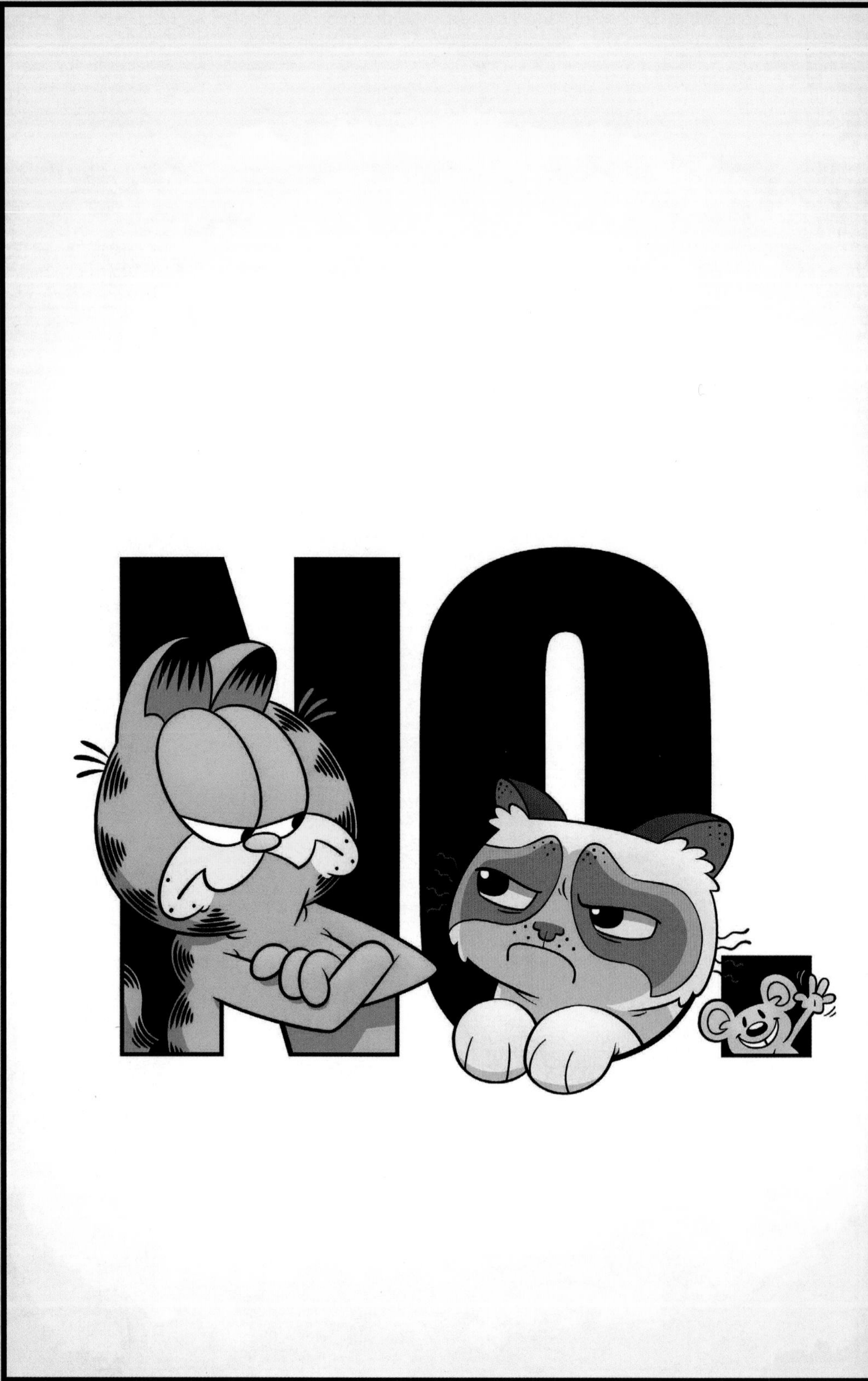
NO.

ISSUE 2 COVER BY: **ANDY HIRSCH**

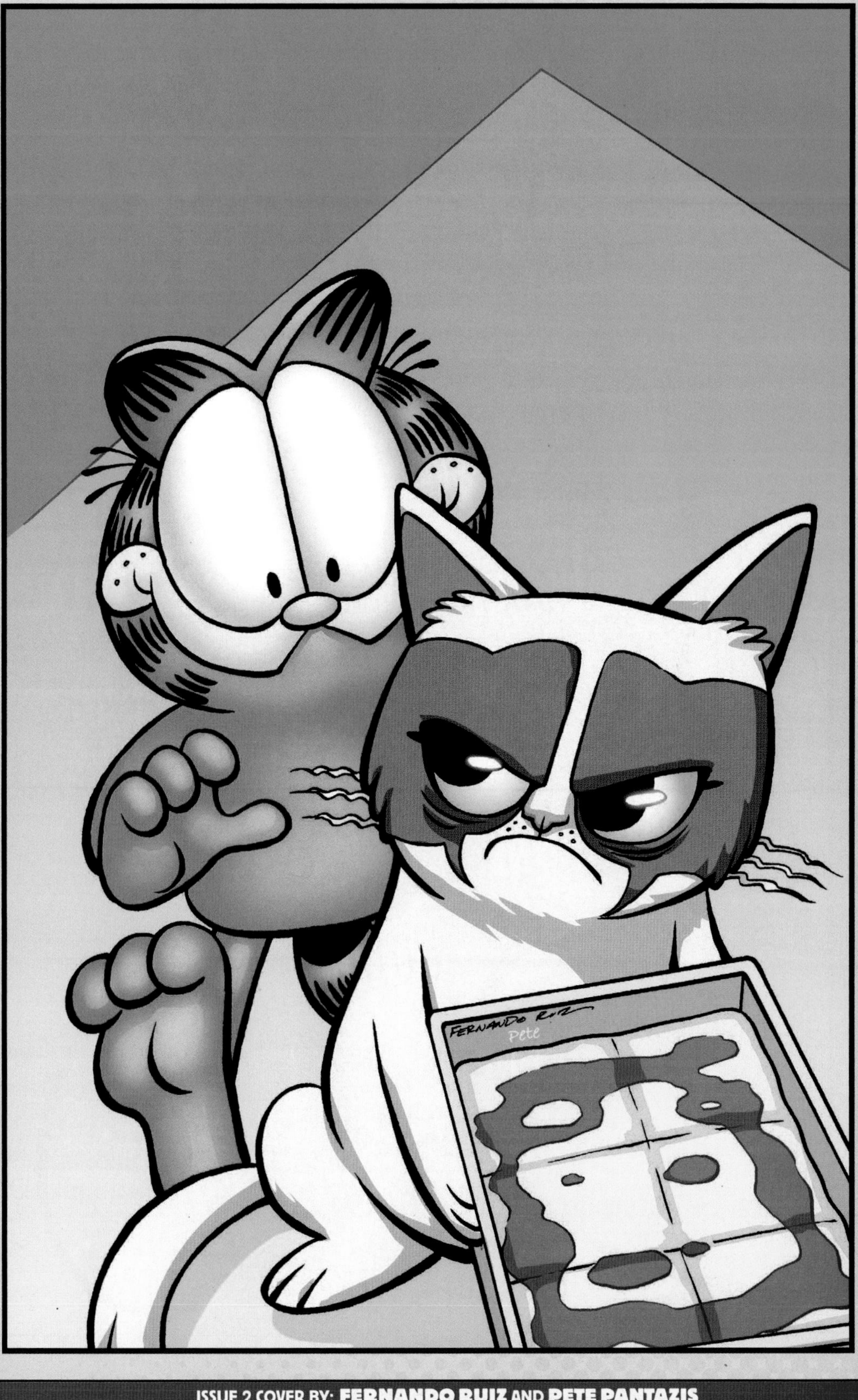
FERNANDO RUIZ
Pete

ISSUE 2 COVER BY: **FERNANDO RUIZ** AND **PETE PANTAZIS**

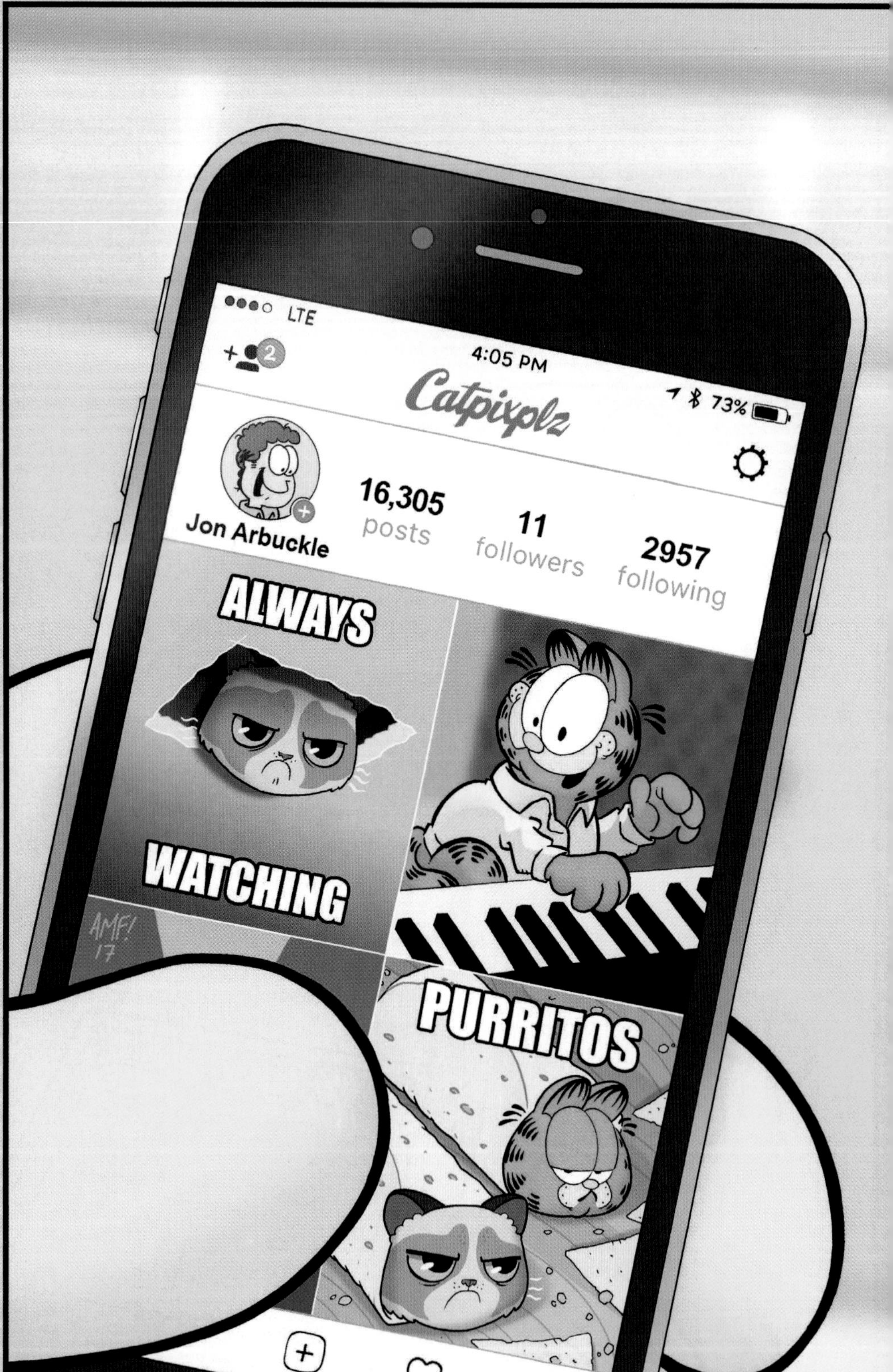
●●●○ LTE
4:05 PM
Catpixplz
73%
Jon Arbuckle
16,305
posts
11
followers
2957
following
ALWAYS
WATCHING
AMF!
17
PURRITOS

ISSUE 3 COVER BY: **TONY FLEECS**

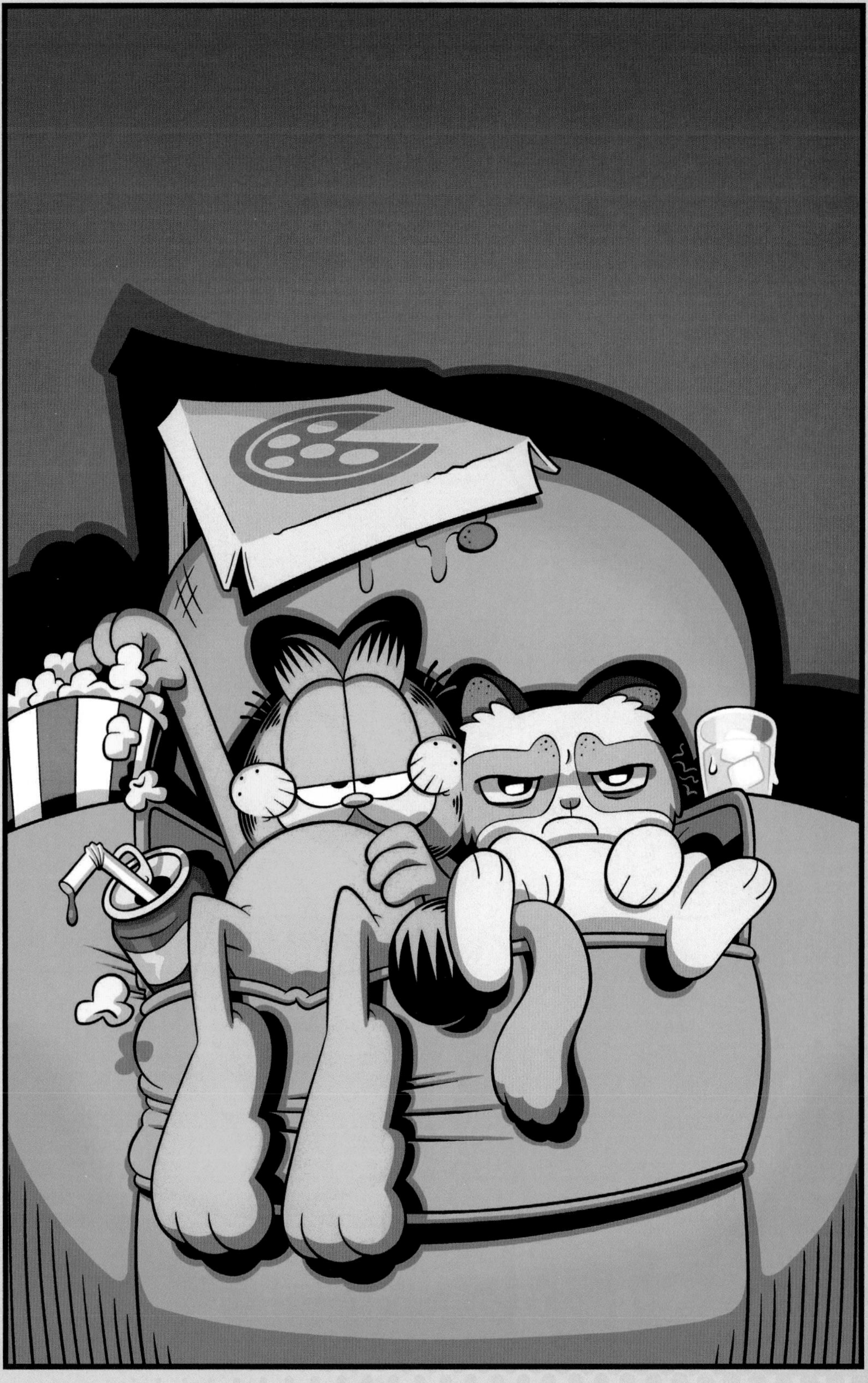

ISSUE 3 COVER BY: **ANDY HIRSCH**

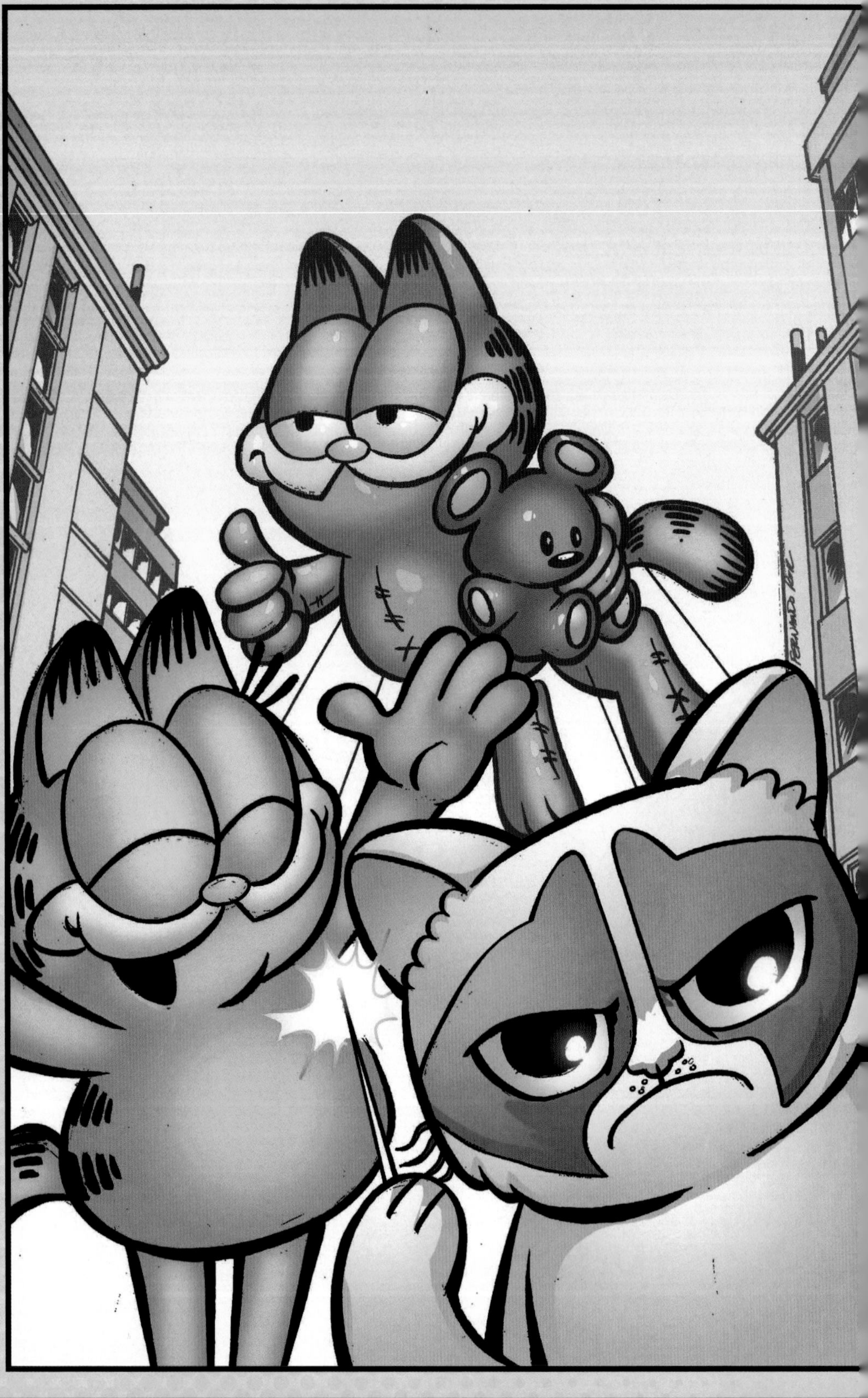

ISSUE 3 COVER BY: **FERNANDO RUIZ** AND **PETE PANTAZIS**

COLLECT THESE OTHER GREAT GRUMPY CAT COLLECTIONS FROM DYNAMITE. IN STORES NOW!

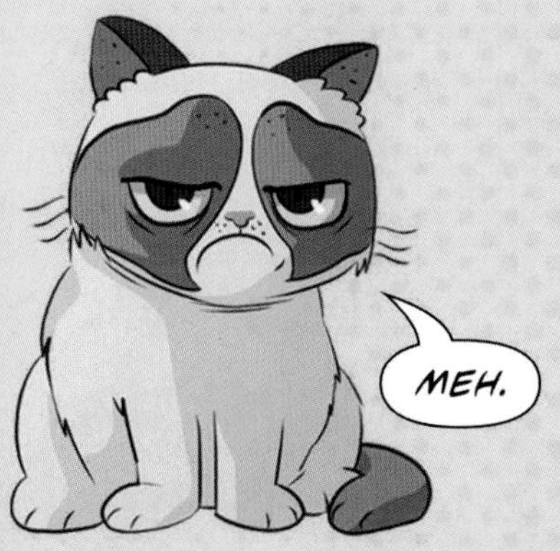
MEH.

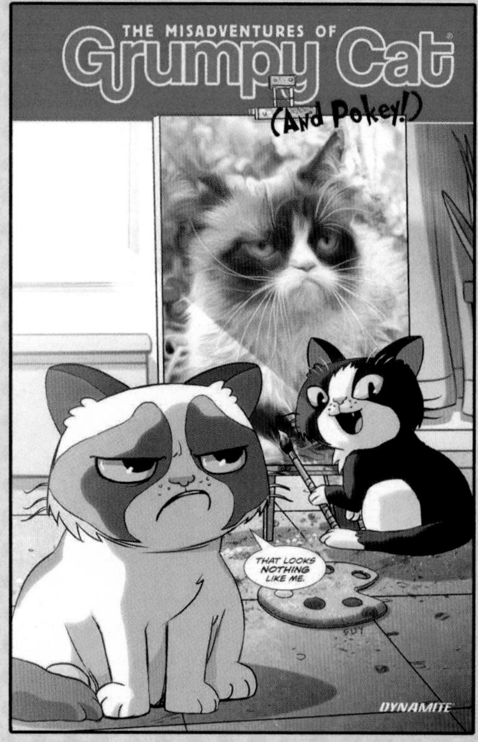
THE MISADVENTURES OF
Grumpy Cat
(And Pokey!)
THAT LOOKS NOTHING LIKE ME.
DYNAMITE

GRUMPY CAT (vol 1)
INCLUDES A REMOVABLE POSTER!
978-1-60690-796-2

DYNAMITE www.DYNAMITE.com

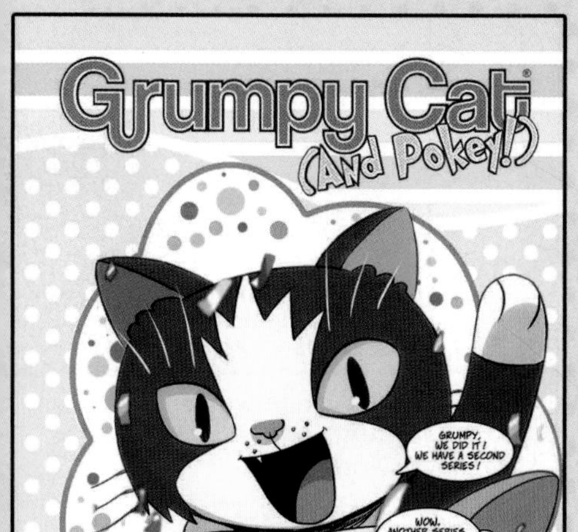
Grumpy Cat
(And Pokey!)
GRUMPY, WE DID IT! WE HAVE A SECOND SERIES!
WOW. ANOTHER SERIES. I CAN HARDLY CONTAIN THE JOY...
DYNAMITE

GRUMPY CAT AND POKEY (vol 2)
INCLUDES A REMOVABLE POSTER!
978-1-5241-0004-9

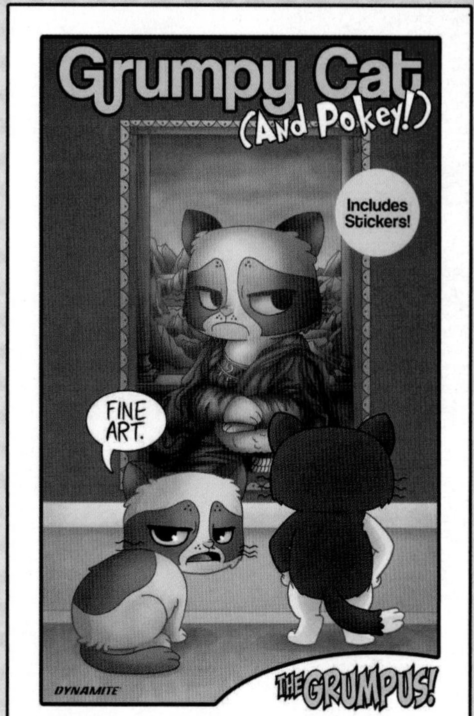
Grumpy Cat
(And Pokey!)
Includes Stickers!
FINE ART.
DYNAMITE
THE GRUMPUS!

GRUMPY CAT AND POKEY: THE GRUMPUS (vol 3)
INCLUDES GRUMPY CAT AND POKEY STCKERS!
978-1-5241-0246-3

DISCOVER
EXPLOSIVE NEW WORLDS

Adventure Time

The Amazing World of
Gumball

Steven Universe
Volume One

Over the
Garden Wall

Garfield
By Jim Davis

Charles M. Schulz
PEANUTS

kaboom!™

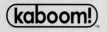

AVAILABLE AT YOUR LOCAL COMICS SHOP AND BOOKSTORE

To find a comics shop in your area, call 1-888-266-4226

WWW.**BOOM-STUDIOS**.COM

Adventure Time

Pendleton Ward and Others

Volume 1

ISBN: 978-1-60886-280-1 | $9.99

Volume 2

ISBN: 978-1-60886-323-5 | $14.99 US

Adventure Time: Islands

ISBN: 978-1-60886-972-5 | $9.99

Regular Show

J.G. Quintel and Others

Volume 1

ISBN: 978-1-60886-362-4 | $14.99

Volume 2

ISBN: 978-1-60886-426-3 | $14.99

Regular Show: Hydration

ISBN: 978-1-60886-339-6 | $12.99

The Amazing World of Gumball

Ben Bocquelet and Others

Volume 1

ISBN: 978-1-60886-488-1 | $14.99

Volume 2

ISBN: 978-1-60886-793-6 | $14.99

Over the Garden Wall

Patrick McHale, Jim Campbell and Others

Volume 1

ISBN: 978-1-60886-940-4 | $14.99

Volume 2

ISBN: 978-1-68415-006-9 | $14.99

Steven Universe

Rebecca Sugar and Others

Volume 1

ISBN: 978-1-60886-706-6 | $14.99

Volume 2

ISBN: 978-1-60886-796-7 | $14.99

Steven Universe & The Crystal Gems

ISBN: 978-1-60886-921-3 | $14.99

Steven Universe: Too Cool for School

ISBN: 978-1-60886-771-4 | $14.99

Peanuts

Charles Schultz and Others

Volume 1

ISBN: 978-1-60886-260-3 | $13.99

Garfield

Jim Davis and Others

Volume 1

ISBN: 978-1-60886-287-0 | $13.99

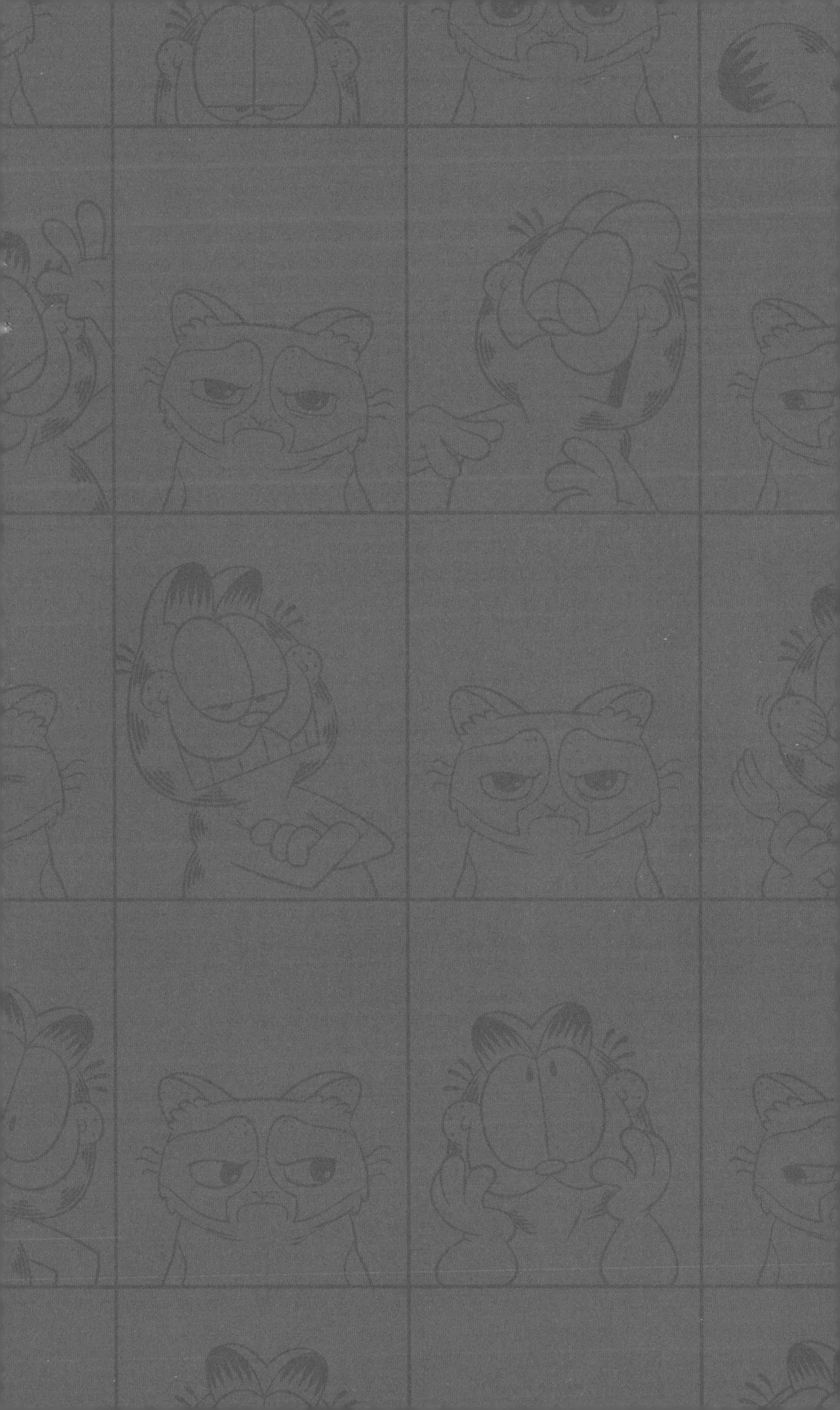

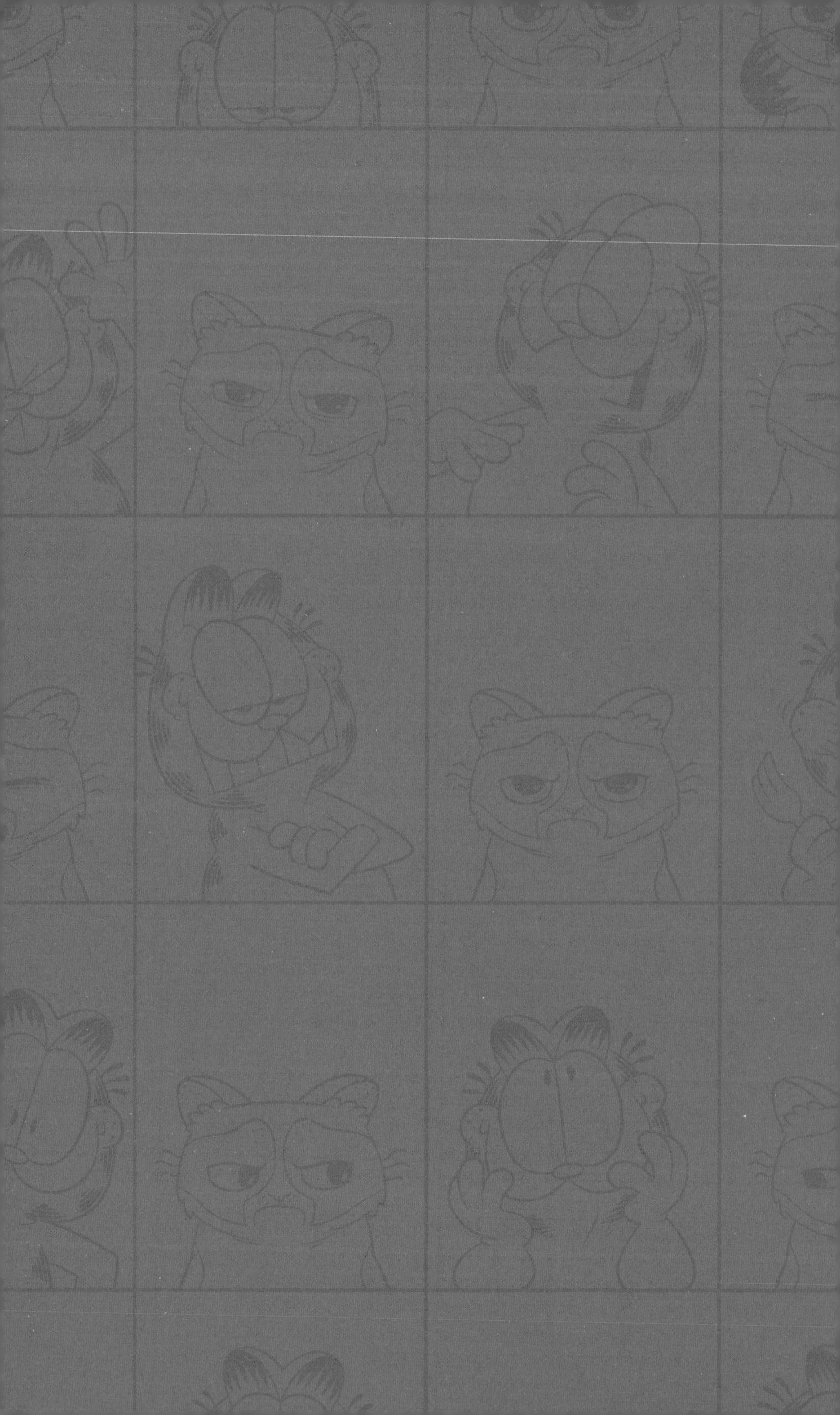